THE HAUNTING SEASON

ALSO BY MICHELLE MUTO:

The Book of Lost Souls
Don't Fear the Reaper

THE HAUNTING SEASON

MICHELLE MUTO

SKYSCAPE

SKYSCAPE

Published by Skyscape, New York

www.apub.com

Amazon, the Amazon logo, and Skyscape are trademarks of Amazon.com, Inc., or its affiliates.

ISBN-13: 9781477847930
ISBN-10: 1477847936

Cover design by Sarah Hansen
Interior design by Paul Barrett

Printed in the United States of America

To my brother Bob, who used to scare the daylights out of me as a kid. Thanks.

CHAPTER ONE

Siler House loomed before them, dark and inscrutable despite the late afternoon sun. Jess couldn't take her eyes from the turrets and spires as her stepfather, Paul, guided the Ford Explorer down the private drive, which was flanked by shadowy old oaks curtained with moss.

In the brochure she'd read, the house had been photographed against a bright blue sky. Now, with the sun beginning to dip below the horizon, the house looked darker, more mysterious. It was as though it harbored something she could only explain as an essence or soul.

Of course, houses or manors, no matter how old, weren't living, breathing things. At times, they only appeared that way—as if the souls of all who had wandered the halls left a bit of themselves behind.

Her younger sister, Lily, pressed her small face against the glass. "Is it really haunted?"

"Nonsense," their mother snapped from the front seat.

"But *all* old houses are supposed to be haunted," Lily protested as she sat back in her seat.

"Especially in Savannah," her stepfather murmured, earning him what her real father used to call *the stink eye* from her mother. Paul wasn't a bad guy. In fact, he'd done everything possible to earn Jess's trust after marrying her mother a couple of years ago. It had been hard on Jess at first. Her parents had divorced shortly before Jess turned fifteen and her mother remarried almost a year and a half later. Until then, Jess had hoped her parents would get back together. But, in her way, Jess had also come to love Paul. Not like she'd loved her father, but Paul was definitely as cool as a stepfather could be. For one thing, he'd been on her side when she'd told her mother she wanted to go to Siler House. Of course, money had been an issue, too. The stay at Siler House was a paid study, which meant she could replenish what her mother had to take from her college fund to pay the mortgage and car loans.

Jess hadn't begrudged what her mother had to do. The company Paul used to work for had laid off the entire engineering department, and it had taken nearly a year to find another job. Still, the money they had taken had wiped out almost half of Jess's college fund. According to the study's contract, the payments would be divided into thirds. One portion to be paid at time of acceptance, one to be paid halfway through the experiment, and the final check would come once the experiment was finished. Her mom had been skeptical since the total amount was rather substantial, but Jess had been adamant about signing up.

"It's *history*, Janice," Paul said. His tone remained upbeat and playful, which was so typical of him. "Savannah has been through war and a few other major tragedies, including a couple of bouts with yellow fever. They buried people in mass graves. Now, hotels, restaurants, and parking lots sit on top of burial grounds. Savannah is *literally* a community built on the dead. It's why they call Savannah the most haunted city in America."

Paul smiled at her mother, but she didn't reciprocate. Jess and Lily exchanged shrugs. They knew when their mother's expressions were all play and when they were a thinly veiled warning. And ghosts were a sore point with her. How many times had Jess been called out for going on about ghosts and hauntings? A hundred times? More?

Stop filling your sister's head with such foolishness. You'll give her nightmares!

"It's beautiful," Jess said as they passed more moss-draped oaks.

Her mother turned in her seat, looking stern. "Remember our agreement."

Jess nodded, although she was eighteen now—even if it was only by a few months. Of course, the agreement she'd made with her mother still held since she had been seventeen when they'd first agreed on the deal. Jess had been raised to believe that promises and deals were something you followed through on. Part of the reason her mother had given in to Jess's participation in Dr. Brandt's study was to prove that ghosts *didn't* exist—that anything Jess thought she had seen was nothing more than a young girl's grief and an overactive imagination. The agreement? If the study produced no solid evidence, Jess would give up her fascination with ghosts. Jess found it both amusing and sad how sometimes promises and deals became more complicated the older she got.

Jess fumbled clumsily for the door handle as Paul pulled the vehicle to a stop. She pushed the door open and got out, still staring at the house.

Siler House was like the belle of the ball, dressed in elegant black, discreetly standing in the shadows and watching her guests. The place looked more like a plantation home or mansion than a regular house. It stood proudly—an expanse of well-kept brick and stone with an angular roofline etched high against the sky and an English garden at its feet. Not just proud, Jess amended. Siler House imparted a certain sense of arrogance. She supposed anything built more than a hundred years ago and still standing had a right to such an exaggerated air of importance. More so, if there was any truth to what Dr. Brandt, the parapsychologist and head of the study, had said. He claimed that Siler House, and the spirits within it, might be the real thing—a channel into the afterlife.

At last. This was it. For a whole month, it would be her, Dr. Brandt, and three other participants roughly her age. And, if everything went well, ghosts. Lots of ghosts.

It was like spring break, only for paranormal freaks.

Car doors slammed behind her. "Jess! Wait!"

Her mother's exasperated tone barely registered. Yes, this was the place. Or, at least she hoped. Jess had been to places on an even grander scale—like the Biltmore Estate back home in Asheville. Even in Chimney Rock there were Victorian homes she suspected were just as old as Siler House. But none of them made a first impression like this. Excitement flooded her senses and she bit her lip. *Please, please let this work.*

"Why can't you wait for the rest of us?" her mother said, the slightest edge of disapproval in her voice. "Why do you always have to be in a hurry?"

What she really meant was that Jess was too much like her father, which was fine with her. Especially since his recent death. Her father hadn't remarried and he'd died alone. How could Jess explain that Siler House was hope, a chance to reconnect with her dad and Grams?

Her grandmother had been her first ghost sighting. After Grams died, Jess doubted that what she was seeing was her ghost. But soon afterward, Jess started to see other ghosts, too. People appeared in the crowd one minute and disappeared the next. Sometimes, they terrified her, like the two women who'd popped up in an otherwise empty department store bathroom. Once, Jess witnessed an angry ghost who was behind a restaurant bar. The ghost somehow caused a patron to spill his drink. But most of the ghosts she saw were perfectly harmless and often shy. A few were even afraid of the living.

Ghosts didn't appear *all* the time, which was probably a good thing, or Jess figured she'd have been sent to the psychiatrist's office a lot more often. Since Grams's death a few years ago, the sightings came and went. Sometimes, weeks went by before Jess saw a ghost. Jess hadn't minded. Ghosts were ghosts, and, by definition, creepy, no matter how social or well meaning.

When her dad had died back in January, Jess had waited, certain she'd see him again. Nights, weeks, and months had passed, but he never came to her. Not like Grams. Not like the others. No word, no sightings, not even a dream. When she'd grown angry and bitter, the rest of the ghosts had stopped showing up and Jess had missed them.

"Jess!"

"Sorry," Jess replied absently. She waited until she heard the wheels of her American Tourister luggage skating against the concrete walk.

"What in God's name did you pack in here?" Paul mumbled. "Feels like a dead body."

Jess smiled, knowing Paul was probably getting the stink eye again. She looked up, searching the windows above.

The act wasn't lost on her mother, who scoured the windows as well. "There's no one there," she said quietly. "Please, Jess. I know it's been hard. Don't do this to yourself." She tentatively reached for Jess's arm, as though she expected her daughter to lash out or break.

Or break down. Again.

"We could put your vivid imagination to good use. Maybe creative writing or something."

Her misplaced imagination.

"We'll go home," her mother continued. "Right now if you want. Just say the word."

Just say that ghosts don't exist. Go back to taking your meds. Admit Dad and Grams are gone forever. We'll return the check.

6

You can get a full-time job and take classes at the junior college instead.

"I'm fine, Mom."

No one peered out from the windows yet, but Jess sensed someone or something watching all the same. Maybe it was her imagination or just wishful thinking, but Jess wondered if the house itself was looking back, regarding her with reserved curiosity. She imagined it inviting her in, envisioned Siler House whispering its secrets to her, showing her how to reopen the passage to the other side.

I'll find you, Dad. I'll find the way like I did with Grams. Like I did with the others. I'll prove to everyone that I'm not some crazy kid with imaginary friends.

Jess walked up the porch steps to the double doors and took hold of the doorknob, feeling the weight of it, the ridges of the tooled, oiled brass in her hand. If she believed hard enough, maybe she'd be able to see ghosts again.

I'm here. At long last, I'm here.

Taking in a breath and closing her eyes tightly, she turned the knob and gave the door a light push.

Please let ghosts exist here. If anyone's listening, help me. Tell me you'll help me connect.

She imagined she heard someone answering—maybe a former inhabitant of Siler House.

. . . We will.

In her mind, men and women dressed in turn-of-the-century attire and anxiously awaiting the new arrivals hurried to look out the windows from the upstairs rooms.

Other than a soft *snick,* the door had opened soundlessly. For a moment, she replayed her last visit with Grams. Jess recalled Grams standing before her, just as real as when she'd been alive. She'd smiled at Jess and issued a gentle warning as she slowly began to fade from sight.

Be careful what you let in, Jess. Promise that you won't come looking for me anymore.

But why, Grams?

Because I'm not the only one who can answer.

Jess opened her eyes and stepped across the threshold.

CHAPTER TWO

There was no small foyer inside Siler House. No small hallway with paintings or flower arrangements or coat racks. The
door opened into a broad space that was part of what the
brochure had called the Great Room. Furniture divided it
into two sitting areas: one in front of the brick fireplace, and
another in the room's middle. A table with a chess set had
been placed in the corner. To Jess's right, a large mahogany
side table with clawed feet stood against the wall closest to a
wide, dark wood-paneled staircase that led to three beveled
windows on the first landing.

"Well, it is elegant," her mother offered.

Jess agreed. The far end of the Great Room hosted a set of
floor-to-ceiling windows that matched the ones on the stairwell landing. The room itself was painted hunter green. A
crystal chandelier the size of a small car glittered high above
the room's center, its prisms casting odd refractions of light

into the corners and illuminating small faces carved into the crown molding. Jess squinted to see them better.

Voices—that of a woman and a girl—carried from around the corner. Was the girl like her? Did she see ghosts? Jess's attention shifted from the odd, staring faces above her to the hallway.

"Aunt Carolyn, *please!*"

"DON'T!" a woman, presumably Aunt Carolyn, replied. "For God's sake, *don't touch me!*"

The source of the voices rounded the corner a moment later—a tired-looking, dark-haired woman in casual slacks and blouse, and a too-thin girl of about seventeen or eighteen with long strawberry blond hair wearing shorts. A man dressed in a black suit and red tie followed behind. Unless Jess missed her guess, he had to be Dr. Brandt.

"Allison, you'll be fine," the man said. "I assure you and your aunt that you'll be safe here."

The woman slowed and turned to offer him a terse smile. "Yes, my husband and I will feel much better when she's here with *you.*" She rubbed her arms as though it were winter rather than late July. "Allison's parents, that is, my sister and her husband, will be in touch, I'm sure. They just need some time." Her eyes darted in Allison's direction and Jess swore she saw fear inside them. Not the kind she'd expect from some weird germaphobe afraid of being touched, but from someone who'd just found a tarantula hanging in front of her, or the boogeyman in her bedroom closet.

Or encountered someone who'd done something to permanently scare the crap out of her.

10

"Well," Aunt Carolyn replied at last, "if that'll be all." She gave the man a cordial nod and hurried past Jess and her mother, almost colliding with Lily and Paul in her rush. Allison's aunt never looked back, slamming the door shut behind her.

The man in the suit approached them, an apologetic look on his face. "Dr. Gregory Brandt," he said. He gestured at the thin, young girl. "And this is Allison Giles. You must be—"

"It doesn't matter who they are," Allison interrupted. "They should leave this place. This instant."

For a long moment, no one spoke. Lily came to stand beside Jess. "*Awk*ward," she whispered.

Allison wrung her hands and managed a smile. Tears glimmered in her eyes. "Are you afraid of me, too? If not, you will be. Just like everyone else."

"No one is afraid of you," Dr. Brandt assured her. A smile spread across his face almost too easily. "Your aunt is uncomfortable with the study, that's all. Nonbelievers usually are."

Allison's eyes cut to Dr. Brandt. "My aunt believes. They all do. How could they *not*?"

Jess opened her mouth to tell Allison that she wasn't afraid of her, even though her aunt clearly *had* been, but Allison shoved past them and hurried up the stairs.

"*Really* awkward," Lily reiterated.

Jess felt her mother's gentle touch on her arm. "Jess, sweetheart. Say the word and you can come with us to Florida. It'll be a nice family vacation. Your cousins will be happy to see you."

The worrisome tone in her voice was too much. Her mother meant well, but Jess found the gesture nearly suffocating and pulled away. She *needed* to do this. Her mother loved her, wanted to shield her, but Jess was stronger now. Hiding the grief and tears had been hard at first, but that, too, had become easier over time. Jess sensed the weight of her mother's stare.

She thinks Allison and I have a lot of potential crazy in common. And maybe we do.

"Allison is just nervous," Dr. Brandt explained. "The relationship she has with her aunt and uncle is a bit strained."

"Wow, I hope she's not my roommate." Jess hoped the statement would go a long way to reassure her mother, although she actually wouldn't mind sharing a room with Allison. Everyone else could call it crazy if they wanted, but Allison might really be in tune with whatever ghosts called Siler House home.

And Allison might be able to help me find the portal, so I can find Dad and Grams.

Paul laughed. "I don't know, Jess. With your luck, she's definitely your roommate. So, what do you say we lug the dead bodies upstairs and find out?" He nodded toward her luggage.

Jess smiled, thankful for Paul's eternal and timely wit.

"Simple case of nerves," Dr. Brandt repeated. "I'm certain Jess and Allison will be fine," he added, essentially confirming that Paul was right about Jess's luck. "They'll be good friends by morning."

Jess's mother finished introducing herself, Paul, and Lily just as the next study mate arrived—a tall, fair-haired guy wearing jeans and a black polo shirt. He held the door for a woman and tall girl who shared his complexion and faded blue eyes. He grinned nervously at Jess and her family before bringing his attention back to what she assumed were his mother and sister. A man entered behind them and Jess noticed that the newcomer's face grew taut. He wiped the palms of his hands against his jeans.

"Ah," Dr. Brandt exclaimed. "Bryan! So glad you decided to join us." He began making the formal introductions around the room. Jess learned that Bryan's last name was Akerman, that he was about her own age, and that his younger sister's name was Erin. The man with his mother was her boyfriend, Alex.

Everyone nodded or shook hands. Alex wrapped an arm around Bryan's mother, and Bryan looked away.

"Bryan, it's okay. Honest," his sister said softly, resting a hand on his arm. Bryan swallowed hard and nodded.

"Sweetheart," Bryan's mother said, excusing herself from small talk with Jess's mother and moving away from her boyfriend. Bryan seemed to relax a bit. "We'll be just fine." She leaned forward and whispered something too softly for Jess to hear clearly, but it was something about finally being happy. Then she turned to face everyone. "It was a pleasure meeting you."

"Hon, do you have the car keys?" Alex patted the pockets on his slacks.

"Bryan!" Erin mouthed accusingly.

"What?" Bryan mouthed back. "I didn't do it."

The boyfriend *seemed* nice enough. At the same time, Jess totally understood. Watching her mother with someone other than her father had been hard at first, too.

"Never mind!" Alex pulled the keys from his right pants pocket. "They're right here."

Bryan shifted his footing and looked toward the door. Whatever ability Bryan had, it wasn't like hers or Allison's. Jess wondered if Bryan's ability was more physical. Telekinesis? Mind control? Something else? Cool.

Her heart skipped a beat. She couldn't wait to talk to her fellow test subjects and get the chance to know more about them and about Siler House. She had been waiting for something like Siler House to come into her life. She looked around at the stairwell and the large, inviting room, and wondered: if houses *could* think, would Siler House feel the same way about her?

CHAPTER THREE

"Are you sure you don't want to change your mind?" Jess's mother asked for the millionth time. "Our last family vacation before you go off to school?" Her eyes darted away from Allison, who had officially become Jess's new roommate.

Ignoring her mother's repeated plea for Jess to leave with them, Jess plunked her suitcase down on the bed closest to the window. Allison sat on her own bed, absently staring into space, her suitcases still untouched against the wall.

The room was a good size, plenty big enough for two girls to share, which Jess thought was saying something. She unzipped her suitcase and pulled out several pairs of shorts and placed them in one of the dresser drawers. "Nice room."

"It used to be a playroom for the Silers' daughters," the maid who had shown Jess and her mother to the room informed them. "If there's nothing else . . ."

It was close to five o'clock, and Jess imagined the woman wanted to finish her chores before leaving.

"No. I'm good. Thanks," Jess replied.

"There's a nightlight in the bathroom, and one for the room, should you need them," the maid added.

"Thanks," Jess replied, as anxious for her to leave as she clearly was. For that matter, she was also ready for her mother to leave.

The maid nodded as she briskly walked across the room to the door. "Take care. Sleep well. My shift's ending and I must be going." Her mother opened her mouth in protest, but the maid was already out the door and halfway down the hall.

With the woman gone, her mother examined the room as though everything about it might be part of some test. She paid particular attention to the lock on the door.

"Mrs. Hirsch has the keys," Allison informed her.

"Mrs. Hirsch?" Jess's mother inquired.

Allison nodded. "I think she's the head housekeeper or something. She was here, right before you came up. She said she'll be living here with us. She's staying downstairs on the second floor with Dr. Brandt and the guys."

Allison wiped at her red, watery eyes, an indicator she'd been crying before Jess showed up. She still couldn't believe the way Allison's aunt had acted. Jess glanced at her mother, who was busy checking the window latch. "I'll be *fine*, Mom. Really. Okay? Every couple of days the maids come in, *and* there's Mrs. Hirsch. She'll be here the *whole time*. Allison and I will be nice and safe up here—alone. Right, Allison?" Jess wanted to bring up that she was eighteen, after all, but decided against it.

"Alone," Allison muttered morosely. Whatever had happened between her and her aunt must have been really something. Allison's shoulders were slumped and her hair needed brushing. She hardly seemed like someone to be afraid of—instead, she was more like someone who needed a friend.

Her mother stood, hesitating. "Well, if you're *sure* . . ."

Jess gave her mother a hug. "Yes! I'm sure. Paul will think you're staying, too, if you don't hurry up. One month, Mom. It's just one month. I'll be home before college starts. We'll have plenty of time together then."

Her mother managed a weak smile. "Don't forget to put your phone on charge. You're always forgetting—"

"I'll put my phone on charge." Jess sighed. "I promise. Now, go before Paul comes up here looking for you."

"One month. Unless you call us before then. Maybe I should go find Mrs. Hirsch. I'd like to at least meet her before we leave." Her mother straightened her blouse and left, leaving Jess alone with her sullen roommate.

Allison stared after Jess's mother for a moment, making the silence between them seem awkward. Jess got up and went to the window. The Red Room, as the sign on the hallway door indicated, had been aptly named. The wall with the window had been painted a vermillion red. The curtains matched their bedspreads, white with red vines. The room overlooked the back lawn.

"Moms," Jess said, turning away from the window. "What she really means is she's going to tell Mrs. Hirsch that I'm prone to imagination and . . ." Jess faltered. She didn't know Allison well enough to tell her she'd been on medication for

17

a supposed nervous breakdown. Not that she *agreed* with the doctors. They just didn't understand. But maybe Allison would.

Jess sighed and flopped onto her bed, deciding that nothing she had to say could come close to the embarrassment Allison had suffered downstairs. "No one believes me. Not even when I told them about a small candy box with some money inside it that Grams had stashed in a dresser drawer before she died. Mom said I must have just forgotten that Grams had already told me or something."

"At least she loves you," Allison replied. "Your mother is here. Mine isn't. My father, either. They had me put away for a while. A mental hospital."

Wow, Jess thought. Allison went one step further than she had. That had to be rough. A mental hospital? When Jess had been seeing the psychiatrist, she'd worried that he would recommend a mental hospital for a short time, too. "I'm sorry."

"It's okay," Allison stated without raising her head. "We've never been close, even before all this. My parents are traveling, so I've been staying with my aunt and uncle the past week. But they're *all* afraid of me." Allison began picking at her fingernails, which were already too short.

"Well, I'm not afraid of you," Jess said. "I think people who are different than us are afraid, sometimes. I'm sure they'll come around."

"I'm classified as borderline schizophrenic," Allison announced casually. "Unless you want to consider the full-on alternative to that diagnosis. Anyway, we've got some real family issues going on. But who doesn't, right? Looks like you've got some issues with your mom. But it's nothing like the relationship I have with mine. So you really think I'm like you?"

Jess shrugged. "Well, sure. I mean, we're all here for the same reason, right? An experiment on the paranormal. Ghosts." Jess didn't want to address the schizophrenia diagnosis, which she found a bit disconcerting. But given her own experience with psychiatrists, she decided to give Allison a chance.

"You see ghosts?" Allison asked, almost as if she was relieved.

Jess nodded. "Yeah. Do you?"

Allison stared blankly at her, making Jess wonder if her new roommate was on some major meds or was really just that strange.

"It used to freak me out," Jess continued. "But I'm sort of used to it now. Sorry about your family. Like Dr. Brandt said, it's because they don't understand. I mean, it's sort of creepy."

"*I'm* afraid of me," Allison blurted out, tears beginning to stream down her face again. "I thought it might all be over, but this *place*! I'm . . . I'm scared. Terrified, actually. I think my family wants something to happen to me. I think they want me put away somewhere permanently. Not that they cared before this, but *now*? *This place*?" She shifted her position on the bed, and took a steadying breath. "Sorry. TMI, right? I don't know you, and you probably don't want to hear all this. But I don't have anyone to talk to usually, and I feel like I'm all alone. Sort of. I mean, I don't think we're *really* by ourselves here." She swiped at her cheeks and let out a half-hearted laugh. "I sound crazy."

Allison might be afraid, but she was hardly crazy. She'd been through a lot, apparently. Still, weren't they all considered a *little* crazy, as Allison had put it, for believing in ghosts and stuff to begin with? Jess shrugged. "Well, yeah. A tiny bit. Which means you're probably at least as sane as I am. So, we see ghosts. Looks like we've got something in common."

Allison managed a weak but genuine smile. "Sure. Ghosts. I guess a few ghosts wouldn't be *all* that bad."

CHAPTER FOUR

Jess finished unpacking, mostly using the dresser draw-ers. Pretty much all the things she'd brought were summer clothes—shorts and cool cotton tops, none of which required hangers. The only thing she had to hang in the closet was a single sundress, which she had packed just in case.

While Jess put away her clothes, she thought about Allison's concerns regarding the house and the experiment. She hadn't anticipated that her fellow test subjects might be unhappy with their ghost-seeing abilities. "Well, ghosts or no ghosts, I think we'll be all right. *Although*," she teased Allison, "I haven't seen Mrs. Hirsch. What's she like? Is she human or some spooky turn-of-the-century chambermaid?"

Allison laughed and the sound made Jess feel more at ease with her new roomie. Sure, Allison had been through a lot, but Jess sort of understood. She'd never really thought about how lucky she was that her family didn't look at her like a *total* freak. Jess never talked about ghosts outside of her family. People didn't understand. But here, at Siler House, they were all the same in some way. They'd all been touched by something supernatural. It was one of the reasons Jess felt at home here.

"She's not a ghost," Allison replied. "But she *is* sort of scary. She's big and kind of mean looking. Carries a huge hoop with a bunch of keys on it. Doesn't talk much, either. When she saw me in the bathroom crying, all she said was that dinner was at six, and I should clean up before then."

Jess put away the last of her clothes. "She sounds awful. We'll stay out of her way, then. Do you want to go exploring? I'm dying to see more of the house."

"I'd rather not," Allison admitted. "But anything beats being in here by myself."

"Seriously? This house gives you the creeps? Do you know the history behind it or something?" Jess asked. "I tried doing some research and didn't find much. It's supposed to be haunted, but so is everyplace else in Savannah."

"Confession. I don't see ghosts. Ghosts don't sound too bad. I see evil . . . spirits. So yeah, I'm creeped out. This place makes me feel like I did when . . ." Allison gave an exaggerated shudder.

"When?" Jess asked.

"You *do* feel it, don't you?" Allison asked, avoiding Jess's curiosity.

Jess took a deep breath and listened, letting the house settle in around her. She supposed it wouldn't hurt to say that what she sensed felt more like hope. The house had a presence, all right. But how much of that was wishful thinking?

How much was because she wanted so badly for Dr. Brandt to prove her right about a connection between the real world and the world beyond? "Yeah," she said finally. "There's *something* here, but I don't think it's bad. Wait. You said you see spirits? *Evil* spirits?"

Allison put her suitcase in the closet on top of Jess's and closed the door. "On second thought, I like your idea about exploring. Can we start outside?"

"Sure." Jess couldn't imagine what it might be like to see evil spirits. It had to be hard on Allison to have experienced what she had. Luckily for Jess, seeing ghosts had always been a gift, not a curse. The entire time Jess had been seeing them, she'd *never* encountered one she'd consider menacing. Pissed off, maybe. Like the ghost who made the guy at the bar spill his drink. But that was about as bad as it had ever been. The idea that all ghosts might not be benign had never occurred to her because it had never happened to *her*.

"We'll go outside while there's still light," Jess said. "Then we'll explore the house after dinner. Evil spirits, huh? Not to pry, but why do you think the ghosts are evil?"

Allison dug through her own clothes, selecting a T-shirt and pair of shorts. "They're not really . . . never mind. It's complicated. I'll tell you later. Probably at dinner. I bet we'll all have to talk about ourselves then."

Jess didn't push the subject further. Allison was already uneasy. Jess wanted to know what had happened to cause such a huge rift between Allison and her family, but decided she'd probably find out soon enough. One thing was obvious, though—this experiment wasn't the best idea for Allison.

After they'd finished changing, they left the room and headed down the hallway.

The renovation crew had done a great job on Siler House. They had refinished the floorboards and put fresh paint on the walls. The whole place looked new—but Jess could imagine it might have looked the same back when the Silers lived here—elegant and grand, and yet charming and comforting. Siler House would make a great bed and breakfast—once all the renovations were complete. For Jess, the next couple of weeks at Siler House held nothing but amazing possibilities.

If Allison would only look at things the way she did—see how beautiful the place was—she might realize the house itself was nothing to be afraid of. Jess wanted to open the door of every room they passed, wanted to take in everything about the house. Once or twice, she absently reached out, letting her hand brush against one of the doorknobs, which might have been original or just a really good replica.

As strange and elusive as Jess found Allison, she drew comfort knowing the other participants would each have *some* strange experience to share, some line of connection.

"Just ghosts, huh?" Allison asked, as they walked out into the stifling heat of the early evening.

The mosquitoes were already out, and Jess swatted one on her arm. She flicked the body of the dead insect off and rubbed at the blood. "Yeah. Not for a while, though. I've been trying to get them to show up again, but nothing's happened since . . . since my dad died right after the holidays. My mom thinks I made everything up. She thinks it's my way of coping with his death, that everything I experienced can be explained some other way."

"I believe you," Allison said, taking a step off the front porch, apparently unfazed by the swarm of insects.

"I hate summers in the South." Jess swatted at another mosquito that had decided her legs made a safer target. "There's got to be millions of these little vampires."

"Run!" Allison darted across the lawn, leaving Jess to chase her.

Jess glanced behind her, seeing nothing but the hovering swarm of insects. She ran after Allison, following her down the length of the yard and around the house's corner, finally drawing up alongside her where she'd come to a complete stop.

"I don't think we outran the mosquitoes," Allison said.

Allison's observation was probably an understatement. But either they'd managed to outrun a few thousand or this side of the house had fewer hordes.

Jess waved away one of the bugs buzzing at her ear. "How come you're not being eaten alive?"

Allison shrugged. "Bad blood, I suppose."

Her voice sounded distant, far off. Jess stopped swatting her arms and legs long enough to see what Allison was staring at. It was a garden. Nothing like back home in Asheville, probably because the hot summer sun scorched the flowers here. Small plants with tiny red flowers, a white hibiscus, and several pots with ferns lined the garden pathway.

At the end of the path was a tall iron fence, complete with arched gate. Inside the gated section was a gravesite with an elaborate monument in the shape of two young girls, carved from marble in amazing lifelike detail. Both girls wore their hair long and loose across their shoulders, with bows at their temples. Both wore matching dresses and ankle-high, lace-up boots. At the base of the monument were more flowers, one sporting soft pink blossoms.

"Wow!" Jess said. "This has to be the most amazing gravesite I've ever seen. Come on."

Decorative, spear-like posts sat atop the iron fence. Jess pulled on the arched service gate, but it didn't budge. "Damn. It's locked."

"It keeps people like us out," Allison replied. "But *wow* is right. I wonder who they were? It's amazing! You can even see their boot laces."

Jess pointed to the base of the monument. "Emma and Grace Siler. April 3, 1899, died August 1909. Twins! But there's no actual date of death, only the month. Kind of weird, don't you think?"

"It's because they're still here." Allison tugged at Jess. "We made a mistake coming out here. We need to go. Now."

"What? We just got here."

"They're here," Allison said.

"I thought you don't see ghosts," Jess said, confused. If ghosts were present, she'd like to see them. She tried to imagine cute little girls with white dresses, each holding dolls or teddy bears. She scanned the area. Nothing.

"There, in the woods." Allison pointed to a section of trees a hundred or so yards from where they stood. "They want us to follow them."

A whitish, shadowy object moved behind a range of trees—or so Jess believed. It didn't look like a person, much less two girls, but she *had* seen something. Hadn't she? Adrenaline raced through her, but she tried to remain calm. Still, it might be the first step in finding her way back to seeing ghosts again. Maybe even Grams and Dad. Her pulse kicked up a beat.

... *Overactive imagination* ...

We're waiting for you, Jess.

The first voice she heard inside her head was her mother's, the second voice her own. Except, this time, the voice didn't *sound* entirely like hers. It almost sounded like a young girl.

Jess took a step toward the woods. "If you say someone's there, then let's follow them."

"No!" Allison pulled harder now, nearly toppling Jess backward. "Never mind. It was nothing. I . . . I was kidding. I do that sometimes—make stuff up. Please, Jess. Let's go. We'll be late for supper. Mrs. Hirsch will be mad."

Jess gave the woods one last look. Nothing moved. If she went to investigate she *would* be late. The mosquitoes were voracious and beads of sweat had begun to trickle down from her breasts to her stomach. "Yeah, sure. Let's go eat. Besides, I'm tired of being dinner for the insect population."

They reached the front porch and Jess opened the door, relieved they were going back inside and away from the hungry insects and humidity.

Allison stared up at the windows, just as Jess had done a short while ago. "It's like this house is watching us."

A thrill ran over Jess's skin. *Yes*, she thought. If any house could be a portal for talking with the dead, Siler House was it. Sure, her excitement contained an ounce or two of fear, but the way Jess saw things, it was like rock climbing or skydiving must be. A little fear and a little risk made life all that more adventurous.

"I suppose," she said to Allison. "But honestly? I don't think there's much to worry about. Trust me a little here, all right? I'm not sensing anything to be afraid of."

Allison was certainly uncomfortable here. If Jess were a glass half-full kind of person, then Allison would be the kind to imagine the glass half-empty, with the remainder tasteless, poisoned water. They stepped inside, and the cool air of the Great Room greeted them along with the enticing scent of food.

"The house has fooled you," Allison said. "It's fooled you into thinking it's something it's not."

"How do you know?" Jess asked, curious. "Have you seen anything here?"

"No—"

"Heard anything?" Jess asked, hoping that Allison had.

"No. I just know, that's all."

"Why don't you give the place a chance? Keep an open mind until something *does* happen?" Jess suggested.

The clock on the fireplace mantel told her they had barely enough time to get ready for dinner. Allison didn't reply to her question about the house as the two of them headed up the stairs. Jess liked Allison, she really did. But she wasn't giving this whole experiment a chance. *Could* bad spirits be roaming the halls at Siler House? Sure. But until someone could prove it, Jess decided to keep a positive attitude. Why was Allison even here if she didn't want to be part of this? Why couldn't Allison's family understand that rational or irrational, her fear was real? She hadn't asked Allison her age, but maybe she was underage and had been forced to come here.

"Sorry," Jess said sympathetically. "But I'm not getting the same vibes you are. I'm not uncomfortable here. In fact, to me, it's just the opposite—Siler House seems warm and inviting."

"It's in the walls and floorboards." Allison's expression became pinched with fear or deep concern—Jess couldn't figure out which. If she hadn't been so determined to keep an open mind, she would have found her words unsettling.

"It's everywhere," Allison whispered. "It's like Siler House is diseased."

CHAPTER FIVE

It wasn't the girls that Gage was keen on observing from the window in his room, although they proved to be a nice distraction. It was the damn graves that had him glued to the window—the ones behind the iron fence. He took a deep breath and forced himself to unclench his fists. His parents had known about those graves. Had to. It's why he was here and why this particular room had been chosen for him. They wanted him to have a good, long look. A constant reminder that his brother, Ben, was gone. A constant reminder of what he was expected to *do* during his stay here. The thought would have made most anyone else shudder. Hell, it should make *him* shudder. What they wanted from him wasn't normal. But then, *he* wasn't normal.

This was his last month before college started up again. His last few weekends of parties and days to sleep in. Why had he agreed to do this study at Siler House at all? It wasn't the money.

It was guilt. Even the late nights, girls, daredevil sports, and drinking couldn't erase it.

Gage recalled the night the men had come to their door. The night when he'd been asked to show them what he could do. And that, along with his parents' desperation, had landed him here.

Didn't they understand his brother was dead? Not just lifeless for the time being, but dead, as in never-coming-back dead? It wasn't Gage's fault. He'd tried to fix it. He'd tried to make it so his little brother could rejoin the living. It just hadn't worked. But his parents wouldn't let it go. Stalemate. What did they think? What did they *all* think? That the two small bodies buried in the cemetery a few hundred yards from the house were some sort of warm-up for bringing Ben back?

No. The men wanted something else, but what? They didn't give a rat's ass about Ben. Something was weird about them. They weren't simply men in suits. One was a lawyer. He had been easy to spot with his jargon and his contract. The other one might have been military, judging by the haircut and the stiff way the dude stood. Both had seemed a bit too serious for the task of signing a college student for a month's worth of paranormal research.

He loved his parents. He'd loved Ben, too. Hell, he still did. Why couldn't they let him put what happened behind him? He wasn't some sort of hero or corporation's science experiment. He was just another college sophomore. At least, that's all he wanted to be. But here he was—at an old, supposedly haunted estate as part of some fucked-up study on

the paranormal—along with a few other freaks with abilities. Except they didn't have a clue what this study was *really*
about. Then again, he wasn't positive he knew everything,
either. He had no proof. His dad said he was being paranoid.
Maybe he was. Or maybe not. But either way, Gage told
himself he'd find out soon enough.

The incident in the backyard with Ben's dog had been a
fluke. Maybe the dog wasn't really dead. Sure. Miracles happened all the time, right? But Ben wasn't a dog or a childhood
pet and his parents' desperation to bring back their youngest
son put the weight of the world on Gage's shoulders. It wasn't
fair. It wasn't *right*.

What to do, though? How to do right by them and be
the son they wanted him to be? He'd let them down before.
He hadn't always been completely reliable. He liked to hang
out with friends until all hours of the night. And he wasn't
exactly dependable boyfriend material, either. His choice in
girlfriends hadn't thrilled his mother in particular. But when
it came to helping his family, he hadn't been able to say no.
Even though he was hoping the experiment would prove to
them once and for all that he didn't have what it took. Not
anymore.

He was Gage. *Just* Gage. He wanted that to be good
enough.

And yet, he never stopped asking himself if he'd wasted
the last of his ability on Ben's dog instead of Ben himself.
He'd have to live with that the rest of his life.

"Checking out the girls, huh?" Bryan said as he joined
Gage at the window.

Gage didn't reply. He'd almost forgotten about the girls. They were talking now. The prettier of the two, a dark-haired girl wearing shorts, which showed off her long legs, and a T-shirt that clung to all the right places, pointed at the gravesite with its carved monument behind the iron fence. The second girl was a bit skinny, but still had a pretty face.

If you gotta be here, you might as well take in the sights, he thought.

He wondered if the girls were here because they wanted to be, or because, like him, they *had* to be. The dark-haired girl seemed more comfortable. More at ease.

"Jess," Bryan said as he stood beside him.

"Huh?"

Bryan laughed. "Dude, the girl you're checking out? Her name is Jess. In case a name matters. I don't know who the other one is yet."

Gage grinned. "Jess? Well, then *hello,* Jess. Hey, this might be a lot more interesting than we thought, right, bro?"

Bryan shrugged.

"What? You don't like the scenery?"

"The scenery is fine. Great even," Bryan replied. "Look, I'm just not like you."

"Meaning?"

Bryan tossed his hands up in a carefree motion and laughed easily. "No offense, all right? I mean, look at you, man. You clearly work out. A lot. Me? Not so much. The girls are fine. Definitely easy on the eyes. Especially Jess."

Gage liked Bryan. Guys like him were easygoing and laid back. Definitely calmer and less demanding than some of the guys back home. This was good. Right now, the less stress the better.

"*Meaning*," Bryan continued to clarify, "I probably move a little slower than you do. So go for it, man. Girls dig the six-pack thing. Besides, my mind is focused on the reason we're all here."

Gage sighed. He knew why *he* was here. His parents expected him to try to bring Ben back—as sick as that sounded. No pressure there. He turned his attention back to the window. Jess tugged at the hem of her shorts.

"I know about reality," he said. "But right now, I'm happy with the fantasy. Ghosts might not be the only spirits we raise around here."

The thin, blond-haired girl gave a frantic tug on Jess's arm. Gage raised an eyebrow. "Afraid of the dead and buried, are you, little sister? Well, I think you've got something there."

Bryan laughed. "If she's afraid of ghosts, then I think she's in the wrong experiment. Or maybe she's afraid of the perv staring out the window at her."

"I told you, I was looking out the window *before* they showed up," Gage explained. He had been. The girls just sort of wandered into view, easing his mind off his dead brother and the heartache he saw in his mother's face every day. There wasn't a day that he opened his eyes, or a night he closed them, that he didn't wonder why he hadn't been able to fix Ben. So, a little distraction? Something to help him forget about the pain for even a moment or two? Sure. He was all over it.

He studied the two girls. Blondie was harder to read, but if she *was* a believer, she didn't seem comfortable with it. Which meant she didn't want to be here.

Bryan glanced over Gage's shoulder, which was easy to do since he stood almost two inches taller. Gage had him pegged at probably six-two.

"The blonde doesn't want to be here, huh?" Bryan commented, unconsciously echoing Gage's thoughts. "Too bad."

"Well, then she and I have that much in common. Her roomie, Jess, seems right at home with it."

"I guess Jess is more like me," Bryan said, grinning and turning away from the window. "Maybe you don't have the edge after all."

Great. He had more in common with Blondie, and Bryan, who seemed like the kind of guy who brought flowers and opened doors, had more in common with Jess.

"Think you can run with the big dog?" Gage glanced over his shoulder and grinned. "Bring it on."

The girls' attention veered suddenly from the graves to a section of the woods. Gage squinted through the glass. He could almost hear Blondie now. Her voice was rising, and he thought he made out the word *please*, but not much else.

Blondie finally managed to pull Jess away, and the two girls disappeared from sight, leaving just the view of the graves again. Gage stared at the markers and the almost life-sized monument of the grave's occupants. He wasn't great at guessing little kids' ages, but the girls on the monument were probably somewhere around the age Ben had been when he died. The image of Ben's small coffin haunted him. He closed his eyes and heard his little brother's laughter as Gage helped him with his pitching arm on summer afternoons. Gage swallowed past the lump building in his throat.

This was one of the good days. Sometimes, he couldn't shake the image of Ben's face as he lay lifeless in the hospital. He opened his eyes again, wishing Jess was still outside, showing off those legs of hers.

"You gonna stare at her all day?" Bryan asked, as he opened a drawer and neatly arranged his clothes inside them.

"The girls are gone, bro. Relax."

Outside the room, the floors creaked, followed by a hard rap on the door.

"Dinner's on the table. Don't be lettin' it get cold." The voice belonged to Mrs. Hirsch, the head housekeeper or whatever she was. The woman looked constantly pissed off.

"They're calling us for dinner," Bryan said. "You coming or what?"

"Yeah. Be right there." Gage drew in a deep breath and took one last look at the monument and graves. He thought of Ben once more. *Sorry, bud. I tried. Really.*

CHAPTER SIX

"Diseased?" Jess stopped and turned midpoint on the stairs. Allison was crazy. Not crazy in a way Jess feared, but enough to make her rethink the roommate situation. Allison's eyes lacked the glassiness of medication. Instead, they were wide and very alert.

She's honestly afraid. Afraid! Of Siler House!

Jess ignored the small voice inside her that had its own reservations. A slight chill traced its way over the nape of her neck. No, this was nonsense. She was reacting to Allison's behavior and nothing more. It was a house, not a person. Not a spirit.

"I get it, Allison, and I'm really sorry you've had such bad experiences. But I didn't have that," Jess said, unsure of how else to handle the situation. "What would you have us do? Leave?"

"Yes! Leave! We should all leave. Right now. We shouldn't even pack."

Jess tried not to look surprised by Allison's outburst. "Why would we do that? I mean, I understand why you might—you're clearly afraid of ghosts and this house. But I've seen ghosts for years. Years! I've never had a problem with them. Ghosts *are* the reason I came here."

Jess had no doubt Allison's fear was genuine, but what was she supposed to do? Freak out because Allison's experiences had been awful while hers hadn't? Believe her about Siler House because she said so, even though it went against Jess's own intuition?

Of course, she hadn't been able to find any information on what had actually happened at Siler House. Had Allison been told something she hadn't? Maybe Allison was reacting to some terrible tragedy that had happened here. Rationally, a tragedy didn't necessarily mean the ghosts had to be bloodthirsty. Scary, needy, persistent, even annoying, maybe. Surely, if the place was as bad as Allison thought, Jess would have sensed *something*. She'd been able to sense when ghosts were in bad moods before, but so far she felt nothing but a sense of peacefulness at Siler House. Whatever lurked here, Jess needed to draw her *own* conclusions.

"Then maybe I'll just leave you here," Allison replied. "Leave all of you here."

"Dinner!" boomed a voice high above them, and both girls craned their heads back in an attempt to get a better view of who had spoken. "Do *not* be late."

"Mrs. Hirsch," Allison whispered, as the woman's shadow loomed large and wide on the stairwell wall. The housekeeper thundered toward them, her girth nearly filling the staircase, a large hoop with keys on it clenched in her thick hand, just as Allison had described. Mrs. Hirsch wore a button-up, baby blue dress and a white apron. Wiry, gray hair hung at shoulder length.

The girls slid over on the stairs to let her pass. Mrs. Hirsch didn't acknowledge them further, continuing methodically down the stairs, into the Great Room, and out of sight.

"I don't think we should be late. There's no telling what she'll do to us if we are," Allison said, seemingly forgetting that she'd been ready to leave. "Let's just follow her."

Jess nodded, feeling a bit better. Allison's rat-in-a-maze nervousness seemed more of a personality issue than a haunted house problem. The girl was afraid of everything, including Mrs. Hirsch. The head housekeeper was intimidating, but hardly scary.

They went down the stairs and through the Great Room, following the scent of food and sound of other voices.

"We weren't supposed to dress up or anything, were we?" Allison asked.

Jess shrugged. "I hope not, but it's too late now."

Dr. Brandt was already seated when they entered the dining room. Bryan was still standing, as though he had been waiting for them to arrive. He held out Jess and Allison's chairs.

On top of being cute, he was downright polite. Jess smiled up at him. "Thanks."

"You're welcome," Bryan replied as he walked past the new guy at the end of the table, offering him what seemed to be an apologetic shrug.

The new guy in the snug T-shirt, who Jess couldn't help but notice, leaned back in his chair. His eyes met Allison's, then hers. "Hello," he said with the faintest hint of a smile on his lips.

Allison seemed to blush, and Jess couldn't blame her. The new guy was hot, but extremely cocky. Jess looked away. No sense in stroking his ego any further. She was all too familiar with guys like him. Sexy, desirable. Until you got too close. She'd been burned by an ex just like him, although he hadn't been quite as hot as this guy. Which meant she'd be smart not to let those eyes and that perfect mouth distract her.

Once everyone was seated, Dr. Brandt tapped his knife against his water glass. "I thought we'd take a moment to introduce ourselves before we eat. Just give us your name and where you're from. Jess, why don't you start?"

Jess introduced herself, followed by Allison—who Jess learned was from Kentucky. Dr. Brandt's eyes cut to the end of the table and the new guy. He was still leaning back in his chair, still looking smug and tempting.

"Gage Jackson. Blairsville, Georgia," he offered.

Simple, to the point, Jess noticed. Right along with those hazel eyes and that totally kissable mouth . . .

Quit staring at him!

"Man," Bryan said in a low whisper from across the table. It made Jess frown. Clearly, the boys had some inside joke going on between them at her and Allison's expense. She'd been caught staring a second too long and Bryan had picked up on it.

Bryan's comment caught the attention of Dr. Brandt, who motioned for Bryan to go next.

He cleared his throat and straightened. "Bryan Akerman from Easley, South Carolina. Nice to meet everyone."

Dr. Brandt slid his chair back a little and all eyes turned toward him. Jess leaned forward, eager to learn exactly what they'd be doing here and how each of them had been selected.

Dr. Brandt situated his napkin in his lap. "As you know, I'm Dr. Gregory Brandt. I work as a parapsychologist at EPAC, a government-funded organization sponsoring this experiment. Each of you has been carefully chosen. And before any of you asks, yes, I honestly *do* believe in the paranormal. At least to an extent. Ghosts, mostly. Also, evil spirits and demons, but not werewolves or vampires—the sparkly kind or otherwise."

Jess and Bryan laughed. Gage smirked. Allison didn't seem to enjoy Dr. Brandt's attempt at humor.

"Which agency? Why is the government interested in us?" Gage asked.

"Why not?" Dr. Brandt replied. "The government funds a lot of studies, ranging from the effects of global warming to various health issues. Why not paranormal activities?"

"What branch of the government?" Gage asked again.

"Various ones, Gage. That's not important right now. EPAC, if anyone is wondering, stands for Experimental Paranormal Activity Coalition."

Bryan laughed. "Paranormal activity. Like the movie?"

"No. This is nothing like Hollywood," Dr. Brandt responded. "Speaking of funding, each of you agreed to the same compensation, so there's no need to discuss the amount. You'll be here for one month. We'll go over the history of Siler House and how it affects our experiment. As for the house itself, you're free to wander except for the few rooms that are locked, and after ten p.m. you should stay in your rooms unless we're all together conducting our experiments. Also, you'll be expected to join the rest of us for meals at the times specified in your paperwork. Please be on time. We wouldn't want Mrs. Hirsch to have to go looking for you."

This brought on a short bout of laughter between the boys.

"No doubt you've already met her," Dr. Brandt said. "The estate once belonged to her family, and she has recently taken on the position of overseeing Siler House. We will meet in the Great Room at eight-thirty every night. During your stay, I will be observing each of you. Also, as explained in your paperwork, there will be no television, no Internet, and phone calls are limited. You'll be allowed to make calls twice a week. You can return calls as needed, but no more than once a day. Tonight's agenda is to get to know one another better—including what brings each of you here. Then, we'll move on to the specifics."

"Dinner is served," Mrs. Hirsch said as she entered the room. "The cook has set up a buffet in the kitchen." She narrowed her eyes as she looked at everyone except Dr. Brandt. "You are expected to clean up after yourselves, as the cook has already left for the day. The entire staff has left. Except for me. I stay on full time. But I'm not your mother, so I don't clean up after you."

Her eyes shifted to each of them again, then she walked steadily out of the dining room.

"She's a charmer," Gage said as they made their way to the kitchen. "In a dour sort of way."

"More like Lizzy Borden," Bryan scoffed. "Maybe at night she carries an axe instead of a key ring."

Jess noticed that Dr. Brandt watched and listened, but did not join in their conversation. Part of the whole observation thing, she supposed.

"There are worse things here," Allison told them once they'd all loaded their plates, filled their glasses, and sat down to eat. The cook had prepared homemade Southern food at its best: fried chicken, buttery corn on the cob, sautéed green beans with onions, and biscuits—no pizza here.

"Is that so?" Gage asked. "So, what spooks you, Allison? Spiders? Mice? It can't be anything supernatural, right?"

A moment of silence went by as each of them waited for the other to speak, to say what they might be afraid of. Jess cut her eyes to Allison, who had apparently decided not to say another word.

Gage seemed to take the hint, so maybe he wasn't trying to be a jerk, after all. "Maybe we all need a history lesson or something, right, Doc? To put us in the mood."

"Perhaps after dinner," Dr. Brandt said, spreading preserves onto his biscuit. "We'll learn a little about Siler House every day. But before we begin, I'd like for us to talk about what brings us here, and what we think of Siler House thus far."

"It's haunted, right?" Jess asked.

"Tell us about the ghosts and how they got to *be* ghosts," Bryan chimed in.

"We could have a séance," Gage suggested. He winked at Jess. "Isn't that what we're supposed to do?"

Oh yeah, Jess thought. Gage was definitely the kind of guy who knew he was eye candy. She returned her focus to Dr. Brandt, who was avidly watching their interactions. It was beginning to unnerve Jess.

"Jess, why don't you start by telling us of your experience with ghosts? Enlighten Gage a little," Dr. Brandt finally said.

All eyes were on her, and her heart raced. She rested her fork against her plate, wondering where she should begin and why Dr. Brandt had selected her to go first.

It's now or never, Jess. Tell them and be done with it. They won't think you're crazy. They're all here for the same reason— because they had some sort of paranormal experience or ability.

"I see ghosts. Well, I *used* to, anyway. The first ghost was my grandmother." She fumbled with her fork. "A little after Grams, I started seeing more ghosts. In restaurants, hotels during family vacation, coffee shops. Almost everywhere. About two years ago, Grams stopped coming around. She said it wasn't a good idea anymore and that if she went away, maybe the others would stop showing up, too. But they didn't stop. Not until later. Like I said, they were everywhere. Then, my dad died at the beginning of the year. I thought he'd show up, too, but he didn't."

And that's when you had the breakdown. Tell them, Jess. Tell them you had the breakdown not because you saw ghosts, but be-cause you stopped seeing ghosts.

CHAPTER SEVEN

Jess felt her face heat. She'd wanted to hear everyone else's story. But she hadn't really thought about what it meant to share her own experiences and innermost thoughts. She hadn't realized it would make her feel so vulnerable.

It's best to leave off the part about Grams's warning, Jess. And it's best not to tell everyone that after years of seeing ghosts, you feel cheated because they all just stopped showing themselves, and now, you're obsessed with them. No one else is particularly happy about what they've experienced. Just you. For you, this study is one of the best things that's happened in years.

Everyone was patiently waiting on her.

What the hell. Just tell them. Tell them everything. Almost.

She stared down at her plate. "A few months after my dad died, the ghosts just stopped showing up."

"So, you can't see ghosts anymore?" Gage asked. "Then why are you here?"

Jess sucked in a deep breath. "Because I'm obsessed with them, okay?"

Because my psychiatrist knew a guy who knew a guy, and they paid me a hefty amount, that's why. I'm here because of my shrink. And the money. Let's not forget about that. What a way to pay for tuition.

"And I miss my dad," she added, trying to put the rambling thoughts in her head into some sort of perspective— some context she was willing to share. "He died of cancer. So, if this place is a conduit, I might get a chance to see him. Talk to him. And I hope the others will come back, too. That's why I'm here. A grief counselor helped me talk my mom and stepdad into it."

It surprised her how easily the white lie slipped from her lips. She waited for Dr. Brandt to correct her, to tell them all that a psychiatrist who dealt with people claiming to see or talk to the dead had suggested she come here, but he didn't.

More surprisingly, Gage didn't say another word. In fact, he nodded as though her explanation made sense.

"I'll go next," Bryan offered, setting down his drink. "My father disappeared. Just vanished."

"Your dad left you?" Allison asked softly. Jess suspected Allison was thinking of her own father—well, both of her parents, actually. Sadly, they'd both pretty much abandoned her.

"I wish," Bryan scoffed. "No, he . . . um, *disappeared*. He and Mom were fighting again. They always fought when he was drunk. He hit her like he sometimes did. I knew something was up when he came home that night. He looked worse than normal. Angrier, more drunk, and he had this

46

look in his eyes I can't explain. Murderous, I suppose. *Insane.*" Bryan's jaw tightened as he stared at the table.

He paused and swiped at his mouth as though brushing away the words he probably wanted to say. "A car door slammed in the driveway, which meant my sister was home from her date. She was an hour late and I knew she was going to be next. She's sixteen—almost two years younger than me. Dad had set her curfew at nine. Not that it mattered. Even when she came home on time, Dad would give her a hard time about stuff. It was worse if she had a date. He'd ask her all sorts of questions. Except they were more accusations than questions.

"Anyway, Dad stormed down the hall, ready to give her hell. I ran after him, hating him even more than usual and wishing he'd just go—that he'd leave us and *never* come back. I wished it with all my might."

Bryan tensed and the tendons in his neck began to stand out. "I'd had it, you know? I'd just reached my limit with him. I swore then that he'd *never* lay a hand on any of us again. *Never!* So, I grabbed a baseball bat I'd hidden in my room, and I ran downstairs."

He paused, cracking the knuckles of his left hand. He shifted his eyes down to the table again.

"He was screaming at my sister before she'd even walked in the door, threatening to teach her a lesson about coming home when she was told." Bryan gave a cynical laugh. "Like *he* didn't stay out until all hours, or not come home for days without an explanation. In fact, he'd get pissed if any of us asked where he'd been. Anyway, I had the bat in my hand when I got downstairs. But he wasn't in the living room like I'd expected. I thought maybe he'd gone out the front door after my sister. But when I got outside, he wasn't there either, and my sister was asking if I'd done something to him. I told her I hadn't."

Bryan raked a hand through his hair. "I was so sure he was hiding, waiting for us, but we searched the whole house— even the garage. His wallet and keys were still upstairs on the dresser. It was winter and he hadn't taken a coat. I swear, it was like I wished it and he was . . . *gone*."

"You're saying you made him disappear?" Gage asked. "As in *poof*, he's gone?"

"Yeah. That's *exactly* what I'm saying."

Gage rubbed his chin. "Is there any chance he just bailed, like you wished for? Maybe he saw you with the bat and left through another door?"

"If I hadn't made other things disappear before and after that, and if he hadn't left his wallet and keys behind, then yeah, I'd say you might be right," Bryan replied. "I can't control it, so don't ask how it works. For whatever reason, it just happens, and not all the time. Before that night, I'd made a bottle of his whiskey disappear. Got knocked around good for that one. He swore I'd hidden the bottle and he wanted it back. But mostly, it's been small stuff. Pens, books, shoes. I can't do it all the time, either. Sometimes nothing happens, no matter how hard I concentrate. And I'd never made a person disappear before, or since. I guess I'm here because the cops put what I said about him vanishing into thin air in their report and all. Somehow, this agency Dr. Brandt mentioned got hold of the report or something. No idea. But here I am."

Car keys, Jess thought, remembering the scene in the hallway when they'd first arrived.

All eyes turned to Gage.

Gage set his knife and fork down, and straightened. It looked like an attempt to appear more confident than actual arrogance. "My folks think I'm a necromancer," he said with a simple, matter-of-fact shrug. "They, um . . . think I can bring back the dead."

Jess's breath caught. Gage had everyone's attention, and why not? He had to be lying.

But what if he could? Could he bring back her father? Grams?

No one could bring back the dead. Still, who wouldn't want the chance to bring back someone they'd lost?

Dr. Brandt shifted in his chair, hanging on to Gage's words, probably aware that the rest of them thought he was psychotic, or at least lying. "Tell us what happened, Gage," he encouraged.

"Look. *I* don't think I'm some necromancer. I don't know what to think. I was only seven the first time I did it." He lowered his voice. "My pet, Leo."

"You brought back the family cat?" Jess asked.

"Not exactly," Gage admitted.

"So, you *didn't* resurrect him?" Allison clarified, confused.

"No. I mean, I *did*, but Leo wasn't a cat," Gage answered, looking a bit uncomfortable for the first time.

A grin crept across Jess's face. Good to know Hot Shot could be knocked down a few pegs.

"So, he was a dog, then?" Bryan pressed. Even he seemed to sense Gage's discomfort and was playing it to the hilt.

Gage coughed and spoke softly. "Hamster."

"A *hamster*?" Bryan repeated with a laugh. Jess had to refrain from joining Bryan, and even noticed that Allison had cracked a smile.

Bryan shook his head. "Sorry. I'm just picturing *you* with a hamster as a pet."

"Hey! I didn't buy him, okay? I was a kid," Gage said. "He was, well, he was sort of lying on his side, and I picked him up. My best friend Stu said I should give him CPR. So, I did. Not like I had a clue *how* to give CPR, but damn if it didn't work."

Bryan laughed openly. "CPR? On a *hamster*?"

Gage gave him a hard stare. "It was twelve years ago. Lay off me. I know my story sounds weird. Anyway, the next time, about a year ago, it was my brother's dog. Some wire-haired mixed breed that followed him home one day. Ben named him Max. About a month after that, Ben got real sick and the doctors diagnosed him with an aggressive form of brain cancer. I found Max dead in the backyard. Ben loved that dog. We swore my brother was only hanging on because of Max."

He paused and took a sip of his drink.

"Max was completely cold. Lifeless. I hated that my brother was dying, and now he'd just lost the one thing he loved most. I don't know why, but I remembered the thing with . . ."

"Your pet hamster?" Bryan added with a snicker.

"Are you going to let me finish?" Gage nearly shouted.

Bryan held up a hand in truce.

"So, I tried the same thing with Max, and at first, nothing happened," Gage went on. "Then, he just jerked awake, like he'd been in some deep sleep. Define irony, man. We still have Max. But Ben died four months later. Never came out of surgery. Damn dog still sleeps in his room."

"You tried to bring your brother back, didn't you?" Allison asked.

Gage looked like he wasn't going to answer.

"Go on," Dr. Brandt insisted. "It's important to tell everyone, Gage. This experiment depends on each of us—"

"Yeah. I tried," Gage interrupted, absently running a finger along the edge of his silverware. "Mom begged me to. How could I say no to that, right? Anyway, I would have tried to no matter what." He stopped fiddling with the silverware, but he still seemed to be in some other place in his memories. He shook his head. "I don't know what went wrong. Sometimes I wonder if I failed because I was afraid it wouldn't work on a person. Maybe I'm limited to resurrecting animals." He shrugged and gave a halfhearted smirk. "You're probably thinking I should have applied to a vet school, right?"

Everyone stayed quiet. No witty comebacks, no teasing.

"Maybe I was too emotional and didn't do it right." Gage briefly closed his eyes. "My parents blame *me* that he's still in the ground. They don't come out and say it, but they keep asking what went wrong. Yeah, like I even know how I'm able to do it at all, and they want to know what *happened*? Like I don't miss him, too. Once, my mother even asked what I had against Ben—that she loved us both. So, I sort of blame myself, too. I'm here because they think I can change what happened."

"Have you ever read 'The Monkey's Paw'?" Allison's voice had taken on that calm, almost trance-like tone again. "Even if you could bring him back, he's been in a casket for a long time. You do know what you'd be getting back, don't you?"

Bryan shook his head, his former playful expression nowhere in sight. "Allison's right. Your brother would be a zombie, dude."

"Or worse," Allison said, still in that odd, detached tone. "You shouldn't call upon the dead. None of us should."

Jess glanced down at her plate. She'd assumed everyone just saw ghosts. She hadn't expected this. The smallest prickle of fear crawled along her nape. She brushed at it, smoothing the hair against her neck.

"Allison, how about if we hear your story next," Dr. Brandt said.

Allison sat for a few minutes, quiet. Dr. Brandt didn't force her like he had Gage, and Jess didn't think she was going to say anything at all. Finally, Allison blinked and took a deep breath, apparently no longer in whatever state of disconnect she'd been in. "I wish ghosts were the only things I had experienced. And I wish I could make things disappear like you, Bryan." Her eyes darted to Gage. "I'm sorry for your curse. All of you, really. You're cursed. We all are."

Bryan frowned.

"My family is afraid of me. They're afraid they'll come back, or that it'll happen again," Allison said softly.

"What will happen again? What is your family afraid of?" Dr. Brandt encouraged. He seemed eager now, watching Allison with an intensity Jess found a bit creepy. It was as though she were some prized find under a microscope.

Allison shifted uneasily in her seat. "Demons. They're afraid the demons will come back."

Evil spirits. So *this* was what Allison had been talking about. Jess could see why her roommate might shy away from anything paranormal. Ghosts were one thing, but demons? Jess nearly shivered. Yeah, she could see where Allison might be freaked out about that.

"Demons?" Bryan asked. "You mean as in possession?"

Allison shrugged. "I guess. Evil spirits. Whatever. It was like they were crawling around under my skin. Then, it was like *I* was the one crawling around under my own skin, and *they'd* taken over. They're everywhere, you know—the demons. You read about them in the papers all the time. Murderers, mostly."

No one dared to ridicule Allison. It was on their faces— her story fascinated them. Jess was glad that all she saw were harmless ghosts. Allison's story about the demons made *her* skin want to crawl.

"Are they still with you?" Dr. Brandt asked.

Allison scratched at her forearm. "Not at the moment. They've been gone for months. But once they've been let in, they can come back. They said so. They know how to find you."

CHAPTER EIGHT

When they had finished dinner, Dr. Brandt scooted his chair back. "Let's clean up, and then we'll talk about Siler House and how its history makes us feel."

Feel? Jess already knew how Allison felt. And, with what she'd said about the demons, probably so did everyone else.

"I get what you're doing," Allison said to Dr. Brandt. "You're playing with our imaginations. But you're stirring things up that you shouldn't."

Take your own advice, Jess thought. *You're the one stirring things up over emotion alone. No one else seems half as freaked out about being here as you.*

"Do you think spirits read our emotions?" Dr. Brandt asked.

"One year, our attic was infested with rats," Allison said. "We had someone come out to get rid of them."

"Rats? You're comparing ghosts to rats?" Jess asked.

"Are you telling us you've got some ghost phobia thing going on?" Bryan asked. "Man, that sucks since you're part of an experiment *with* ghosts. You do realize that's why we're all here, right?"

Jess nodded. Maybe if she cleared up a few things about ghosts—at least what she knew of them—Allison might relax. "You do know ghosts are supposed to be disembodied, right? It's not like they can do anything to physically harm you."

"You don't know that!" Allison threw her napkin on the table. "Just because it's never happened to you!"

Ouch! Jess thought. She was just trying to help. She didn't mean for Allison to rip her head off.

"Easy, ladies," Dr. Brandt interrupted. "I'm certain we'll all be fine here. There's nothing to worry about."

Jess tensed. Why did she feel so uneasy about his response?

"Let me get this straight," Gage said. "We all know we've been brought here as part of a study on the paranormal. Jess communicates with the dead. Allison has demons on speed dial. My buddy Bryan here sends stuff to the Twilight Zone without return postage. And I've got a knack for making my own zombie zoo theme park. Fun times. To add to all this *fun*, we're actually sitting here talking about how we feel about a house?"

"We're merely going over the history and legend of Siler House, both of which suggest that it has an effect on those who stay here." Dr. Brandt got to his feet. "There's a lot to cover, so let's get this cleaned up, shall we?"

Kitchen detail didn't take long with the five of them. While Dr. Brandt opened drawers and cabinets looking for the right place to put things away, Jess and Allison washed the last of the dishes that didn't fit into the dishwasher while Gage and Bryan dried them.

Overhead, floorboards creaked, as though someone was pacing on the floor above them. Allison rubbed her arms.

"It's probably Mrs. Hirsch," Bryan said. "She likes to walk the halls a lot."

Allison nodded, hesitantly.

"Well, everything here is reasonably tidy," Dr. Brandt announced at last. "Why don't we go into the Great Room and continue our conversation?"

Dr. Brandt and Gage left, leaving Jess and Bryan with Allison. Allison continued to stare upward, oblivious when Bryan flicked the lights a few times. "Come on! Wouldn't want to be late for campfire stories."

"Allison," Jess coaxed. When Allison didn't budge, Jess grabbed her by the arm and pulled her from the kitchen, flicking the lights off a final time as they left.

Whatever hang-up Allison had with Mrs. Hirsch, she had gotten past it by the time they settled onto the sofa nearest the unlit fireplace. The boys took up the other two chairs, and Dr. Brandt moved another nearby chair closer to them.

"Before we dive into the history lesson I'd like everyone's impression of the house," Dr. Brandt said.

"It's old," Gage said. "It's just an old house."

"Nothing else?" Dr. Brandt asked, jotting stuff down in a notebook, making Jess feel more and more like a lab rat. Writing down their responses and actions made this discussion seem like a therapy session. Been there. Done that. Nearly had the straitjacket.

You're in my office because your family worries about you, Jess. Tell me. Why do you think you can see ghosts?

"No," Gage replied with a laugh. "It's *just* a house, man."

Jess noted that so far, neither Dr. Brandt nor Gage thought Siler House was evil. Only Allison.

"And you?" Dr. Brandt asked Allison.

"Why ask me?" Allison wanted to know. "I already *told* you. I hate this place."

"Are you upset that you're here because of what's going on with you and your family—the disagreements?" Dr. Brandt crossed his legs.

"It's because this *place* scares me," Allison replied.

He resumed writing in his notepad. "And why does it scare you, Allison?"

"Because it's . . . can't *anyone* else here feel it? Can't *any* of you?" She pulled her feet up under her as though something might be lurking beneath the couch.

Gage and Bryan both shook their heads, indicating they felt nothing unusual.

Yep, it's only Allison. No one else feels what she does.

"How about you, Jess? Do you think there's something wrong with Siler House?" Dr. Brandt asked.

All eyes were on her.

Ghosts aren't real, Jess. You're in what is called denial. I'm going to help you with that.

Jess pushed her former psychiatrist's words aside. Ghosts *were* real. But a house wasn't a ghost. As much as she'd like to believe Siler House had a soul, deep down, she agreed with Gage. It was a house. She hated to admit that, but what were the alternatives? Say that she *wanted* to think of Siler House as a person? Allison would feed off every word as though they were proof.

"No," she replied. "It's a great old house. It's settled. I think it has history, is all. Maybe something paranormal exists here. I hope so. But I don't feel anything weird. I don't sense anything bad. If anything, I'd say the house has . . . *personality.*"

Gage laughed, and the grin on his face looked playful. "Why do girls assign human characteristics to things?"

Jess folded her arms in mock annoyance. "You mean like cars?"

He grinned. "Touché."

Dr. Brandt kept writing. "What do you think of Siler House, Bryan?"

He shrugged. "I dunno. I'm with Jess and Gage, I guess. It's old and big, and sort of drafty in places, and the floorboards creak, but I don't feel anything weird here, either. Why all the interest in how we feel about this place?"

"I hope we're not supposed to group hug after this," Gage quietly commented to Bryan.

Dr. Brandt wrote for a moment more before laying the pen on the notebook. "It's been rumored that Siler House is haunted in a way no other house is."

Gage and Bryan exchanged dubious glances.

"How's that?" Bryan asked. "You said the house has an effect on people?"

Dr. Brandt smiled faintly, and Jess didn't like it. It wasn't a stretch that he knew more than they did. She didn't like the way he wasn't sharing that information.

"It's rumored that Siler House has a way of getting to people," Dr. Brandt explained. "Supposedly, those who stay here for too long . . . change."

Gage cocked his head and stared at Dr. Brandt. Jess couldn't have agreed more with his skepticism. "Like how?"

"He *means*," Allison said, "that this place gets under your skin. You begin to crave it."

Bryan raised his eyebrows. "You mean like a drug?"

Dr. Brandt nodded. "Something like that. An addiction of sorts. I'm not sure how it works, exactly, except that those who've experienced things here tend to stay, regardless of how frightened they become. Regardless of how much they tell themselves they want to leave."

Allison turned her head to stare at Jess as if saying *I told you so.*

Hearsay, Jess thought. Although the idea fascinated her, she preferred to make the call for herself. What raised her suspicions at the moment was that Dr. Brandt might trick them into some group psychosis, fueled by Allison's fear of Siler House. If the legend had any truth to it, and Siler House had some power of its own, she'd see evidence of it soon enough. What did Grams always say? *Believe nothing you hear and half of what you see?* Was it possible? Sure, and Jess hadn't gone all skeptic, believing in only ghosts and nothing else. It was more like she wanted to experience Siler House and everything in it for herself, in her own way. Not secondhand. It'd be like going on vacation and everyone telling you everything about a place before you saw it yourself. Still, a house with a soul or presence might be pretty cool.

Or really scary.

Dr. Brandt set his pen and pad aside. "Okay. Short history lesson, as promised. Siler House was built in 1904 by banker Jonathan William Siler for his wife, Catherine, and their two young daughters, Gracie and Emma. The house has three aboveground floors, four if you want to count the attic, which the Silers converted to a dance studio and music room for their daughters. Mrs. Siler loved ballet and piano. Siler House has thirty-five rooms, ten of which are now bedrooms. There's a basement, which is mostly storage space and a pantry. The stairs to the basement are through the kitchen. There's the main staircase connecting the three top floors, and another separate staircase from the third floor to the attic. All told, Siler House is over twenty-two thousand square feet, including the basement, and sits on almost thirty acres. The estate sat deserted for years, and only recently has anyone decided to renovate it, mostly because the descendants of the Silers refused to refurbish it, live in it, or even sell it. That changed when there wasn't money enough left to continue paying the taxes. The last living heir to the Siler estate finally agreed to sell last year—Mrs. Hirsch. But the event, the reason we're all here, happened in August of 1909. It was the week before the start of the fall hunting season."

Jess nudged Allison. "The graves!"

Dr. Brandt smiled. "I see you've been exploring. Gracie and Emma were murdered when they were ten years old.

Their bodies were found in a clearing in the woods by hunters the following week."

"Did they find out who killed them?" Allison asked.

Dr. Brandt nodded. "Oh, yes! They did."

"Did the parents do it?" Gage asked. "One of the servants?"

"No," Dr. Brandt replied. "The parents were very kind, very loving. They doted on their daughters. Nothing was too good for them, as Jess and Allison can attest. Their graves are remarkable."

"So, the house has been sitting empty for about a hundred years?" Bryan asked. "Seems like a waste."

"It's what the family felt best at the time," Dr. Brandt said.

"Just because of a couple of murders?" Bryan asked, shaking his head in disbelief.

Allison rubbed her arms again. "See? The house got to them, didn't it?"

"Enough!" Jess nearly shouted. "Would you stop it? You don't actually know that's true!"

Gage exchanged a glance with Bryan as though he thought the girls might break into a fight. Jess glared at him.

"Relax, okay?" Gage said. "Don't get so uptight about it."

Allison withdrew, balling herself up and continuing to rub her arms.

"I'm sorry," Jess repeated, more quietly this time. "I didn't mean to yell. But Siler House didn't kill Gracie and Emma and dump them into the woods. As much as I believe in the supernatural, that's impossible. It had to be someone close to the family, or some random stranger. Maybe the killer was someone tied to Mr. Siler's business?"

Allison looked away from Jess.

Great. Now she'd done it. But what else could she do? Allison wasn't dealing with the facts, just emotions. If she weren't careful, they would consume her. Jess wasn't ready to admit that she had her own observations about being watched when she'd first arrived—as though the house really *was* alive in some odd way. In all honesty, though, if something had been watching her, Jess was more inclined to believe that it had been a ghost who hadn't wanted to show himself yet. Gage was right; anything else would be assigning human characteristics to an inanimate object.

"As it happens, however, Allison *is* correct," Dr. Brandt said. "The house did get to the Siler girls. It got to them all in one way or another, or so the legend goes. But the question remains, is the legend metaphorical or literal? Does Siler House have a way of putting people under its spell? Is such a thing possible? And, will any of you think the deaths here had anything to do with the paranormal? Or did the Siler family merely experience a string of bad luck?"

CHAPTER NINE

The first night with Allison had been nearly impossible. Jess awoke on more than one occasion to find her roommate sitting upright in bed, rocking back and forth. Trying to ignore her, Jess turned over and faced the window. Sleeping in a strange place the first few nights bothered most everyone, she figured. Hotels were the worst because of the noise from elevators, doors, and neighbors in close proximity. Jess put old houses right up there on the same list. But Siler House was a good distance from noisy highways and the sounds of city life. The chirp of crickets and chorus of bullfrogs in a nearby marsh had filled the night, and eventually lulled her to sleep.

It was only when the crickets and frogs stopped that she awoke. She blinked, trying to adjust her eyes to the dark. She turned back over, expecting Allison to be either still sitting up, or asleep. But her bed was empty and Allison stood in front of the dresser, hands at her sides, staring at the mirror. Alarmed, Jess sat upright.

"It's happening again," Allison said.

"Huh?"

"The spirits. They're back. I can see them."

Jess rubbed her eyes as a spark of uncertainty and a moment's worth of fear rustled somewhere deep inside her. "They're there, in the *mirror*?"

"Yes."

Jess got out of bed and tentatively stood next to Allison. She looked at the mirror, then behind her. Nothing. Uncertainty gave way to disappointment. The mirror cast back only the shadowy figures of Allison and herself, their faces made pale by the moonlight streaming into the room. They were alone, as far as Jess could tell.

Damn it! Why couldn't *she* see the ghosts? Were they here? Disappointment gave way to a pang of envy.

"You don't seem as upset as you were before," Jess said. "If they're back, aren't you afraid they'll take over? Possess you?" She wasn't making fun of Allison. Something horrible *had* happened to her, and she was probably more sensitive to the supernatural than Jess was.

"Yes, I'm afraid," Allison replied calmly.

The way Allison spoke seemed at odds with her words. The hairs on Jess's arms tingled, but not because of any ghosts she couldn't see. Right now, the only thing creepy in the room was Allison. The girl had been possessed, after all.

Allison turned her head to look at Jess, her expression unreadable in the shadows, even this close up. "He collects souls."

Jess peered harder into the mirror, trying not to show Allison she was indeed afraid. "He? Who are you talking about?"

"He's looking at you. I can't make out what he's saying. But see?" she pointed to the mirror. "He wrote his name."

Fear and a healthy dose of agitation rose inside Jess. Fear, because someone staring at them from inside a mirror was downright scary. Agitated, because she couldn't see anything, and Allison's continual freak-outs were wearing on her. After a long day getting here, she was exhausted and just wanted to sleep.

"Allison, I don't see anything! He? *Who* are you talking about?"

"*Riley,*" Allison whispered.

"Riley? Who's Riley?"

Allison stood just as still as she had upon Jess's wakening. "He lives here. With the others."

"Others?" Jess stepped closer to the mirror, leaning against the dresser to get a better look. Her breath fogged it enough to reveal a single name, written backward: Riley.

Jess's heart and feet leapt in unison. "Oh my God! Oh my God!"

"See? I told you," Allison said, still speaking in the same monotone voice.

Jess gulped in a breath and approached the dresser again, her heart still hammering in her chest. Shadows shifted eerily inside the mirror, but Jess told herself it was just the light refracting off the angular ceiling. She leaned even closer. She had to be sure. *Wanted* to be sure. The name was there, but she hadn't actually seen anyone write it. Allison had been standing in front of the mirror before Jess woke up. What if she'd written the name herself?

What if she hadn't?

Ghosts can't hurt you. They've never hurt you—or anyone you know of, Jess tried to reassure herself.

"Hello?" Jess whispered. She squinted, bringing her face closer to the glass, trying to seek out any movement, any form deep within the mirror.

Allison grabbed her arm and jerked her backward.

"Allison! Ow!"

"Ignore him, Jess. Don't talk to him. Don't talk to any of them. It just makes them stronger. We'll have to tell Gage and Bryan not to talk to them, either."

Jess opened her mouth to say Allison was scaring her again, but snapped it shut. If there were ghosts here and Allison wanted to be afraid of them, fine. Not her. Not *yet*, anyway. A name in the mirror didn't mean the ghost was evil.

"Allison, did you write that?"

Allison reached up and wiped at the name with her fingers. The name didn't smudge. "If I had, don't you think I'd be able to erase it?"

"Oh my God," Jess repeated. She paced in front of the mirror, rationalizing this out. "Okay, so a ghost wrote his name on the mirror. That doesn't necessarily mean he's evil."

"But he is," Allison said. She still hadn't budged an inch.

"Then maybe it's a demon. Did the demons follow you here?" Jess asked. The thought of demons in their room *did* scare her.

"No," Allison answered.

That was a huge relief. So Allison had only seen a ghost. One that tried to communicate with her and startled her. "Did he hurt you?"

"No."

"Threaten you?" Jess asked.

"No."

Jess resumed pacing. Allison had no real *proof* the ghost meant anyone harm. She couldn't make out everything Riley said. She'd said so herself.

She didn't doubt Allison had seen a ghost, just that she knew for certain it was evil. Allison was quick to freak out, quick to judge without good reason. Understandable, given her history, but no one else, not Jess, and neither Bryan nor Gage, had felt anything inside the house yet—especially anything bad. Weren't they also sensitive to the paranormal?

"I don't mean to sound bitchy, but why is it just you, Allison? Help me understand. Why are you the only one who thinks something is wrong here? How come the rest of us don't sense anything in the house is evil?"

"I *told you*," Allison said. "It's fooled you. It's fooled you all."

Jess took another look into the mirror. No ghosts. No one named Riley stared back at them. She wished she could see what Allison did. Maybe then she could help her with her fears.

"Allison?"

"Yes?"

"Is it possible that you're afraid of Siler House and ghosts because you've had such a bad experience? I mean, demons . . . that's worse than anything I can imagine."

Allison didn't respond. Maybe Jess was getting somewhere. "Ghosts are spooky," she continued. "I get that. They pop into and out of a room so quickly and so quietly. Sometimes they shimmer, or flicker. Sometimes they stand there and stare without saying a single word. I'd call that scary if I didn't know better—if I hadn't come across them as often as I have. I've seen hundreds! And not one of them ever threatened or hurt me. And ghosts aren't the same as demons, right?"

"I don't know," Allison said, still staring into the mirror. "Until now, I'd never seen a ghost. We need to warn the others. Gage. Bryan. Dr. Brandt. Even Mrs. Hirsch."

Jess nodded slowly. "Fine. We'll tell them what you saw, okay?" They'd tell the others, all right. And if Allison's behavior got any stranger, she'd insist on her own room. Jess was exhausted and if it wasn't already so late, she'd find another room right now. If Allison saw a ghost, Jess believed her. But Allison wasn't listening. Jess *wanted* to see ghosts again—no, she *needed* to see them, even if Allison didn't. It was the first step in a process of closure for Jess that Allison would never understand. But it wasn't just Allison. No one seemed to understand how important this was to her.

"Sorry. Go back to sleep." Allison turned away from the mirror at last, and crawled back into her bed. "I think he's gone now, but I'll stay up and watch for him. If you want."

"No," Jess said. "We should *both* go back to sleep. If you say he's gone, then he's gone. We'll tell Dr. Brandt about it first thing in the morning. Will we be okay until then?"

The odd, trance-like state Allison had been in was finally gone. "You think I'm crazy, don't you?"

Jess struggled for the right words, but came up short. It had been a long day. Her brain couldn't rationalize anything right now except sleep. And she was worried that there might truly be something wrong with her roommate.

Like there's not something wrong with all of us, Jess thought.

Allison laughed. "I wouldn't believe me, either. The girl who sees malevolent spirits in mirrors." She turned to face Jess. "I'm sorry about grabbing you so hard. I don't want you to be afraid of *me*. But we've got something in common, don't we? We've both been to a psychiatrist. You're like *me*, Jess. People think we imagine things. They may not say it out loud, but they think we're crazy, you and me both."

Jess wanted to disagree, to say that seeing ghosts or whatever didn't necessarily make them crazy. But she couldn't, because Jess *had* felt that her parents and everyone else who knew about it *did* think she was crazy.

She communicated with ghosts, or at least, used to. Allison had demons on speed dial. Bryan sent stuff (and people) to the Twilight Zone, and Gage reanimated the dead. Yeah. To most people, they had a lot of crazy in common. What if this whole experiment was about them, and how madness sets in? How people begin to hallucinate, see things others didn't? Claim that things happened that never did?

70

Allison's eyes were pleading now, and her voice began to quiver. "Everyone is *always* afraid of me. Please don't be scared of me, Jess. You're all I have here. You're the only person who can understand."

CHAPTER TEN

Morning came a bit too bright and early. Jess glanced at the alarm clock. It was close to seven-thirty. Breakfast wasn't until nine. Allison was still sound asleep. Jess slid out of bed, dressed as quietly as possible, and padded across the room, thankful none of the floorboards creaked. She opened the door, again relieved it didn't make a sound. Oddly, it'd had a slight squeak to it the day before, but Jess passed it off as the door expanding and contracting with the temperature. She stood in the hallway, listening to the sounds of the house. She imagined it breathing, stirring awake along with the birds and the wind. Of course, that was ridiculous. Siler House was wood, brick, and stone. Not blood, bone, or soul. Just like she'd said last night.

It was definitely time to do some exploring. Dr. Brandt had said they were free to roam. Some of the rooms would be locked, he'd told them. But any room *unlocked* was hers to check out.

Jess walked across the hall to the room opposite hers. The doorknob turned easily in her hand, and she pushed the door open enough to see inside. Sheets blanketed a roomful of furniture, making it look like some ghostly convention. Dark yellow-gold paint covered the walls. Heavy brocade curtains hung at the windows. Jess stepped inside and gently closed the door behind her, taking in the musty smell of the stored furniture. Making her way around the room, she pulled aside the sheet draped over a tall piece of furniture and found a floor-length mirror. It was old and the glass pitted and dark. She stared at it for a moment, examining it, curious and scared at the same time.

"Riley?" she said softly, not surprised when no one answered. She'd let her imagination run the show again.

She let the sheet slide back over the mirror as she walked to the window. The curtains made most of the room impenetrable to the morning light. She pushed one of the panels aside, although it took some effort. The material was dense and heavy. Jess squinted against the light that spilled onto her face. As she did, she swore someone shrieked. The sound was faint, but it had come from within the room, she was sure of it. She spun, looking for whoever might have entered—a maid, perhaps. Even Allison. But she was alone. The light from the window had momentarily hurt her eyes, but now she noticed the sunlight did little to chase away the dark shadows resting in the corners.

"The house, I suppose," she said. The thought both pleased and set her senses on edge. It sounded like something Allison would come up with.

It'll be our secret.

The voice was in her head, but it wasn't hers. It sounded younger.

Her mother's words echoed in her head. *Admit that ghosts don't exist . . .*

But Jess wanted there to be someone here. There had to be. Just had to.

"Who's here?" she whispered. "Are you a ghost? Riley?"

Why she'd said Riley instead of Emma or Gracie, she didn't know. She wasn't even sure who Riley was, except that Allison had said Riley was a boy, not a girl. Dr. Brandt hadn't mentioned that the Silers had a son.

She waited a minute or two for a reply, but none came. Jess left the room, careful to close the door behind her.

"No one goes in there!" Mrs. Hirsch announced loudly. She stormed toward Jess, mouth pinched.

"Sorry," Jess said. "I didn't touch anything."

Mrs. Hirsch narrowed her eyes and stared at Jess as though searching for a lie.

"It wasn't locked," Jess explained.

Cold gray eyes glared at her. "Bobby pin? Sewing needle? What do you have? I locked this door myself."

"Neither. Nothing. It wasn't locked."

Mrs. Hirsch opened the door. "Didn't touch nothing, did ya?" She pushed past Jess and into the room. She thundered to where the mirror stood. The sheet covering it had somehow slipped off onto the floor. Mrs. Hirsch threw the sheet back over the mirror and turned to Jess. "You're messing with things you shouldn't."

"The mirror?" Jess asked. Cold pooled in her stomach as she recalled how Allison had sworn she'd seen someone in the dresser mirror. "What's wrong with it?"

"It ain't yours to be messin' with is what's wrong with it! What's wrong with *you*, girl? Ain't you got the common sense not to be touchin' stuff that don't belong to ya?" She turned to Jess, hands planted firmly on her hips and a scowl on her face. "Well, what the blazes are you waitin' for? Scat."

Jess turned and ran back across the hall to her room, leaving Mrs. Hirsch behind.

Allison was now awake and dressed. "Hey," she said, offering a thin smile. "I was looking for you. I thought you might be downstairs, but you weren't. Just the guys and Dr. Brandt. You went exploring without me."

"Yeah, well, Mrs. Hirsch ended that," Jess replied, leaning against the door.

"She's weird. She freaks me out," Allison said. "I think we should go downstairs."

"Allison, *everything* freaks you out."

"The guys want to go exploring outside today," Allison said, ignoring the dig. "Not sure what there is to do, but maybe we should tag along." She grabbed a hair clip from the dresser and swept her hair up into it. "I heard one of the maids say that it's going to be in the nineties today."

"Good thing for cool showers. I hate summers," Jess replied.

"Come on. You can shower after breakfast. Let's get out of here before Mrs. Hirsch decides to check up on us."

Jess couldn't agree more.

* * *

Dr. Brandt was already at the table, just as Allison said he would be, drinking coffee and going over more of his notes. "Morning!" he called out cheerily. "Fresh coffee in the kitchen. Bagels and pastries as well."

The girls went into the kitchen and grabbed cheese Danishes from the buffet. Allison poured a glass of juice, while Jess made a cup of coffee.

"That stuff isn't good for you," Allison said, motioning to Jess's cup. "I read it somewhere."

"Yeah, well, *I'm* not good without it," Jess kidded as they left the kitchen.

"I suppose you'll want to hear about our first night here," Allison said to Dr. Brandt. She unfolded her silverware from the cloth napkin.

"From each of you, yes," he replied. "But I think we should wait until Bryan and Gage join us. Gage went to shower and Bryan stepped out onto the front porch to return a phone call. I'm sure they'll be here soon. If not, I'll send Mrs. Hirsch to look in on them."

Jess grimaced.

"Is there a problem, Jess?" he asked.

"No. Not really, just that I've already seen Mrs. Hirsch. She doesn't seem very cheerful today."

"She's not so bad," Dr. Brandt said. "She just takes her responsibilities seriously."

"Dr. Brandt," Allison interrupted. "Have you ever heard anything about mirrors and the paranormal?"

"Do you mean about breaking mirrors and bad luck?"

She shook her head. "No. Not breaking them. About seeing things in them."

He eyed her for a moment. "Superstition has it that to look into a mirror is to see your own soul. It explains why, in folklore, vampires cannot see their own reflections. In Greek mythology, reflections can foretell the future. In some cultures, when someone dies, all the mirrors in the house must be covered to prevent the soul from being trapped behind the glass. Then, there are some who believe mirrors are portals into the world of souls. Some people have sworn they've seen the image of a dead person in a mirror; others claim they've seen evil spirits. And finally, according to a few demonologists, demons, being the vain creatures they are, sometimes like to see their own reflections. Does that help?"

Jess nearly spilled her coffee. Last night, Allison had stood in front of the mirror, staring into it. Given her history, or at least her story about possession, she couldn't help but wonder exactly what Allison had been looking for. The demon she believed had once taken her over? Had it followed her?

"Yes, thanks, that does help," Allison replied calmly and took a bite of her Danish.

Dr. Brandt set his pen down. "Did you see something in a mirror, Allison?"

Allison didn't appear as though she wanted to answer. She chewed on her breakfast and then chased it down with juice.

"Allison? What did you see?" Dr. Brandt pressed.

"Riley," Allison replied matter-of-factly.

He blinked and fumbled with his coffee mug. "How do you know about Riley?"

"Who is Riley?" Jess asked Dr. Brandt. She turned to Allison. "A demon? Is he the one who possessed you?"

"No," Allison replied. "I don't speak his name."

"Bael," Dr. Brandt said as he continued to stare at Allison. "A demon commanding sixty-six legions. He's the one who possessed Allison."

"Don't say it!" Allison slammed her hand on the table, rattling the dishes. "Don't call him."

"My apologies," Dr. Brandt replied. He picked up his pen and began writing.

Jess looked from one to the other, not sure which direction she wanted to go—whether she should try to get more information on the demon Allison wouldn't talk about or learn what she could about Riley—the boy in the mirror Allison also wouldn't talk about. But maybe Dr. Brandt would.

"So, who is Riley, Dr. Brandt?" Jess asked.

He removed a small voice recorder from his pocket and placed it on the table. He pressed a button and a red light flickered on. "Tell us about Riley, Allison."

"I thought we were going to wait for Gage and Bryan," Allison replied.

"It's okay. Just tell us about Riley."

She sighed. "He lives here. There are others here, too. He trapped them and now they can't leave." She turned to Jess. "You can't help them, Jess. The souls Riley has kept here are his now. It's too late for them."

"It's too late for whom?" Dr. Brandt asked.

"The others. And the girls. He killed them. Riley told me." She took another bite of her pastry.

"You could have *researched* that much," Dr. Brandt said.

Jess took a thoughtful sip of her coffee. Allison hadn't told her Riley was a murderer. A small shiver danced along her spine. She thought of the two girls, their souls held captive by some evil being. They were the same age as her sister, Lily!

If I find a way to talk to ghosts again, maybe I can help them.

Jess didn't have any ideas on just how she'd do that, or even why the thought occurred to her. The idea of helping the girls escape their murderer made her uneasy, but if they'd been trapped this long and no one else had helped them, Jess figured she and the others were the girls' best hope.

"Did he tell you how he killed them?" Dr. Brandt asked.

"No," Allison said. "I didn't want to know. At first, I was afraid he was a demon, because he looks that way. He doesn't look entirely human anymore."

"Why didn't you tell me he'd killed them?" Jess asked.

Allison laughed, but it was more cynical than humorous. "I didn't want to scare you more than you already were. Don't look at me that way! I know what you think of me. All you've ever seen are normal ghosts. I see the kind like Riley. Once you're touched by darkness, it follows you. No matter where you go."

Careful what you let in, Jess . . .

The chill spread from her spine down her arms as she remembered Grams's warning, but Jess shoved the thought aside. She wouldn't let Allison spook her. Fear was paralyzing, and Jess refused to let Allison's fears keep her from the very reason she was here—to break down whatever barrier was keeping her from seeing ghosts on the other side. But the ghost of a murderer was enough to make her a bit more cautious.

Maybe Dr. Brandt knew of some way to banish evil spirits. He was an expert in the field, after all. Surely he knew how.

What was she doing? Considering going up against something she couldn't see? A demon or something else? Jess was barely starting to learn to take care of herself, make her own way, and now she was considering how to get rid of an evil spirit?

She'd had the thought before—that she was holding on to this whole ghost thing as a way to believe that death didn't really matter. That Grams and her father were still with her and always would be. It was a way of holding on to the past as though nothing had happened—that Grams hadn't died. That her parents hadn't divorced. That her father hadn't died, either.

That life wasn't moving too fast.

You want ghosts, but what you need is something real to hold on to.

Jess shook the thoughts from her head. Ghosts *were* real. So was the past. She wasn't ready to set those memories aside just yet.

Baby steps. Stick to the plan. See if I can talk to ghosts again and prove I'm not going mad. Get my college fund back. THEN go to college and get a normal life. Whatever that is.

"Allison? Did Riley follow you here?" Jess asked.

"Oh no, he's been here a long time," Allison replied. "And before that, he wasn't Riley. Although that's what he calls himself."

"Go on," Dr. Brandt encouraged.

"There are others here," Allison said, moving the discussion away from Riley.

She had mentioned this before, but her tone unnerved Jess. Even if Allison managed to hold it together long enough to help her find and talk to the girls, even if she found some way to help them find their way out of Siler House, what scared her most was *not* the ghosts of the girls or anyone else. Dr. Brandt kept asking Allison whom she was talking about, but Jess began to wonder if maybe it was more of a *what* than a who.

The guys had entered the room while Allison was talking, but Dr. Brandt had motioned for them to keep quiet. They each took a seat and listened, too.

"Allison, who was he before he became Riley?"

"A demon," she said.

"Which demon, Allison?"

Allison began to tear her paper napkin into tiny pieces. "They don't like to give up their real names, and bad things happen when you try to force them. People die."

CHAPTER ELEVEN

Gage took a seat quietly, as Dr. Brandt had motioned for him and Bryan to do. Allison was at it again. Demons. Evil spirits. The girl needed to let off the crazy pedal. Okay, so they *all* had some sort of experience and, as he saw it, had time to come to grips with it before they'd come here. It wasn't like they'd all been invited here for a picnic.

Sure, it was a bit freaky. But if Allison didn't chill, she'd soon find herself on the fast track to the funny farm. He'd hate to see that happen.

Jess sat at the table a bit too stiffly. Gage offered her what he hoped was a reassuring smile. He could see Allison's nervousness was wearing on her. In fact, the whole topic of Siler House had begun to cause a rift between the two girls. It didn't take a genius to figure it out. Jess loved Siler House— so much so that Gage sometimes thought she and the house could use some alone time. It was the way she looked at everything, the way she studied it and touched the furniture and art. It was even in the way she listened so intently when Dr. Brandt talked about the place.

In contrast, Allison hated the house. Feared it. Even said it had done bad things. And *that* was a bucket full of crazy.

Gage had come to grips with the fact that there probably were ghosts, as well as ways to make weird shit happen—like make stuff vanish or . . . reanimate things that had been alive. But a house was just a house. Just walls and floors and a roof. It didn't have a soul or a spirit. It had never been alive and therefore, couldn't die and haunt people. Maybe Allison meant the house was haunted as in *ghosts* were haunting the house.

He and Bryan listened as Dr. Brandt quickly filled them in on what happened last night. Ghosts in mirrors? That was some weird, freaky shit.

"If Riley is some sort of demon or evil spirit, do you think he's hurting them? The girls and the other ghosts?" Jess asked.

"They're dead, Jess. If they're really ghosts, they're not feeling anything," Gage pointed out softly.

She glared at him, which definitely wasn't the response he'd hoped for. So much for trying the reassurance route.

Bryan rubbed his chin. "Maybe we could talk to them. Find out if they're in any sort of danger from Riley."

Jess's pretty eyes lit up in Bryan's direction.

Grrrreat! Leave it to Bryan to say exactly what Jess wanted. And the doc just sat quietly, scribbling down notes and watching everyone's interactions like a hawk. Gage didn't trust Dr. Brandt. Of course, he didn't trust this whole experiment, but until he checked out what Brandt was writing, he didn't have any real proof. Yet. First step, see what buttons to push.

"Wait . . ." Gage said. "How do we know any of this is true?" He glanced at Dr. Brandt. "You said you wanted to see how we'd respond to what you *say* is a haunted house. We don't actually know the house is haunted. Yet."

Dr. Brandt set down his pen. "And what do you think is happening here, Gage?"

Gage didn't want to say that *maybe* Brandt was setting them up to look like the Scooby Gang meets the Ghostbusters. "I don't know! Group psychosis? You get all of us to start joining in—seeing what Allison says she sees. So far, I haven't seen a thing. I haven't felt a single thing."

Allison slammed her hand on the table and glared at him. "I am NOT lying!"

"She's got a point. Just because *we* haven't seen any ghosts doesn't mean they aren't here," Jess chimed in.

"Whoa!" Gage leaned back and extended his palms outward. "I wasn't saying there couldn't *be* any ghosts. It's just that only Allison has seen one so far. And this Riley dude was inside a mirror. In the dark, in the middle of the night. Jess didn't see him, right? So, don't you think that *maybe* just maybe at least one more of us should see something first? Especially Jess. She's like the Ghost Wrangler or whatever. Has anyone else seen, heard, or sensed *anything* since we've been here?"

"Fine." Allison crossed her arms tightly. "The house is haunted when *you* say it is, jackass."

Jess and Dr. Brandt sat silently. Bryan was busy covering up a smirk. Gage sighed. He'd hoped to get a rise out of Brandt, not everyone else, and least of all, Jess.

Riiight. He was the jackass. They were all supposed to take Allison in Freaking Wonderland's word that the house is twin to the hotel in The Shining *because she said so.*

Jess stared at him, daring him to say something. Gage held his tongue. He'd have to give in until he found something in Brandt's room. It wasn't that he didn't believe the house wasn't haunted, he only knew Brandt wasn't telling them everything. If he could prove there was something weird going on with the study, then maybe his folks would also give up on bringing Ben back. Maybe then they could accept his death.

"What about those ghost-hunting devices?" Bryan asked. "Do you have any of those?"

"Yeah," Gage added, motioning to Bryan. "What he said."

"Yes," Dr. Brandt said. "And we'll be using those tools starting today. First, let's finish up with the history of Siler House, shall we?" He motioned to the kitchen. "Why don't you and Bryan grab some breakfast before I begin?"

Bryan and Gage nodded and headed for the kitchen.

"So, there really was some kid named Riley?" Gage asked on his way out of the dining room. "You're not messing with us?"

"I'm not messing with you," Dr. Brandt replied.

Dr. Brandt busied himself with more notes. Gage tried to see what he was jotting down, but without standing over the dude's shoulder, he couldn't read dick.

Gage grabbed a plate of food and returned, immediately digging into his plate of scrambled eggs and bacon. Dr. Brandt stopped writing and pushed his chair back. He took a final sip of his coffee, which had to be cold by now, but he didn't seem to mind.

"Riley was their nephew," Dr. Brandt said. "In 1906, the Silers took him in. The boy had suffered seizures and delusions for years. Doctors claimed he was mentally disturbed. Even at a young age, Riley talked to people no one else could see. When his parents asked who these people were, Riley became sullen, angry, even growling and striking out. He rarely demonstrated affection, unless he found himself in trouble. His mother often made excuses for him when members of the staff found dead farm animals on the property. Since her son had a *medical condition*, as she called it, he didn't understand his own strength, or right from wrong. She believed he hadn't meant to kill any of the animals and insisted some of the livestock deaths were purely coincidence. Riley never showed any remorse or guilt for his actions."

"How could the Silers ever let him around their children?" Jess asked. "At least, without someone around to watch?"

Dr. Brandt raised a hand. "I'm getting to that. When Riley was thirteen, his father tried to kill him. This is where stories differ. Some think Riley killed his mother. When his father found out what Riley had done, he went to fetch his shotgun, then shot Riley. Without his family, some think he turned the gun on himself. Catherine Siler didn't believe this. She thought a superstitious farmhand shot the whole family after Riley complained of strange creatures that came to visit him in his room at night. On more than one occasion, Riley said the creatures sat at the breakfast table with the family. At any rate, Riley survived. Catherine wouldn't let her sister's only child go to an orphanage. Jonathan Siler agreed, but with conditions. The Silers hired a woman to watch after all three children, but Emma and Gracie were her first priority. Jonathan Siler gave the staff strict orders to keep an eye on Riley and not to let him out of their sight. And, for a while, that worked. At least for three years, no harm came to the girls."

"Why do I get the feeling that wasn't true for everyone else?" Bryan said.

Dr. Brandt gave a nod of agreement. "The first death was ruled a suicide. A pastor who came to say blessings over the house. He didn't die here, though. He was found hanged in his own church."

"That's awful," Jess said. "What happened? Was there an exorcism?"

Allison inhaled sharply and her eyes darted from Bryan and Gage to Jess, and then to Dr. Brandt. "I don't think I want to hear any more right now."

"Not at first," Dr. Brandt went on, ignoring her. "Not until after the servants started to complain of cold spots and doors opening or closing on their own. One reported hearing Riley talking to someone, but found the boy alone, sitting on the floor facing his opened armoire. She swore that its doors slammed shut right after she'd entered the room.

"Other occurrences made the hired help nervous, too, like a large amount of dead sparrows in close proximity to the house, and dead, shriveled plants that had been vibrant and alive the day before. Riley often sat on the stairwell and stared at the maids as they cleaned. They'd order him outside to play, but that also meant one of them had to go with him to ensure the girls' safety. Since none of them wanted to be alone with the boy, even outside, they let him stay."

Dr. Brandt paused for a sip of his coffee. He had Jess and Bryan's full attention, Gage noticed. Allison stared at the floor. Only when Dr. Brandt paused did she steal a glance in his direction, waiting for him to go on with the story.

Dr. Brandt obliged and sat his coffee cup down. "A few of them became so nervous around the boy, they became accident prone. One of the maids fell from a ladder while cleaning a chandelier and broke her neck. Later on, another maid swore Riley had locked her in a room while she was cleaning, although no one had actually seen Riley near the room at the time. A cook quit after he cut off a finger while making dinner. The boy had come into the kitchen asking for a snack at the time of the accident."

"Finger food?" Gage scoffed.

Jess winced and Allison began to rock in her chair in seeming discomfort, but Dr. Brandt didn't notice. "Then, Riley began to have seizures. They terrified everyone who witnessed them. He sometimes spoke in strange voices, foaming at the mouth and twisting in ways that should have broken a few bones. Finally, the Silers talked about having Riley sent to a hospital that could more easily care for him. That's when the seizures stopped. Almost everything stopped. The accidents, the odd voices. But the cold spots didn't stop, nor did the reports of doors opening and closing on their own, or the occasional sound of footsteps in empty hallways during the night. For whatever reason, most of the staff stayed on despite these reports. No one quit or talked of leaving. That is, until 1909, when Gracie and Emma were murdered."

Allison leapt from her chair. "I said I don't want to hear this!" She turned and fled from the room.

Jess shot Dr. Brandt a harsh glare, although she'd seemed as interested as everyone else in learning what had happened. Again, Dr. Brandt didn't pay her much attention.

"Allison!" Jess called out before running after her.

Bryan seemed ready to go follow the girls.

"It's a girl thing. I suppose," Gage offered. "Let them talk it out."

Bryan seemed unsure. "You think so?"

"Hell if I know, but sure. I just know I wouldn't get up and run after *you*, bro." Gage grinned. "If you didn't want to listen to the story because it freaked you out, don't look to me to hold your hand." Although Gage wanted nothing more than to go after Jess, to make sure *she* was okay.

The corners of Bryan's mouth twitched. "You're such a jerk, man. But do you think one of us needs to see if they're okay?"

"Only if you wanna be one of the girls." Gage gave him a cockeyed smirk. Bryan laughed and settled back into his seat.

"Do you think we could take a look at some of the equipment?" Bryan asked. "Might as well, since the history lesson is on hold, right?"

Dr. Brandt stood. "Let me refresh my coffee. Anyone else?"

Gage and Bryan shook their heads.

"I'm good," Bryan replied.

"Hey," Gage called to Brandt. "Let's pick up where you left off. So, the girls died in 1909. Then what?"

"That's when a lot of people died," Dr. Brandt replied as he returned from the kitchen. "It just started with Gracie and Emma."

CHAPTER TWELVE

Jess found Allison in their room, sitting on her bed, knees tucked against her chest as she rocked back and forth.

"Allison, it's okay," Jess said quietly as she sat next to her.

"I want to go home," Allison cried.

"Can you call your parents or your aunt to come get you?" Jess asked, knowing they weren't likely to answer Allison's call, much less come and get her. Not if the incident yesterday was any indicator.

"No one will come get me," Allison said, sniffling. "They all wish I'd go away. Or that Dr. Brandt will tell them I'm nuts enough to go to the psych ward again. They'd all prefer to have me locked up until I'm eighteen, at least. Then, they can force me to stay away from them. They wouldn't have long—just another few months. I think it's why they're happy I'm here. It's one less month they have to deal with me."

Jess patted Allison's back. She wanted to say her parents wouldn't send her away, but she didn't think Allison had lied about her family.

"I'll talk to Dr. Brandt. Tell him you need more time—"

"I don't need more *time*. I need to get out of here. But I can't." Allison swiped at her tears.

"I'm sorry," Jess said. "But if this place scares you so much, maybe if I talked to Dr. Brandt—"

"No! I can't leave because if I do, you'll all die. They'll kill you." Her eyes met Jess's. "They want to, you know." She began to laugh. "It's doing it. The house."

Jess frowned. "Doing what?"

"Keeping us here, that's what!" Allison said. "It's started already. I found Dr. Brandt sitting in the Great Room this morning. He kept staring at the picture above the fireplace. He told me Siler House was the most incredible, most beautiful house he'd ever been in. Don't you find that weird? He's been all objective and scientific, but suddenly, he's infatuated with the beauty of the place?"

Jess withdrew her hand. Allison had seriously lost it, and her behavior scared Jess more than anything Dr. Brandt had said about the murders or Riley. Yeah, it was odd to see a man so infatuated with a house—but that didn't mean the house was doing anything to him. And his behavior wasn't exactly alarming. Maybe old homes were his thing. It was Allison who made her feel uncomfortable. She'd have to talk to Dr. Brandt about the sleeping arrangements.

"I'm *not* crazy!" Allison insisted as though reading Jess's mind. "He's in there," she said as she motioned toward the mirror. "He's in *all* of them. You *know*, Jess. Deep inside you know what I'm telling you is true. But you doubt yourself. You know we're being watched. The house is plotting against us."

"I don't see anyone," Jess said, feeling a bit unsure. Was someone watching them? Or was she letting Allison get to her again? Why couldn't *she* see them? "Allison, you have to stop doing this."

"Stop doing what, Jess? Scaring you? Don't you see how frightened *I* am? I'm staying for *you*, Jess. You and the others. I'm the only one who understands what we're up against. I've done enough . . . *bad* things that maybe before I die I can set them right." She took a tissue from the nightstand and wiped her nose. "If you believe in ghosts, then why don't you believe what I tell you?"

What could she say? Allison had a point. Still, her weirdness and insistence that everything was demonic and out to get them didn't sit well with Jess, especially since Allison had said she was staying for her? For Gage and Bryan, and Dr. Brandt, too? And what bad things had she done? That bit of information wasn't exactly helping her see Allison's cause. Maybe if she stayed calm. Maybe if she tried some logic, her roommate would relax a little.

"Allison, *please*. Understand that not all of us are afraid. We haven't gone through what you have."

Allison laughed again and pressed her hands into her face in frustration. "Oh, I suppose all ghosts are perfectly harmless!"

"I'm not saying they're *all* perfectly harmless! It's . . . it's just that I've never had *your* experience," Jess said in as calming a tone as possible. "Why don't you tell me about the ghost who hurt you?" Jess couldn't help but think she sounded like a shrink. But she had to calm Allison down.

"I've never seen one of *your* ghosts," Allison said. "I told you, I don't see ghosts!"

"Just evil spirits, like demons?" Jess asked. In her experience, all ghosts were like her grandmother and the others. Not like the demons Allison had encountered.

Careful what you let in, Jess.

"They're evil! *All* of them! Every. Single. One. Ugh! *Why* won't you believe me?" Allison wailed.

"Because I don't think every ghost out there *is* evil!" Jess shot back.

Allison stared at her like she had three heads. "Sure, Jess. Whatever." She got off the bed, shoulders slumped. "I'm going to take a shower. Then I guess we'd better start planning out what we're going to do."

"Good idea," Jess replied, although she wasn't sure what Allison had in mind as far as plans went. Or what she was actually going to plan for.

Allison set her clothes on the bed and headed to the bathroom. Jess waited until she heard the shower start before collecting her own set of clean clothes and toiletry bag. Since there were more guest rooms, she thought she'd take advantage of one of their bathrooms and take a shower, as well. That way, they'd be ready for whatever Dr. Brandt had scheduled for the rest of the day—if anything. She hoped to finish and head downstairs to talk to him without Allison. It also gave her the chance to scope out a possible new room for her to stay in. Right or wrong, Allison's emotional outbursts were exhausting.

A few of the doors were locked, including the room Mrs. Hirsch had caught her in. Eventually, Jess found an available room down the hall from hers and Allison's. The room faced the back lawn and Jess had a clear view of Gracie and Emma's gravesite. Jess locked the door behind her and set her clean clothes on the corner of the bed, stripped down, and headed for the shower.

The bathroom was smaller than the one she and Allison shared, and although the window shades were closed, Jess peeked outside to make sure the back lawn was void of voyeurs. Not that anyone would be able to see up to the third floor and through a shuttered window, but still . . .

It felt as though she wasn't alone. "Hey! Some privacy, please?" she called out in case any ghosts happened to be around.

She turned on the water and stepped into the shower.

Once showered and feeling clean again, she towel-dried her hair. If a ghost had been in the bathroom with her, they'd gone somewhere else.

. . . *your imagination. Your misplaced imagination* . . .

Allison had mentioned Riley being in all the mirrors. Jess pushed that disturbing little thought from her mind.

She gasped when she stepped into the bedroom. Her clothes lay in a heap on the floor as though someone had snatched them off the bed and thrown them there. Allison. She was clearly still upset.

Jess glanced around the room. Empty. Clutching the towel around her, she checked the door. Still locked.

"Hello?" she tentatively called out, uncertainty beginning to pool in her stomach.

No response.

Harmless. Ghosts were harmless. They couldn't touch people much less throw things around. It had never happened before. It had to be Mrs. Hirsch. Jess gathered her things from the floor, considered the mirror for a moment, then hurried back to the bathroom to fetch another towel and threw it over the mirror. She dressed quickly, putting on her underwear and bra, then throwing her T-shirt on and sliding the pair of shorts over her hips as quickly as possible. The idea of a ghost in the room didn't frighten her as much as one seeing her naked. She hadn't thought about how weird that would be until now. Okay, so maybe she was a little afraid. But that had been Allison's influence.

After she collected her things, she opened the door and stepped quickly into the hallway, half expecting to find Mrs. Hirsch waiting for her, but it was empty. She padded toward the room she shared with Allison, and entered. No Allison.

"Allison?" she called out. She checked the bathroom. No Allison there, either. She must have already gone downstairs without her. Jess turned and walked back into their room.

"You shouldn't be here," said the little girl standing in front of the dresser.

Startled, Jess took an involuntary step back. She thought she'd be used to the way ghosts appeared and disappeared by now, but she wasn't. Probably would never get used to it. The girl wore a pretty white dress and black shoes. The dress was tied around the middle with a red bow that matched the one in her curly, dark hair.

She's a ghost. She's the ghost of either Gracie or Emma Siler, Jess thought, aware of her quickening heartbeat. Finally! Her first ghost sighting in months! The girl looked young and sweet, so why did she feel so jumpy? Probably because her roommate would have her believe the small girl sporting dimples and curls was Satan in disguise.

Damn you, Allison!

Her face didn't look anything like Jess would have expected of a child who had been murdered. The girl's complexion was healthy, with a glow like that of a living ten-year-old. Not one who had been dead for well over a hundred years. But ghosts were like that—appearing how they wanted you to see them, or so she believed. Or, maybe it was how they saw themselves. Jess had never thought to ask.

She could still see ghosts, which meant there was hope—hope of seeing Grams again and her father, too! Jess's unease began to fade.

The girl waited patiently for her to do or say something.

"Hello," Jess said softly.

"Hi," the girl replied.

"I'm Jess. Are you Emma or Gracie?"

The girl smiled. "I know who *you* are. I'm Gracie."

Jess tried to keep the remaining nervousness from her voice. "Thanks for letting me see you, Gracie. I like ghosts."

Gracie's smile faltered. "You're still a little scared. I can tell. Are you here to hurt us? To make us go away?"

97

Ghost or not, Gracie's words melted Jess. Hurt her? Never. Jess knelt down in front of Gracie. She reached out for Gracie's arm, realizing she couldn't actually touch the child—the gesture was simply automatic. Gracie stepped back, her arms still at her sides.

She thinks I'm going to hurt her, Jess thought. "No, Gracie. I'd never hurt you. In fact, I'm here to help you."

"You're very kind," Gracie said, looking down at her shoes.

"I try to be," Jess replied.

Gracie's head jerked toward the mirror, then back to Jess, her eyes wide. "I have to go now. You should go, too."

"Is someone there, Gracie?"

She nodded.

"Who's there? Is it Emma?" Somehow, she didn't think it was Emma at all.

Gracie frowned. "It's Riley. He says I can't talk anymore right now."

Jess stood and looked in the mirror. Once again, she saw nothing but her reflection and oddly, Gracie's, in the old mirror. Unease seeped back into Jess's skin.

"I'll help you, Gracie. You and Emma. I promise," Jess said, although she had no idea how to do that yet. She turned back to the child, but Gracie was gone.

Slowly, as if a child were writing it from the other side of the mirror, the word *hurry* appeared. And underneath, *we need you.*

CHAPTER THIRTEEN

"I believe you," Bryan said, looking up at her from the sofa. "Do you want me to take a look, or do you think we should tell Dr. Brandt first?"

Jess looked around the Great Room. Neither Gage nor Dr. Brandt was there. Fleetingly, she wondered where Gage was. What did it matter, anyway?

Bryan grinned. "I don't think you've got anything to worry about, Jess."

She frowned. "You mean about the mirror? The ghosts? Yeah, I tried telling Allison—"

Bryan laughed. "No, I mean about Allison and Gage."

"I wasn't worried—"

"Look, I'm not blind. I see the way you look at him."

Jess eyed Bryan, unsure of what to say. She hadn't meant to be so obvious. But Bryan was mistaken. There wasn't anything between them. "It's not like that. Honest."

Bryan let out a small laugh. "Yeah, model-perfect dude is sort of a jerk, so I can understand if you'd prefer someone like me."

"*What?*"

"I'm kidding. Sort of. I'm not that much younger than you. What? A few months?"

Jess stared blankly. This was awkward.

Bryan sighed and slowly shook his head. "Look, he's been checking you out, too, if that makes you feel any better."

Butterflies somersaulted in her stomach. This wasn't the conversation she'd come down here for. She'd hoped to find everyone here, together. But truth be told, she *had* been disappointed not to see Gage.

Bryan got up from the couch. "So, back to your ghost spotting. Like I said, I believe you. What do you want to do about it? Dr. Brandt is walking through the house, somewhere. He's been wandering around the past couple of hours. It's like he's doing some home inventory thing. That, or he's just really into the place."

"Really?" Jess said, recalling what Allison had told her about Dr. Brandt's weird obsession with the house.

He shrugged. "I think he's somewhere here on the first floor in one of the locked rooms."

"Okay," Jess said. "Dr. Brandt really should see this."

"*I'll* tell him," Mrs. Hirsch said as she came into view. Keys in one hand, she fumbled with some pendant around her neck. Jess couldn't make out what the object was—just that it looked like it was made of dark metal. "I don't need the other of you two sneaking off someplace."

100

Other of you two?

"We'll be in Allison and Jess's room," Bryan said. He grabbed Jess by the wrist and headed to the stairway.

Mrs. Hirsch frowned, but Jess didn't wait to hear her reply. She allowed Bryan to tug her up the stairs, trying not to think about Allison and Gage taking off together.

"Where did she come from?" Jess asked.

"Kitchen. Basement. Somewhere from that direction," Bryan said, still holding on to Jess. "I don't know, but it's like she's always going through the house. I don't think she trusts us."

"I guess," Jess replied.

"Don't sweat it. Allison isn't his type. She just said she needed to show him something."

They'd reached the third-floor landing when Bryan finally released her.

"Right," Jess replied.

"I'm serious," he said as they walked down the hall. "She had her phone with her. I think she took it from Dr. Brandt's room. At least, that's the direction she came from—our rooms."

Bryan paused when they reached Jess's room.

"Why Gage?" Jess asked. "She seemed pretty pissed at him when he didn't believe her earlier."

"I think she wanted to prove him wrong. Allison is a bit touchy, or I would have asked to see it, too. But I know Gage will fill me in later. And Jess?"

She looked up at him.

"This thing you've got for Gage? I'm serious. The dude's got it for you, too."

Jess laughed. "You're telling me to go for it?"

He shoved his hands in his pockets. "Yeah, I guess I am. Only if you wanted to, of course."

Jess felt herself blush. "Well, let's go back to the ghost for now, okay?"

Bryan nodded toward the room. "Want me to go in first? Check the mirror out?"

She shook her head. "I'm not afraid, but sure, go ahead."

He opened the door slowly and took a look around. Jess followed him into the room. They stood side by side in front of the mirror.

"Where did you see the message?" he asked.

"Right here." Jess leaned forward and breathed on the mirror. It fogged up, but revealed nothing.

"I swear, it was right there!" She stepped back, blinking. "It was *right* here!" The floorboard creaked outside the room.

"What is it? What happened?" Allison asked, entering with Gage.

"Writing," Jess said, trying not to look at either Bryan or Gage. She didn't need to see Bryan's expression to tell he was probably smirking.

"Like the other night?" Allison asked.

Jess nodded. "Except one of the girls wrote it. Gracie was here. We talked for a few minutes and then she said Riley wouldn't let her stay anymore. Next thing I knew, she was gone and the writing appeared on the mirror, like she was writing it from the other side."

"How about using some of that fancy equipment?" Gage suggested. "Like an EMF reader or whatever. Maybe it'll pick up on something." He gave Jess a gorgeous half-smile.

Was Gage saying he believed her, or that he didn't? It sounded as though he was giving her the benefit of the doubt. At this point, she didn't think he actually doubted her, anyway. If he'd been a jerk before, it was probably just because he was trying to establish some weird power-play, testosterone thing. Guys sometimes did that. She tried not to think about what Bryan had told her about Gage. She tried not to think about what his lips would feel like against hers. "Yeah, the equipment. Good idea."

"I like it," Bryan said. "This looks like the perfect opportunity to get my geek on."

Dr. Brandt set a box on the Great Room's coffee table. He took out three devices, handing one to Jess and the other to Gage, keeping one for himself. "One per team. Sorry, you'll need to share. These are EMF meters, also known as electromagnetic field detectors. Not only will they give us readings, but they also have alarms."

"So, if there's a particular threshold and we're, say . . . in the dark, it'll let us know?" Bryan asked.

"Exactly," Dr. Brandt replied. "Better, the display is backlit so even if you are in the dark, you can see what the reading is."

He pulled a few more devices from the box. "For each of you, there's a flashlight, a digital thermometer, and voice recorder. And we also have a full-spectrum video camcorder that allows us to film in the dark."

"Cool," Gage said, hand extended. "Do you mind?"

Dr. Brandt handed the device to him. "Pass it around."

The guys spent a few minutes going over the equipment before handing it to Jess. She had no real idea what she was looking at, aside from the camcorder itself, which seemed like any other handheld video camera. "You mean this works in the dark?"

Dr. Brandt nodded. "Yes. It does. Well, we could've added an IR booster, but this should suffice for our purposes. And, it still gives us some light to see by."

"What else have you got?" Gage wanted to know.

Until now, Jess hadn't noticed how quiet Allison had been. She was staring at the box on the table. "No," Allison said. "You shouldn't have brought that here."

Dr. Brandt gave her a puzzled look. "Brought what, Allison? Do you know what's in the box?"

Allison nodded. "It's either Tarot cards or a Ouija board."

"You can't possibly know that," Jess said. "Can you?"

Allison gave a disinterested shrug. "It's all pretty standard stuff, actually."

"But it's not standard," Dr. Brandt said. "At least, not exactly." He pulled out a Ouija board. It was old, the oldest Jess had ever seen. Not that she had seen that many, but this one wasn't plastic, small, or glowing. There were creepy people illustrated in the lower corners, each one appearing to be using the board.

"It's an antique," Dr. Brandt explained.

"Is it as old as the house?" Jess asked.

He smiled. "No, not quite. This board is from the early forties. It's the oldest I could track down." He reached back into the box and withdrew a wooden object with a point on one end. Jess recognized the device as the piece that spelled out the answers. Except this pointing device, also wood instead of plastic, had a hole toward the pointer itself, along with the Ouija logo stamped on it. For some odd reason, that silver dollar–sized hole made the object more menacing.

"Now *this*," Dr. Brandt exclaimed, "*this* is the planchette from the Ouija board first used in the 1910 séance here at Siler House. A maid destroyed the original board. She burned it in the fireplace."

"What happened to her?" Allison asked.

Dr. Brandt frowned. "What do you mean?"

"She's dead, isn't she?"

"Well, *probably*," Gage said. "1910? I don't think the Ouija board was her personal fountain of youth."

"Don't be such a dick," Bryan said. "This is cool stuff. Listen."

"Kidding, dude," Gage said, sounding somewhat sincere. "But seriously? All this equipment is a lot cooler. The full-spectrum camera, the EMF meter. This . . ." He touched the Ouija board, spinning it on the table. "This is old school. It's Hasbro, man."

"Actually," Dr. Brandt corrected, "this one was made by the William Fuld Company, which made the boards from 1890 until 1966."

Gage laughed. "Sixty-six?"

"True story," Dr. Brandt said. "As for what happened to Ms. Evans, the chambermaid, she fell down the stairs. The fall broke her neck."

"You puttin' us on?" Gage asked.

"No," he said. "But keep in mind that people fell down stairs and broke their necks or died of head injuries without ever having to touch, much less set flame to, a Ouija board, Gage. You just have to ask yourself if you think the house, the spirits . . ." He observed the planchette for a moment before setting it down directly over the word GOOD-BYE, and Jess could see the letter Y through the hole in the planchette. ". . . or if the board had any part in her demise."

"You're saying this was used here?" Jess asked. "After the girls' deaths?"

Dr. Brandt nodded. "Yes. Several times. Catherine Siler swore her dead daughters first started talking to her through the Ouija board."

"Portals," Allison said, drawing her legs under herself. "The last time I touched one . . ." She shook her head. "Keep it away from me. I won't. You can't make me."

There she went again. If Jess weren't inclined to believe her, she'd think Allison really was as crazy as she appeared.

"That's fine," Dr. Brandt replied to Allison. "Perfectly understandable. You won't have to. You're welcome to watch, of course. Although I think it's highly unlikely your experience had anything to do with the Ouija board."

Gage frowned. "What is she talking about?" He turned to Allison. "What about the Ouija board, Allison?"

"Wrong," Allison said. "That's *exactly* how the demon found me." She lowered her head, glaring at Dr. Brandt as though the two of them shared some intimate knowledge. "You don't want to use that board in Siler House."

Bryan frowned. "Huh?"

Gage tapped the board. "What she's saying is that using it in this house is like waving a steak in front of whatever's here."

CHAPTER FOURTEEN

No matter how much Jess argued or pleaded the next few days, Allison wouldn't budge on her stance regarding the Ouija board. Nothing the others said had made a difference, either.

During their group sessions—the ones revolving around each of their abilities—Dr. Brandt spent more time with Allison than anyone else. Bryan tried to make things disappear that were larger than a set of keys (he'd made a potted plant disappear the day before), while Dr. Brandt encouraged Jess to concentrate on detecting the presence of ghosts. Although Jess had sensed that someone or something was present during the sessions, she was unable to convince a single entity to materialize. Not even Gracie and Emma would make an appearance. Jess thought the girls' shyness might have something to do with Allison or Dr. Brandt's presence.

"I think they're mad at me," Jess suggested. It was better than telling the truth, and she didn't want to upset Allison. "They haven't been to see me since yesterday morning."

Dr. Brandt finished his examination of a vase from the fireplace mantel. The guy couldn't quit touching everything—pictures, furnishings, walls. It was as though he was more obsessed with the house than she was with ghosts. "What happened yesterday morning?" he finally asked.

"I tried to get them to tell me why they won't show themselves to all of us."

"Apologize," Dr. Brandt instructed as he returned to his seat. "Gain their confidence." He scribbled down a few more notes. Jess exchanged glances with Gage, who she knew distrusted his note taking as much as she did.

"I'd like you to work on that before our next session, Jess. It's very important. I'd like you to visit each room today. Call to Gracie and Emma. Get them to come to you."

"All right," Jess replied, resigned. Gage gave her a slight shrug as Dr. Brandt jotted something else down. It wasn't lost on Jess that the looks between them lasted longer than they probably should and she wondered if Bryan had said something to Gage.

"Allison, let's start with you next," Dr. Brandt said, turning Jess's thoughts to the discussion at hand.

"Let's talk about the demons. Let's talk about when the demons were inside you, Allison. There were times when they *weren't* controlling you. Where did they go?"

No answer.

"Okay, let's try another question," Dr. Brandt said, undaunted. "Was there ever a time when you thought the demons listened to you? Did as you asked?"

Still no answer. Allison was having none of it. She simply sat and stared at him. Yesterday, she'd at least been argumentative.

Dr. Brandt jotted down more notes and once again, Jess found herself looking toward Gage. This time, he raised an eyebrow with that smile. *I know, right?* At least that's what she imagined him saying. Jess did her best to wipe the smile from her face and pay attention to the group discussion.

Dr. Brandt tapped his pen on his notepad. "Okay, Bryan, your turn. Have you been practicing with the objects I've given you?"

"Too much," Bryan replied. "It's giving me a headache."

"I'll get you some aspirin. Were you able to make any of the larger objects disappear?"

"Not really."

Jess frowned. Didn't work? He was lying! "You pushed a book off the coffee table last night," she offered. She started to mention the potted plant but something in both Gage and Bryan's expressions kept her quiet. Why were they lying?

Dr. Brandt went back to writing more notes. "Take the aspirin, Bryan. Keep hydrated, too. And keep practicing. I know you can do it." He turned his focus to Gage. "I've got something I'd like for you to try, Gage."

He retrieved a shoebox from the floor beside his chair and placed the box on the coffee table. He opened the lid, revealing a dead mockingbird. Jess and Allison grimaced.

Gage merely shrugged. "No thanks, trying to cut back."

Bryan laughed.

"Funny," Dr. Brandt said, and he smiled briefly as he placed an old, worn book on the table. A glossy bookmarker stuck out of its middle. "All of this is important to the study, Gage."

"You want me to bring back a bird?" Gage said. "Why is that so important?"

"With a little help," Dr. Brandt said, ignoring the question. He pushed the book toward him.

Gage looked at Dr. Brandt, his eyes narrowing for a moment. He flipped the book open to the bookmarked page. "Is this Latin?"

"Yes. It's a spell to raise the dead," Dr. Brandt replied. "Since your concentration doesn't work every time, I thought this might help."

After a few moments of contemplation, Gage cleared his throat and did his best at reading the incantation. Dr. Brandt reached down into the box beside the chair and pulled out the Ouija board and planchette.

"No," Allison said. "I'm done with this. I am *so* not going there." She got up and walked out of the room. Everyone stared after her.

"Go talk to her," Dr. Brandt told Jess. "We need her participation. You're all stronger as a group."

Jess glanced at the guys. Bryan shrugged as if to say he had no idea what was up with Allison this time. She got to her feet and headed toward the stairway.

* * *

111

"I don't get it, Allison," Jess said, collapsing on her bed. "We'd *all* be there. If something bad happened, you wouldn't be alone. We'd fix it."

"How?" Allison shot back. "It's not just about the dead bird or Bryan's cute magic tricks. I'm so tired, Jess. No one listens. It's better if I don't say anything else." She reached to her nightstand and grabbed a book sitting there. The dust jacket was gone, but the hardcover was in fair shape. It was like some of Grams's old books, the cover made out of some sort of pale blue fabric. Allison flipped the book open and pretended to read.

"You're not really reading that," Jess said. "And I *am* listening. Talk to me, Allison! You were right about Riley being in the mirror. And, I think you're right about him being evil. At least, I agree he doesn't have the best intentions."

Yeah. Riley was a murderer and a psycho.

Allison eyed her for a moment and Jess waited patiently. Finally, Allison closed the book. "This whole thing . . . it's not just about finding your dad. You know that, right? There are *other* spirits here. The Ouija board, that book Gage was reading from? We're just asking for something to happen. We can't control it. You think you can, or at least Dr. Brandt thinks so. But you *can't*. Not really. You can tell whatever it is to go away, and maybe it will. But not if it doesn't want to."

"They got rid of the demons in *you*," Jess said.

"But the demons can come back! Remember when Gage said I had them on speed dial? He's not too far off."

"But they *haven't* returned, have they?" Jess countered. "How much of that might be because you keep thinking about it? And, if you keep thinking about them, then sure. They might be able to find you. What if you try not thinking about them so much? Would that work?"

Allison sighed, looking either defeated or beyond frustrated. Jess wasn't sure which. She was only trying to help, but it was as though Allison didn't want alternative viewpoints. Did she *want* to stay freaked out?

Allison narrowed her eyes. "You wouldn't be so eager to do this if you'd been through what I have. Like I said, this isn't just about your dad, Jess. Or your grandmother."

"But we could focus only on them," Jess offered. "Or Gage's brother. They'd *never* hurt any of us. They're *not* evil."

"See? You're *not* listening!" Allison let out an exaggerated sigh. "Even if we somehow channeled your dad, the others are already right there, waiting. They're likely to come through the portal before anyone else. And Bryan might not be able to send them all back. Not in time, anyway. All. Ghosts. Are. Evil! If your dad's a ghost, then I wouldn't trust him, either."

Jess took a steadying breath. Calling random ghosts evil was one thing. Saying that her father was evil was something else entirely. "Have you ever lost someone?"

"What?"

"Has anyone in your family died? Anyone that you loved?" Jess asked.

Allison shook her head. "No, and I'm really sorry—"

"Then you *don't* know what it's like!" Jess spat. "You have *no* idea how painful it is to be so close to getting a chance to find out if you can talk to them again—even one last time." She got up from her bed and grabbed some of her things.

This argument was going nowhere and Jess couldn't imagine spending another night in the same room with Allison. "We need a break."

"Where are you going?" Allison asked.

"Down the hall," Jess replied curtly.

She didn't take much, just her hairbrush, toothbrush, her pajamas, and a change of clothes. She left the room and walked down the hall as quietly as possible, careful to avoid the creaky floorboards in the center. She stopped in front of the room she'd showered in the other day, fumbling with her things and freeing up a hand to turn the doorknob.

It turned easily. Jess pushed the door open, stepped inside and flicked on the light switch. A quick search told her the room was empty. She quickly closed the door behind her. Mrs. Hirsch would be angry if she came along and found the door opened and Jess sleeping in a different room.

She retrieved a towel from the bathroom and put it along the base of the door to keep the light from spilling into the hallway. Then, after changing and brushing her teeth, Jess turned on the lamp beside the bed, removed the towel from the base of the door, flicked off the overhead light switch, and climbed into bed. She reached over and turned off the bedside light and shut her eyes. Maybe for once since being here she'd get a decent night's sleep. After a few minutes, she felt herself falling into peaceful slumber.

The creak of a floorboard woke her sometime later. She listened, thinking she'd imagined the sound. Had it come from the foot of the bed? She reached to the nightstand and fumbled with the light. Part of her was afraid it was Mrs.

Hirsch, or Allison. The other part of her was disappointed it wasn't Gage. But her first squinty-eyed sweep of the room revealed no one, and Jess figured she imagined it.

She shook her head and wiped her tired eyes. "Get a grip," she said softly.

She sighed and looked up to find Gracie and Emma standing in the middle of the room, staring at her. Jess nearly shrieked.

"Hi, Jess," Gracie said. Emma remained quiet. The only way Jess could tell the two girls apart was that Gracie was a little thinner and she had curlier hair than her sister.

"Sorry," Emma said. "We didn't mean to scare you."

Jess checked the clock on the nightstand. It was two-thirty in the morning.

"You can leave the light on," Gracie said. "Mrs. Hirsch is sleeping. We checked."

"How did you find me?" Jess asked, realizing how stupid that must sound. "Ghosts. Never mind."

"We were waiting for you," Gracie said.

Jess frowned. How long had the girls been watching her sleep? Is that what they meant, or was she supposed to have met them someplace? "Waiting for me?" Jess wiped at her eyes again.

"We don't sleep," Emma said, leaving Jess to wonder if that was an explanation or a statement. The girls weren't always the most animated when they talked. But then, she figured with Riley still around, they didn't have a whole lot to be happy about.

Gracie fidgeted a bit. "We want to help you."

Jess pulled the covers back and sat with her legs under her. "You do? Help me with what?"

"The Ouija board," Gracie said.

"How did you know about that?" Jess asked. "Were you spying on us?"

"Don't be silly," Gracie replied. "Of course we did."

Well, that's unnerving, Jess thought, and wondered how many ghosts had been present, but never showed themselves over the years. "Then why didn't you show yourselves? Everyone else is here to see ghosts, too."

"The other girl *has* seen us," Gracie said. "And we don't think she likes us very much. She doesn't like any of us."

"We like you the best," Emma said and her sister nodded. "We know you want to help us, too. That you aren't here to hurt us."

"I thought you two might be mad at me," Jess said.

"We've been here the whole time," Gracie said. "Riley's kept us busy."

They were unusual girls. Sort of quirky. Jess supposed that being dead for over a hundred-plus years did that to them. And of course, Riley. If he was holding them here, that explained a lot. She wished she could send them into the light or heaven or wherever ghosts went when they were at peace.

"Yeah. About that. How am I supposed to help you? Do you know of a way?" Jess asked them.

The girls nodded in unison.

"Use the board to cross Riley over," Emma said.

Jess didn't like that suggestion much. "But I don't have the board and I don't like the idea of bringing Riley out into the open. Even if we did, then what?"

"We'll help you," Gracie said. "We'll help all of you."

She didn't like the way the girls spoke so sparsely. Sometimes they didn't make much sense. But then, Grams and a few of the other ghosts had been the same way. Maybe it was hard for them to be seen *and* heard at the same time. The idea seemed logical, since sometimes, Grams had been transparent, other times solid, and occasionally, like the girls, she flickered or rippled when speaking. But if the girls thought Allison would take part in using the board, they were wrong.

"So you think we can do it? Cross Riley over?" Jess finally asked. The idea of making Riley a ghost that could appear front and center instead of lurk in mirrors or walls was terrifying, and she'd need to ask Dr. Brandt about banishing ghosts.

Again, the girls nodded.

"From the shadows into the light," Gracie said.

The comment about sending Riley into the light or wherever ghosts went should've made Jess feel better, but it didn't. Not entirely. "Do you want to tell me what happened?"

The girls shook their heads.

"Why not?" Jess asked.

"It's all *here*," Emma said, as though that explained everything.

"Here? You mean Siler House? What's all here? Are there clues?"

Gracie lowered her head, but her eyes still met Jess's. "We can show you."

Emma looked over her shoulder. "We have to go."

"Where? Where are you going?" Jess wanted to know.

"To help you," Gracie replied. The sisters turned, took each other's hand, and disappeared through the door.

CHAPTER FIFTEEN

Gage found Jess sitting against the huge oak tree closest to the graves. Its trunk had to be about six feet across by Gage's estimate. Judging from the distance from the gravesite, the tree had probably been planted around the time of Gracie and Emma's funeral.

Allison, it seemed, was nowhere to be found. It hadn't surprised Gage. The girls, who had seemed to enjoy each other's company the first day or two here, had grown more distant. Especially since the Ouija board incident. Girls. Go figure. One day, they're bonding and BFFs, and the next day? Well, they were like this—all moody and nonsocial.

Of course, that was mostly a front. What they usually wanted was company. With any luck, *his* company. He liked Jess. A lot. Smart, kind, and sexy as hell. The way she looked at him sometimes nearly took his breath away. Unless he was dead wrong, she'd noticed him, too.

Siler House might be haunted, even though he'd yet to see a ghost, but now seemed like a good opportunity to spend some alone time with the girl who'd been haunting *his* dreams since they'd been here.

Besides, Gage knew what was really bugging Jess. At least he thought he did. It wasn't Allison herself, and it wasn't because Allison didn't see eye to eye with Jess on the whole house and ghost business. They each had their points. Allison saw demons. Jess wanted angels.

"Hey," he said as he sat down next to her. "Is this side of the tree taken?"

"No," Jess said with a halfhearted smile.

"This experiment isn't turning out quite like you expected, is it?" he asked, sitting close enough that his shoulder almost brushed against hers. It was a good lead-in.

"I'm not sure *what* I expected," Jess replied without taking her eyes from the graves.

"Sure you do. You're looking to find someone. And, unless I'm wrong, it's not the ghosts of those two little girls. Well, not really." His eyes met hers. "It's not exactly your grandmother, is it? You mentioned that your dad died."

She looked at him then, as though determining how serious he was. Gage didn't look away. "Feel like talking?"

She shrugged and tucked a strand of hair behind her ear.

"I know what it's like to lose someone you love, Jess. I get it. I loved my little brother."

"How did it feel?" Jess asked. "How did it feel when you couldn't bring him back?"

"Like crap," Gage admitted. "Like I'd let him down. Hell, like I let my whole family down." It felt good, how easy the words came out. How easy it was to tell her.

Her expression softened, the pinched, worried look gone, and Gage couldn't help but notice her natural beauty.

She stared out into the open field. "My dad died about a year ago. Cancer. I wasn't there when he passed away. I'd been going every day after school. Mom was going to take me to see him right after dinner, but then . . . they called and . . ." Jess closed her eyes, clearly fighting back the memory. "He died alone."

Gage resisted the urge to reach out and touch her face, instead resting his elbows on his knees. "Sorry. That really sucks."

Jess offered him a sad smile. "For you, too. Especially since your parents think you can undo your brother's death."

"There are days when I'm not sure what's really expected of me. Do they think he'll just show up good as new— as if nothing happened? Or do they think I can summon his ghost?" He sighed and raked a hand through his hair. "Problem is, I've never seen a ghost. Now, *you*, on the other hand . . ."

"So, you believe me? You don't think it's just my imagination?"

"Oh, I believe you," Gage said. And he did believe her. He wasn't lying about that. Hell, he hadn't lied to her about anything. "I guess I don't have to see one myself to believe that you can. At first, I thought that maybe you were just a little too eager. But I think you're the real deal. Allison, too."

He smiled. "Not so sure about Bryan, though. The largest thing I've seen him make disappear is a plate of food," he kidded. It made her smile, which got him smiling, too.

"Nah! That's not true," he quickly amended. "Bryan is a good guy and he's got one scary talent. Anyway, I say that we see about getting out that Ouija board. Give it a try. Just you and me. What do you think?"

"You'd do that?" Jess asked, turning those golden brown eyes his way once more.

He would. Not just because he'd like to one-up Bryan, but because if he was going to do this, he needed to prove it to himself and his parents once and for all that whatever hocus-pocus mojo he might have had wasn't there anymore. Okay, and it wouldn't hurt to impress Jess, too.

He shrugged. "Hey, we've both got something to prove and nothing to lose. That's the way I figure it. We use that Ouija board to make the connection, I'll see what I can reel in, and you do the talking. Because otherwise, we're just going to walk around with all this equipment and get nowhere. Bryan and I tried it out after you and Allison went to your room last night. Other than a few EMF readings and cold spots we didn't get much."

"Dr. Brandt said we'd use the board with or without Allison by the weekend. He just wants to give her a little more time."

Gage cocked an eyebrow. "You don't want to wait until the weekend, do you? You're miserable just sitting around."

She stared at him, apparently considering his offer. He nudged her with his shoulder. "Come on. No one will really care. Maybe they won't even have to know, if you're more comfortable with that."

Please say yes.

Jess's smile widened. "Okay, I'm in."

"Then I say we get started." He stood and reached down a hand. Jess looked up at him and took his hand into hers, sealing their deal and allowing him to help her up. When she was standing in front of him, he was almost reluctant to let it go. With those eyes and that smile, she really was a beauty. The guys back home might have thought she wasn't his type, but they'd have been wrong. Deep inside, he liked girls like Jess over the flashier ones with the tough-chick attitude. Those were easy to come by. And for Gage, easy to get. He had learned early on how to turn on his good looks and charm. But girls like Jess were fun, easy to be around. And definitely worth his best effort.

Jess gave him a faint smile. "How are we going to get the board?"

"Come on," he said, squeezing her hand gently and pulling her with him. They headed toward the house. "I've got a plan."

Which to him, was an understatement.

CHAPTER SIXTEEN

Jess laughed as Gage tugged her across the yard. She didn't even mind him holding on to her hand. In fact, she rather enjoyed it. The grass was cool beneath her bare feet, despite the day's humid warmth. For the first time in a couple of days, she felt like everything was moving forward again.

She told herself that her lightened mood had nothing to do with Gage himself, just his offer to help.

And why not let him? He could be right—the two of them might have the abilities to pull this off. Gracie and Emma had said they'd help with the board, too. She hadn't told Gage that part, mostly because she wasn't sure what the girls had meant.

He pulled her close as they stopped by the front door, and she thought he intended to kiss her. For a moment, Jess forgot to breathe. Her gaze wandered from his hazel eyes down to his mouth. Not that she would have minded a kiss.

Except Gage knew how hot he was. Not pretty-boy model handsome, but more ruggedly sexy.

He's probably a jerk in the romance department. Don't let him see what he does to you. How you light up inside when he's around.

Then again, they weren't going to be here that long. A kiss didn't have to mean anything else. Surely it'd never develop into much of anything. Just a summer attraction. Jess didn't have a boyfriend back home—well, not anymore. She forced herself to breathe again, to stop looking at his totally kissable mouth so temptingly close to hers.

One kiss. Just one . . .

"Ready?" he asked. The corners of his mouth twitched into a grin.

"Now?" she eked out.

Gage's grin widened. The jerk had to know he was teasing her, but Jess didn't have the guts to lean in and kiss him. "Why not?" he said. "First, we've got to see where everyone else is, especially Mrs. Hirsch."

"Who's to say she isn't walking the halls?"

"I'm sure she is. That's why you're going to be the diversion."

"*Me?* She's already caught me in one of the rooms."

"Hey, I can't think of a better diversion," Gage murmured, making her think about that kiss again. "As for Mrs. Hirsch? It's even better if she catches you. Do it again. Try the same room or find another one. Just don't be quiet about it."

They stared at each other. He was killing her, but she refused to make the first move. They'd done nothing but stare at each other their entire conversation. Jess forced herself to look out into the yard. "I think you're way too good at this," she finally said.

"Yeah, well, what can I say? Where do you think Allison is?"

"No idea." Jess didn't want to mention that she hadn't stayed in the same room with her last night.

"Now, we'll just have to find Dr. Brandt," Gage said, opening the front door.

Jess couldn't believe she was going through with this. It was one thing to try to persuade Dr. Brandt into using the board or doing a séance without Allison or Bryan, but something else entirely to enter his room and take the Ouija board without asking. Yet, it also seemed the right thing to do. What if the ghosts had a hard time showing up with all the equipment and Allison's negativity? Allison had made it clear she wanted nothing to do with ghosts, and wasn't fond of anyone else having anything to do with them, either.

She found herself staring into Gage's eyes again.

Why couldn't she stop staring at him?

Gage held the door and followed her into the foyer. They found Allison sitting in the Great Room reading a book and Mrs. Hirsch in the dining room, polishing the table. She had no idea why, since maids came in twice a week, but it didn't matter. At least she wouldn't be wandering the halls.

Jess didn't ask how Gage was going to get the Ouija board up into the attic unseen, but in a way, the less she knew the better.

He leaned in and whispered, "Meet me in the attic, after dinner."

She loved the feel of his breath against her ear. Before she could even nod, he was already halfway up the stairs. Damn him!

Allison looked up from her book and glanced from Jess to the staircase and back. She raised an eyebrow.

"Where's Bryan and Dr. Brandt?" Jess asked, avoiding any questions about Gage. Mrs. Hirsch was too close and bound to be listening. The last thing Jess wanted was for her to start following either of them around, thinking something was going on that shouldn't be. Not that they had to answer to her.

"Third floor," Allison said. "They're checking out some of the rooms that are normally kept locked. Bryan is enjoying all the ghost-hunting equipment a little too much."

"Do you want to join them?" Jess asked, already knowing the answer.

Allison shook her head and went back to her book. Mrs. Hirsch was standing on a step stool, using a duster on an extended pole to clean the room's molding. Jess couldn't help but watch, taking note again of the strange, carved faces.

"Problem?" Mrs. Hirsch said, not bothering to stop her chores.

"No," Jess replied. "Just looking at the faces. It's like they're watching."

Mrs. Hirsch stepped off the stool and moved it to another area. She reached inside her blouse and pulled out a silver chain, then rubbed its dark gray pendant before tucking it back inside. "That's the point."

Jess frowned.

Mrs. Hirsch began dusting again. "Catherine Siler had the molding installed after the murders. For all the good it did."

"Good?" Jess asked.

She got down from the stool and gave Jess an exasperated glance. "In some areas of the South, it's believed molding like this prevents the corners of a room from harboring evil spirits. She even had a lot of the walls and ceilings painted sky blue, another method used for scaring off spirits." She moved the step stool again. "Guess it didn't work."

Jess waited for the rest of the story, but Mrs. Hirsch didn't say another word as she removed cobwebs from a corner. Then, with a small huff, she picked up the stool and disappeared into the kitchen, probably to check on what the cook was preparing for dinner.

Convinced Mrs. Hirsch was otherwise occupied, Jess thought joining Bryan and Dr. Brandt might be a good idea. She could at least keep them on the third floor a while longer, hopefully giving Gage more time in Dr. Brandt's room.

"I'm going to go find Bryan and Dr. Brandt," Jess said.

Allison put the book down. "On second thought, I'll join you."

Jess hadn't expected Allison to tag along, especially since ghost hunting wasn't her thing, but she figured it was a good idea to keep her with her instead of having her catch Gage going through Dr. Brandt's things.

They left the Great Room and headed upstairs. On the second-floor landing, she caught the shadow of a man on the wall. The shadow moved around the corner and down the hallway. "Gage?" Jess called softly, hoping the sound of her voice would give him a heads-up that they were nearby. But if it wasn't Gage?

Jess started down the hallway, aware Allison had stopped following. The corridor was empty and she turned back to her. "What? Did you see someone?"

Allison was staring at the wall where the shadow had been. So, she'd seen it, too. If it wasn't Gage, Bryan, or Dr. Brandt, then who? Jess tried to think back to all the ghosts she'd encountered in the past. Had any of them been able to cast a shadow?

"Allison? Tell me you saw the shadow of a man?" Jess whispered.

Allison continued to stare at the wall. "*I saw a man upon the stair. I saw a man who wasn't there. He wasn't there again today. I wish the man would go away.*"

"That's really creepy," Jess said.

"Don't worry," Allison said, taking a deep breath as she started up the third flight of steps. "It's an old poem or something."

Jess looked behind them, then followed Allison. "It's still creepy. But you did see a shadow, right?"

"Yeah. There really *was* a man on the stairs."

CHAPTER SEVENTEEN

When she and Gage caught up with one another two hours later, Jess tried not to think of how close he was as they sat on the sofa in the Great Room. "So, the Ouija board isn't in his room?" Jess asked. She could have sworn Dr. Brandt had left the board and the planchette in the supply box, and according to Gage, he'd taken everything back to his room that night.

"Nope," Gage replied. "I looked everywhere. Weird, isn't it?"

"Maybe he put it someplace else."

"I guess, but why would he have taken the Ouija board out of the box? I found everything else in his room."

Jess frowned. "You don't think Allison might have already taken it, do you? You know, to keep all of us from using it?"

Gage shrugged. "I don't know."

"Well, regardless of whoever stashed the Ouija board, I think the basement is a good place to start looking for it. That, or a locked room," Jess said.

Gage grinned. "I know just how to do it without being too suspicious."

She gave him a curious glance.

"We drag out the equipment," he said. "Go on a little ghost-hunting expedition. We'll even rally the troops. Bryan hasn't had a chance to use the video recorder yet, and this would be the perfect opportunity. All that equipment gives us license to dig around. Look behind some closed doors, scope stuff out. I like your idea of the basement. Let's start there."

It hadn't taken much convincing to get everyone in on the ghost hunt. And after the incident on the stairs, Jess was eager to see what the equipment might tell them. Gracie, Emma, and Riley weren't the only ghosts here, after all. She'd sensed them and the girls had confirmed that much. Jess wasn't sure if it bothered her that the others hadn't shown themselves.

Dr. Brandt handed out the equipment—flashlights, EMFs, and the voice recorders. Even Allison was complacent enough to at least accompany them. She'd said anything was better than sitting alone.

Bryan seemed happy to be in charge of the full-spectrum camera. One thing Jess had noticed about him was how much he liked anything technical.

"Leave the lights off!" he said excitedly as they all headed down the basement stairs. "I want to see how the night-vision feature works."

Behind her, Gage pulled the chain on the overhead light, momentarily putting them into semi-darkness. The only light came from the camera.

Jess groaned. Boys. They'd break their necks. The stairs were steep and oddly shaped. People must have had smaller feet in the early 1900s. She flicked on the flashlight Dr. Brandt had given her and pointed the beam at the steps. The light was dim, providing barely enough visibility to see just past Bryan. It only brought the shadows and dusty cobwebs more to her attention. Jess smacked the base of the flashlight a few times.

"They're low-light," Gage explained. "It's how they're designed."

"Oh," Jess replied.

Up ahead, Dr. Brandt turned on his flashlight. Small sections of the basement came in and out of view as he panned the beam of light—brick and stone walls, shelving with an assortment of items stacked on them, and paint cans and hand tools.

"Hey!" Bryan alerted them. "You guys are going to mess up the infrared!"

The temperature in the basement felt ten degrees cooler than on the main floor—Jess didn't need to check a temp reading on her EMF reader for that. Basements were always cooler, though. This was the first time she'd come down here, and she ran a hand over the walls, enjoying how cold the stones were to the touch. She inhaled deeply, taking in the delightful scent of earth and damp stone, the scent of Siler House itself. Up ahead, Dr. Brandt appeared to be doing the same.

Allison glanced over her shoulder at Jess. "See?" she mouthed.

Gage made a sweep with the EMF detector and Bryan recorded the action.

"Is the EVP on, Allison?" Dr. Brandt asked.

Allison checked on the voice recorder connected to the lanyard around her neck. "It's on."

Dr. Brandt reached up and pulled a chain, snapping on the overhead light. Darkness receded into the corners of the basement, and as the lightbulb swung back and forth, the shadows danced.

"What did you do that for?" Bryan complained.

"Food storage," Dr. Brandt explained. "I don't want any of us to crash into the shelves. There's a lot of jars and canned goods. The rest of the basement will be plenty dark. We won't turn on any more lights."

Dr. Brandt led them past the shelving that housed countless jars of sauces and cans of who knew what, as well as an area with a large freezer and refrigerator, and a section for the housekeeping staff that held organized cleaning supplies and fresh linens. The next section was an open area with even more odds and ends. It looked like the staging area for the renovation crew—extra baseboards and molding, a workbench, some plywood, and lots of stuff that must be original items pulled from the rooms.

"It's like a museum of old junk," Bryan said, panning the camera over a small area of furniture, some covered with dusty sheets, some without. Jess caught a glimpse of a chair with rotting upholstery. An old bike and several dolls with antique, waxen faces sat in another section. Nothing in Siler House had given Jess the creeps as much as those dolls, and she felt the fine hair rise on her arms. She had never liked dolls, and these were especially awful. For one, they were sitting on top of an old dresser, facing toward them as if waiting for someone to show up. A blond-haired doll in the middle looked the worst of the bunch. At some point, it appeared to have been a child's favorite. The dress was dirty and the hair, which must have been golden and in perfect ringlets at one time, now looked frizzy and dull. Worse, a fairly large spider had built a web between it and the dresser mirror. The pale light from her flashlight cast shadows, illuminating white stripes on the spider's legs. Jess quickly panned the flashlight upward, making sure the spider didn't have relatives overhead.

She almost wished they hadn't come down here.

Gage's EMF meter whirred to life as he panned it past the dresser. Everyone's attention turned toward it and the dolls. The spider, which sat in the middle of the web, retreated, scrambling down into the doll's hair. Gage stepped closer to get a better EMF reading but Jess reached out and took hold of his arm.

He glanced down at her hand, which she removed, and he gave her a playful smile. "It's okay. Just a bunch of old dolls. *Creepy* dolls, but it's not like they're going to come to

134

life or anything. Trust me, I don't work my voodoo magic on inanimate objects, okay?"

Jess mustered a nervous smile.

"Afraid of spiders?" Bryan asked. He moved the video camera aside. He closed his eyes and took a deep breath. Jess watched in amazement as the spider scuttled out of its hiding place and onto the doll's face before fading into . . . nothing.

Gage grinned. "Show-off."

"Hey, you guys feel that?" Bryan asked.

Jess rubbed her arms. She felt it all right. While the basement had been noticeably cooler, this area had suddenly grown quite cold.

Dr. Brandt took out his own digital voice recorder. "Bryan, record this."

Bryan panned to Dr. Brandt, who held up a thermometer. The readout began to drop. "Fifty-six degrees," Dr. Brandt said. "Which is unusually cold for any basement in Savannah during the summer. There is no draft, just a sensation of cold."

Gage's EMF device went off, the needle jumping back and forth wildly. "Hello?" he called out. "If there's anyone here, can you show yourself? Talk to us?"

Dr. Brandt recorded his next note. "Gage's EMF reader has picked up a strong reading in the area, as well. Readings quickly fluctuating between two and five milligaus, indicating we may be in the presence of a spirit or spirits. Reading is not typical of electronic interference."

Everyone grew silent, waiting. Allison looked absolutely terrified and Jess wrapped an arm around her. The action helped Jess, too. Until now, she hadn't realized how hard her heart had been pounding in her chest. Ghosts in restaurants in full daylight were one thing. But ghosts in dank, spider-infested basements were something else entirely.

Gage's EMF meter went silent. No fluctuating needle, no whirring sound, no red light.

"Maybe the spirit moved off to another spot," Dr. Brandt said.

From somewhere farther in the darkened basement, somewhere amid the piles of furniture, lamps, and assorted old appliances, a child's xylophone began to play—the song clear and unmistakable:

Three blind mice.
Three blind mice.
See how they run.
See how they run.
Then, silence.

"Holy shit!" Bryan exclaimed as he nearly dropped the camera. He righted it, panning the basement far too fast to actually film anything.

Dr. Brandt slowly scanned the basement with his flash-light. He and Bryan set off in the direction the sound had come from. Gage gave Jess and Allison a quick glance and they followed him, clinging more tightly to each other than before.

"It's just the girls," Jess whispered to Allison, hoping that was true. "They're just trying to say it's all okay." Jess wasn't sure she believed her own words, but the idea mildly comforted her. Just the girls. Nothing else.

Allison trembled. "They all ran after the farmer's wife, who cut off their tails with a carving knife," she sang softly. She stepped away from Jess and pointed back to the dresser with the dolls.

The mirror was different. It reflected another room, one Jess recognized as one of the locked ones from the third floor. Someone lay in the bed, sleeping. Except the person wasn't really sleeping. Something glittered on the red bed coverlet. Jess stepped closer, her breath caught in her throat. What she had mistaken for a bed cover wasn't a quilt or covering of any kind. It was blood. A large knife protruded from the woman's chest. A couple of smaller knives lay around her, blades pointing inward.

"Guys?" Jess called out, voice shaky. "Whatever it is, it's back over here."

"In a minute," Gage's voice called back. "We found the xylophone."

"No, really," Jess answered. "You need to see this."

Inside the mirror, something moved. From a shadowy corner emerged a boy approximately her age. Riley. He had to be Riley. He grinned, revealing thin, dark teeth. Something awful and dark and soulless lurked behind his black eyes. Riley made his way to the mirror, head slowly cocking from side to side.

A scream caught in Jess's throat.

Someone threw a sheet over the mirror—Allison. "I warned you not to talk to them," she hissed.

Gage returned to her side. "What happened? Jess! Are you okay?"

She shook her head and pointed at the mirror. "Riley. He's in the mirror."

"Riley?" Dr. Brandt asked. "You saw Riley in the mirror?"

"Y-y-yes," Jess choked out. No ghost had ever shown her part of their past before. None of them had shown her such violence, or looked and felt as malevolent. "Someone else was there, too. A woman. He killed her. There were knives everywhere."

Bryan turned the camera on Jess. Dr. Brandt placed his hand on the sheet.

"Don't!" Jess nearly shrieked. "He's *in* there. And he sees us." She realized how much she sounded like Allison. She jumped when Dr. Brandt peeled back the sheet. His hand gently caressed the frame.

The mirror reflected nothing but her reflection and the others', ghostly and shadowy in the low, greenish light from Bryan's camera.

"It's okay, Jess," Dr. Brandt assured her. "No one is there now. See?" He turned to face her, his back exposed to the mirror. Jess wanted to scream a protest, to tell him not to stand so close to it. Her eyes darted to the mirror, still reflecting nothing but them and the basement. Images from the here and now. Nothing from the past at all. The dolls stared blankly outward.

"I'd like to go upstairs now," Allison said.

"Sounds like a good idea," Dr. Brandt agreed.

"You sure you're okay?" Gage asked.

Jess nodded. "I'm fine now," she lied, taking a deep, steadying breath. This wasn't supposed to happen. Ghosts weren't supposed to behave like this. Whatever Riley was, he couldn't be a ghost. He had to be something more. As the others turned and headed out of the basement, Jess couldn't resist training the flashlight back one last time. The light bounced off the mirror, revealing nothing. But Jess swore the doll in the middle winked.

CHAPTER EIGHTEEN

"Who was she?" Jess wanted to know. "The woman in the room."

Dr. Brandt sat at the dining room table, fingers steepled across his lips as he contemplated Jess's question.

"Julia Alcott. Gracie and Emma's personal nanny. A chambermaid discovered her the day after the search party found the girls' bodies."

"So, they caught Riley red-handed?" Gage asked.

"Red-handed." Bryan laughed. "Funny, Gage."

"No," Dr. Brandt said. "While Ms. Alcott's death was most certainly Riley's doing, no one caught him. Ms. Alcott told her employers that Riley was pure evil—that he had the soul of a devil. She threatened to leave unless they did something about him."

"No surprise there," Gage added. "I'm sure the Silers had to see that one coming a mile away."

"True, but those aren't words you'd kill someone over," Jess said.

"Riley wasn't exactly sane," Bryan offered.

Dr. Brandt smiled. "Oh, Riley *was* sane. I think he only pretended to be insane. To answer *your* question, Jess, Ms. Alcott's comments about Riley having the soul of a devil didn't get her killed. Recommending an exorcism *did*. She even supplied the Silers with the name of a priest."

The pieces clicked together for Jess. "That's what happened the first time. That's how Riley's parents died. They tried to exorcise him."

Dr. Brandt nodded. "That's *exactly* what happened. Ms. Alcott's uncle was a priest. She'd told him about Riley, about what he'd done, and he suggested an exorcism. Catherine Siler didn't take a lot of persuading, not after what happened to her sister and now her own children. She wanted Riley dead as much as her husband did at this point, but a servant told her that unless they exorcised the demon in her nephew before he was tried and executed, the evil inside him would only transfer to someone else."

"So how'd that work out for them?" Gage asked.

"It didn't," Dr. Brandt replied. "The priest arrived, saw Riley for a few minutes, then fled the house. They discovered Ms. Alcott's body soon afterward. So I'd say the exorcism didn't work for them at all. But a shotgun blast did. Riley was dead before nightfall. Where Riley's father failed, Jonathan Siler succeeded. Without an exorcism, the deaths and other strange happenings continued at Siler House. Lights turned on and off. The piano in the music room played at night."

"The nursery rhyme," Bryan said, replaying the video. "The kid's xylophone. How did it do that?"

"Anyone check the thing out?" Gage asked. "Make sure no one tampered with it?"

"You think someone's putting us on?" Allison said. She seemed angry, upset. Scared. "You heard it! We all did. Jess and I weren't having some group hallucination. No one tampered with the xylophone *or* the mirror, Gage."

He held up his hands in a truce. "Okay, okay. It was just a suggestion. I'm not saying the paranormal doesn't exist. I know better. It's corporations and studies I don't trust." He and Allison stared at each other for a long minute and Jess wondered what had been said between them. Whatever Allison had shown Gage, neither of them had told anyone else.

Gage finally looked away. "We all heard it. Just trying to rule stuff out. Any chance it was the girls, Jess? Could Gracie and Emma do that?"

Jess shrugged. "I guess the thing with the xylophone was possible, but I don't think the thing with the mirror was. That was a pretty gruesome scene. That was Riley's doing."

Allison shook her head. "They aren't helping us, Jess."

"They've promised to help. They're just little girls. Riley killed them! I don't see how they'd side with him." Jess looked at Gage to try to see disbelief in his expression, to see if he would mock her. But he sat there, calm and unreadable. At least he didn't seem to think she was crazy.

"They said they'd help? With what? Your dad? Ben? This experiment?" Bryan asked, sounding excited. "That'd be pretty cool."

Allison went back to shaking her head. Jess could be upset with Allison all she wanted, but deep down, she felt bad for her. This place terrified her and she shouldn't be here. Yet, no one seemed to care.

Dr. Brandt turned on his digital recorder. "What happened? What did they say, Jess?"

Jess shrugged. "Just what I said. They said they'd show me things. I suppose the music came from them. Maybe they wanted to warn us about Riley in the mirror."

"So, what next?" Gage asked. "Do we wait around to see if something else happens? Do we have a séance?" He paused, giving Allison a quick glance. "Do we revisit the idea of using the Ouija board?"

"They're getting stronger," Allison said. "It's because of all of us. It's our combined energy. Who we are and our experiences with the supernatural. A séance or the Ouija board will only make it worse. You *don't* want them to get stronger."

"What if we can help the girls?" Jess asked. All she could think of was her sister—that if something so horrible had happened to Lily, she'd want someone to help her. The idea of spending eternity with the person responsible for your own death was unfathomable to Jess. "After all this time, don't you think they deserve some peace?"

"That's the problem," Allison said. "They've been here for too long. Messing around with this isn't going to help matters. They're not the same girls."

Jess's jaw went slack. "They haven't done anything to suggest they're against us. They're *not* Riley. I'm not saying they're perfect angels, and they *can* be a bit strange, but still—"

"Fine," Gage interrupted. "I say we have a séance. We'll skip the Ouija board. We don't need the Ouija board to conduct a séance." He gave Allison another quick glance.

"I agree," Jess said.

"Sure, I'm in," Bryan added.

Allison gave Bryan a dark look.

Dr. Brandt nodded. "Allison, we've been over this. No one will make you touch the Ouija board. You only need to be in the room. Jess has a point about Gracie and Emma. Some ghosts become trapped. I've freed others in the past, sent them on their way to peace."

Without waiting for a response he turned to the others. "There's a few things I'll need to take care of first. We'll work on the plans tomorrow over breakfast. I think everyone has had enough for one night and I need to transcribe some notes and copy the video onto the laptop along with the voice recordings."

The boys got to their feet, ready to head back to their room.

"Allison? Jess?" Dr. Brandt called as the girls slid from their chairs, too. "I'd like a quick word."

He waited until both the boys had made their way upstairs.

"I don't want you two separated at night," he told them.

"Why?" Jess asked. "I'm not afraid."

"I'm not asking," Dr. Brandt said. "I thought if I gave you two some distance from each other you'd work things out. I'd like the two of you back in the same room."

He glanced between the two of them. "I'm serious, ladies. Do we need to discuss what's going on between you two?"

Allison shook her head. "No. We're fine. My insomnia keeps Jess awake. I'll try harder to be quiet." She offered Jess a smile.

"Good," Dr. Brandt said. "Go work out whatever you need to. Tomorrow, I want you two back in the same room."

Jess followed Allison upstairs. When they were out of earshot, Allison said, "He's right. If they get any stronger, we'd all be better off making sure we're with someone."

"You think they're getting stronger?" Jess asked. "Weren't they like this before we came here?"

"Sometimes, spirits feed off people's energy, and there's never been anyone like us here before—at least not *four* of us. And haven't you noticed we each have a unique ability? It's not a good combination to have in Siler House all at once."

Jess thought about it as they walked down the third-floor hallway. She had no intention of going to their room. Not tonight. Tonight she wanted to see if she could talk to the girls. Ask them a few more questions. "So, we're different. What does that mean in relation to the house?"

"They're drawn to people like us," Allison explained. "I've told you." Exasperated, she left Jess standing in front of the other guest room and continued down the hallway to the room they'd shared. "Ask Gage why we're here. He knows."

Gage? So he and Allison *had* been talking about all this. She'd ask him what they'd found out tomorrow. Jess entered the guest room and closed the door. No Emma. No Gracie.

"Girls?" Jess called out. "Hey, I need to talk to you."

Nothing. No creaking floors from Mrs. Hirsch, although Jess had no doubt she'd be along soon enough.

"Really, guys! I need to talk to you. Emma? Gracie?"

Nothing. Maybe Allison had been wrong about them being stronger. Or, Riley was keeping them from showing up. Bastard!

Jess kicked off her shoes and shed all her clothes except her panties and tank top and crawled into bed. She lay there in the dark, listening to the sounds of the house settle down for the night. The crickets and frogs were once again in full chorus. After what seemed like an hour, she finally drifted to sleep.

A soft tap on the door woke her. She listened for a moment or two, thinking she'd dreamed it.

Someone softly tapped at the door again.

"Allison," she muttered, getting out of bed. Who else? Mrs. Hirsch wouldn't be tapping lightly. Jess opened the door, expecting Allison to be standing there in her night-gown. Instead, she found Gage in a pair of jeans and a dark shirt. "Oh!" she exclaimed and closed the door. "Give me a minute." Her cheeks flushed with warmth—not just because he'd made no attempt to look away when he'd clearly seen her in nothing more than her underwear and tank top, but because the warm, tingly sensation wasn't limited to only her face.

"Meet me in the room across from Allison's," Gage whispered through the door.

"It's locked," Jess replied. She scrambled across the room to retrieve the denim shorts she'd left on the bed. Quickly, she smoothed out her hair, turned out the light, and opened the door. No Gage. Didn't he hear her? Mrs. Hirsch kept the door locked. She crept down the hall, hoping the floorboards wouldn't creak.

For the time being, and despite her every effort, ghosts were the last thing on her mind.

CHAPTER NINETEEN

The door opened with a soft snick. Gage waited, remaining hidden behind some furniture until he was sure it was Jess. She looked around the room, missing his shape entirely before she closed the door behind her and walked toward the window.

"See? Not locked," he said softly, stepping from the shadows and standing close to her. "Glad you showed up."

He didn't really think she *would* have stayed in her room, or at least, he'd hoped she wouldn't. The fact that she'd met him here in the middle of the night told him Jess was at least curious. With any luck, her curiosity extended beyond why he'd asked her here. He thought about her far too much lately. He couldn't get Jess out of his mind.

"How'd you do it?" she asked.

"The door, or getting here without anyone seeing me? The door was easy to pick. All the doors here are. And Bryan is keeping his mouth shut."

"Why didn't he come with you?"

Gage grinned. "I told him I was meeting you."

Jess's eyes met his for a moment, then he looked toward the door and said, "He's a little envious, I think, but he's cool with it."

"I—"

Gage's eyes met hers again. "I know you didn't meet me here for that. Not that I'd mind."

Jess smiled softly. He tried to tell himself their close proximity made it easier to hear each other and not be overheard by anyone else who happened to pass by the room, but that'd be a lie. At least on his end. He hoped on hers, too.

"Why are we here?" she asked. He glanced at her lips, thinking of what it'd be like to take her in his arms and kiss her, to show her the most important reason he'd asked her here. "I suppose you want the real reason?"

Jess fidgeted and the corner of his mouth tilted upward again. She gave him a look, clearly indicating he'd better start talking. Gage sighed.

"Allison thinks Dr. Brandt wants to free whatever is trapped here. I agree. She also thinks the place is evil, and whatever lives here is evil, too. All of it."

"I know most of that," Jess said.

"I'm not sure if Dr. Brandt is really into the experiment anymore, or if he's just saying he is. He might still think there's a way to control evil spirits, but he's changed somehow. He's less interested in the experiment for EPAC's sake. EPAC isn't going to be happy. Brandt is supposed to be sending them reports on our progress. No company funds an experiment like this—pays us what it has without wanting something. Like a way to control the stuff of nightmares."

Jess studied his face as she considered his explanation. Gage hoped he hadn't sounded too crazy.

"You think that's what Brandt was sent here for? But how can anyone *control* ghosts? Or demons or the dead? It's sort of far-fetched, Gage. Don't believe everything Allison tells you."

He'd have to tell her. There was no other way. "I went through some of Dr. Brandt's notes."

"What?"

He grimaced. She must really think the worst of him—breaking into rooms, smarting off, trying to get her alone. It was all true, but not the way it appeared. "Look, Allison has been snooping in his office. She's the one who told me the conspiracy theory. I always thought the goons who showed up at my parents' house were up to something. Remember when I went through his things looking for the Ouija board? Well, I sort of came across his notes in a locked drawer."

"Locked drawer?" Jess shook her head. "You picked the lock?"

"Seemed pointless to suddenly grow morals on picking a locked drawer when I'd already picked the lock to his room and gone through his stuff."

"Why didn't you say something earlier?"

"Because I hadn't finished going through his notes yet. I needed to be sure before I said anything, and I wanted to put everything back where I found it."

"Wait. You're kidding, right? You *took* his notes?"

"Yeah, but like I said, I put them back," Gage replied. "Bryan and Allison watched the hallway for me. At first, I thought Allison was a little crazy, but I think she's telling the truth—at least about the experiment and EPAC. Anyway, Jess—some of what I read—it's about you."

She blinked. "Me? Why were you going through *my* files?"

"Not files, notes. I only read a few days' worth of notes because I needed to have them back in his desk drawer before he went to his room for the night. Those notes just happened to revolve around you. Mostly," he said. "Well, you and Allison. But since Allison already knows, I figured I'd tell you."

"Why didn't Allison tell me?" Jess asked.

"Would you believe her if she did?" He didn't want to tell Jess that Allison *had* wanted to tell her, but he'd convinced her to let him do it. Alone. Allison had smiled at that, which meant no matter how crazy everyone thought the girl was, she was at least observant. Then again, it was hard *not* to see he had a thing for Jess.

She chewed on her bottom lip. "No. I guess not."

"So, do you believe me?"

Arms folded, she smiled warily. "Depends on what you have to say about the notes."

Gage nodded. It was fair enough. "Seems this whole paranormal thing interests the military."

"Military?" Her eyes widened.

"I'm not kidding," he said. "I know it's only one page of notes, and some suspicions based on a few visits from men in black to each of our homes, but the real takeaway here is that EPAC is a private-sector company that works with military intelligence. I'm not sure what they want. I can only tell you what I read."

Jess shook her head slowly, as though taking all of it in. Good. She hadn't stormed out or called him paranoid yet. He couldn't prove any of this to her without stealing Brandt's notes again, but so far, so good. He had a chance.

Jess walked toward the window. "Are you sure?"

Gage went to stand alongside her. "Positive. For some weird reason, he doesn't have a password on his computer. Brandt's been corresponding to some *Colonel Blackwell*. It wouldn't be the first time the government has tested ESP, telekinesis, or even mind control. Who knows what they've dug up? At any rate, it's not anything they'd share with us, right?"

Jess bit her lip again. He really liked it when she did that. It was sexy as hell. He tried to stay focused on the conversation. "You believe in ghosts, right?"

She eyed him suspiciously. "Of course I do."

"Do you think Allison lied about the demons? Was I lying? Or Bryan?"

She shook her head. "No."

"Then don't you think someone might want to figure out a way to use abilities like ours?"

Jess closed her eyes and nodded. Finally. She was starting to understand. "Yeah. I guess they would. Not exactly what we thought we were signing on for, is it?"

"You got that right. Except Bryan doesn't seem to mind some of it. He's kind of looking forward to seeing if he can do it, I think. Make stuff vanish. But not necessarily in front of Brandt. Like us, he's leery about the government wanting to tap into his talent. But if he can make other stuff vanish, it'll prove he made his dad disappear. Deep down, he's afraid he's not really gone. That one day, he'll show up again. He didn't tell anyone else, but Bryan's dad threatened to kill them all if they ever called the police on him again. I think he still has nightmares. He's sort of messed up about it."

"You're saying Dr. Brandt is keeping information from us? More than he's told our families? I can't say I'm surprised, but . . . wow."

Gage nodded. "There's a huge grant for this. It's why we were all offered such a large check, and why we all had to sign nondisclosure agreements. Someone way above Dr. Brandt's pay grade is behind this."

Jess frowned. "How do you think they were able to go through all our psych records without court orders?"

He rubbed a hand through his hair. "I have no idea. Big Brother and all that crap, I suppose. As for why they'd conduct such an experiment, think of it from their perspective. If the four of us can actually talk to, conjure, bring back whatever is on the other side, then send it back again, that'd be pretty handy."

Jess took a deep breath. "Okay, so back to the notes about me. What did you find out?"

"That other than Allison, you show the most promise. Brandt's initial notes said EPAC is going to be thrilled to finally have a communicator to deploy."

"Communicator? *Deploy? Are you sure?*" Jess asked. "I never agreed to anything like that in the contract!"

Gage shook his head. "Siler House is a testing ground for them. Honestly, I'm not one for conspiracy theories, but I figured something was up when some guys sporting official badges came to the house one day. Wanted to talk to my parents about Max."

"Max?" Jess said. "Your brother's dog."

"Yep. Seems after the funeral, Mom started talking about it. About me. No one really believed her, though. The town thought she was just too grief-stricken. I came home from school for the summer to help around the house and to help get their minds off Ben. About a month ago, these guys showed up in suits and asked a few questions. They left, not really saying much. Then I got a letter in the mail."

Jess nodded. "One that mentioned a federal grant, a study into group psychosis and the paranormal."

Jess seemed to be thinking about what he'd told her. Probably putting together her own pieces to the puzzle. Not that any of them *had* all the pieces, Gage thought. Whoever sat at the top of the food chain wasn't likely to come clean. Why would they? Well, except in the case of Allison. From what she'd said, her family was banking on her never coming back.

They both looked out the window at the moon shining down on the back lawn. Jess rubbed her arms and stood a little closer to him.

"And back to Dr. Brandt, this whole thing about not pushing us as much?" she asked.

"Allison has a theory about that, too. But you already know it. She thinks the house is getting to everyone."

Jess smiled. "Yeah, she told me. It can't be true, can it?"

Gage didn't want to think so. It was just a house. But then, he didn't know *what* to believe anymore. "We'll all be okay," he said, carefully wrapping an arm around Jess. She didn't seem to mind. He'd dumped a lot on her; the least he could do was try to reassure her they'd be okay.

Besides, he couldn't help himself, and holding her felt right.

Down the hallway, a floorboard creaked.

"Mrs. Hirsch!" Jess whispered.

Gage took her by the arm and gently pulled her behind a bulky armoire wedged in between some other pieces. Sheets draped the furniture, and best of all, it was in the darkest corner of the room.

"Quiet," he whispered into her ear.

More footsteps. Definitely Mrs. Hirsch's. They were louder now, just outside the room. Jess drew closer to him and he nearly stopped paying attention to Mrs. Hirsch. Outside the door, her key chain rattled.

Gage pulled Jess closer, lifting a corner of one of the sheets and letting it fall over them. He brought Jess even nearer, moving them to the center of the furniture they were hiding behind. The sheets hung thicker here, blocking out even the moonlight filtering into the room. Jess was pressed up against him in the small space. How he wished Mrs. Hirsch would go away.

The door opened with a loud creak. Jess started to take a deep breath and Gage placed a finger against her lips.

"Don't breathe," he mouthed. Reluctantly, he returned his hand to his side, although not before brushing against Jess's collarbone and shoulder.

Mrs. Hirsch's footsteps drew closer as she walked into the room. She paused somewhere in the middle of it, judging by the sound.

Gage's pulse picked up when Jess leaned into him, her face mere inches from his. He carefully wrapped his arms around her waist, keeping her as still as possible. They could only wait either for Mrs. Hirsch to find them, or for her to walk out of the room.

After another minute, her footsteps indicated she was leaving. Even then, Gage didn't relinquish his hold on Jess. Not that she seemed all that anxious to move away from him, even when the door closed and the floorboards creaked as Mrs. Hirsch walked away.

CHAPTER TWENTY

Jess listened as Mrs. Hirsch's footsteps grew more distant. She should move, step back. But she didn't want to. Gage stood in place, staring at her. It was now or never. She leaned forward and kissed him gently, savoring the feel of his mouth on hers. He eagerly kissed her back as he pulled her more tightly against him, sending heat and adrenaline coursing through her body, and apparently through Gage's, as well.

His breath quickened as he kissed her lips, her neck. "Jess," he whispered, sending her pulse into high gear. She ran her hands over his well-defined arms as his hands twined through her hair, cupping her head. Jess didn't want to ask herself what she was doing—she hadn't known Gage that long or that well. She simply couldn't resist. Being so close to him, feeling his breath against her skin, tasting those lips she found so inviting . . .

Her hands traced their way up his well-muscled chest. She leaned back a little as his mouth traveled down her neck again to her collarbone. Jess let out a groan of pleasure.

"Beautiful," Gage whispered as his hands slid up under her top. She tugged at his shirt.

It took a second before they both registered the commotion, breaking the moment between them.

"What the hell?" Gage said somewhat breathlessly.

"Someone's yelling," Jess replied.

Gage was already in motion, out from under the sheets, with Jess right behind him. From somewhere in the house the screaming and yelling continued. The furniture became an obstacle course as they made their way across the room. Finally, they ran into the hallway. Above them, the floorboards creaked with Mrs. Hirsch's footfalls.

"Quick!" Jess said, carefully closing the door behind them, the soft snick of the door latch louder than she'd hoped. They ran down the hallway and raced down the stairs and to the room Gage shared with Bryan. Gage pulled up as he reached the doorway and Jess collided into him.

Bryan lay on the bed, surrounded by knives. Jess had no idea how many knives the kitchen had, but it looked like every one of them was here on the bed, tips pointing at Bryan. Jess's knees wanted to buckle beneath her and her hands flew to her mouth. The scene reminded her of the vision in the mirror, except that Bryan was alive.

Dr. Brandt paced the room. "Make them go away, Bryan. Do it!"

"I—I can't!" Bryan yelled. "It's Allison! Make her stop it!"

"It's not me!" Allison shouted. "I'm trying to make *him* stop!"

"Bryan," Gage said calmly. "Just get up. Nice and slow . . ."

Bryan shook his head. "I don't think I can," he replied, voice shaky.

"What happened?" Jess asked, her eyes darting to Allison, who sat in a chair in the corner. She still wore her pajama shorts and top and her arms were wrapped tightly around her legs.

Were the demons back? Was Allison somehow doing this to Bryan?

Mrs. Hirsch burst through the doorway, shoving Jess and Gage aside like bowling pins. Her eyebrows were knitted together, making her perpetual scowl even more pronounced. "What is going on here!" she demanded. She eyed them all darkly.

"It's perfectly fine, Mrs. Hirsch," Dr. Brandt said. "We have a little experiment going on. It's all under control."

"Under control? Well, you're taking it too far!" She reached out to retrieve one of the knives but they soared upright, their blades hovering directly over Bryan.

She gasped, then clutched the chain around her neck and the pendant that hung from it. She spun around to face Dr. Brandt. "Freaks!" she spat. "I warned you! I said bringing them here wasn't a good idea, that you should call the whole thing off!"

"Mrs. Hirsch," Dr. Brandt said, his tone edged with warning. "Go back to your duties. Or your room. Now."

Her eyes narrowed. Without another word, she stormed from the room.

Everyone turned their attention back to Bryan and the knives dangling above him.

"Make her stop it," Bryan said, motioning to Allison.

"I told you I'm not doing it!" Allison repeated.

"Then why were you here? You were here when I woke up!"

"Because I knew *he'd* be here!"

"Who?" Jess nearly shouted. "Who'd be here?"

"Slow down!" Gage said. "We'll figure it all out, but first, let's work on getting the knives away from Bryan."

"And us," Dr. Brandt added. "Wouldn't take much for the knives to change direction."

"Allison?" Jess said as soothingly as she could. "Can you put the knives down someplace safe?"

From upstairs, the sound of piano keys echoed, the house seemingly using the air vents as its own speaker system.

She cut off their tails with a carving knife,

Have you ever seen such a sight in your life . . .

"It's the same tune from the other day in the basement," Jess said, no longer able to keep her voice from trembling.

"Allison, it's okay. No one is going to hurt you," Dr. Brandt coaxed. "Just make it stop, okay? You can control them. Bryan can't focus on this many objects at once."

Or under this kind of pressure, Jess thought.

Allison shook her head. Tears streamed down her cheek. "I'm not possessed! It's Riley. *He's* doing it."

"There's no one else here!" Bryan said. His outburst caused the knives to drop a few inches closer.

"Chill, okay?" Gage said, taking a step toward Bryan. "Let's all stay calm."

Jess believed Allison—she wasn't doing this. If the demons were back, Allison would have said so—that much, she was sure of. It had to be Riley. "Where is he, Allison? Where's Riley?"

"In there." Allison raised a trembling hand and pointed toward the dresser mirror.

Gage shook his head. "I got nothing."

Jess stepped closer to the mirror despite the pounding in her heart telling her to stay away. The same dark hair and eyes that had looked back at her in the basement stared at her from within *this* mirror. Riley's skin was pale and his complexion gaunt. Jess looked over her shoulder, but found only Dr. Brandt and Gage standing behind her. Allison still sat in the chair. The knives still hung over Bryan. The only difference was that in the mirror, Riley was crouched on the end of Bryan's bed.

"Oh my God," Jess said softly.

"Lord Riley would have sufficed, but . . . if you insist," Riley said. He twirled a finger and the knives spun around, too.

"No one else sees this, do they?" Jess asked, keeping her eyes on the mirror. She didn't want to turn her attention from Riley. His features seemed *off* just enough—just a little here and there. His eyes were solid black, void of the whites around his irises. His face seemed too long, the cheekbones a bit too pronounced. His facial features human, but *not*.

"Allison is telling the truth. She's not doing this. Does anyone else see Riley?" Jess repeated.

"No," everyone replied. Everyone except Allison.

"Is it the demons?" Dr. Brandt asked. "Allison? Are the demons back? Are you sure one isn't inside you? Maybe Riley is a demon now. Tell him to put the knives down. You can do this," Dr. Brandt said. "Order the demon to do as you ask."

Inside the mirror, Riley growled. The sound was neither human nor animal and fear danced up Jess's spine.

"I *can't*!" Allison wailed. Her eyes turned to Jess and then to Bryan. Dr. Brandt paced some more, his expression both frightened and yet . . . exhilarated. Jess gave Gage a quick glance.

His expression was a definite *told you he was losing it.*

Corporation, government experiment, the house taking over Dr. Brandt, or whatever else it might be, Jess couldn't allow Riley to hurt Bryan. Her heart raced wildly. Every part of her wanted to turn and run, not take a step closer to the mirror. "Leave him alone, Riley!"

Riley grinned. His teeth were dark and thin.

"Now!" Jess demanded.

Almost instantly, Riley stood directly on the other side of the glass, his dark eyes glittering. She could see Bryan lying on the bed behind Riley's image. "What will you give me, *Jessss?*"

"What do you want?" She tried to sound defiant, but took a step back.

Riley grinned. "Why, a queen, of course. For now, I'm just a dark prince. But if I had a queen, I could be king. You'll do. *So pretty.* Is it a deal? A kingdom isn't complete without a queen. Help me become king, Jess*sss*. We'll rule Siler House and all those within."

"Stay away from me!" Jess managed to say.

"Don't you want a family, Jess?" Riley leaned against the mirror and it pitted where his fingers touched the glass. "Don't you want a family that will always be there for you? We'll never die, Jess. No one here will ever leave you. Not like your father or grandmother. We'll all stay here. Together. Forever."

"Look at the fingerprints!" Dr. Brandt exclaimed. "My God, he's really there!" He turned to Jess and Allison. "You've done it, you've actually done it!"

Jess wasn't sure who made her flesh crawl more—Riley or Dr. Brandt. He didn't seem scared. He seemed overly excited at the prospect of finally getting Riley to show himself.

"Jess?" Gage stepped closer to her. "Talk to me, Jess."

"Why don't you have lover boy bring me out?" Riley coaxed. "Oh, yes! I *know*." Riley bent forward and his eyes glittered beneath stringy hair. "I didn't see it since . . ." He tapered off, the smile fading from his lips. "But I can hear through the walls. It sounded like fun." His mouth crooked into a menacing grin. "Are you having fun, Jess*sss*? Are you having fun with Gage?"

Jess hated the way he said her name with the snake-like hiss at the end. She stepped back, coming to rest against Gage.

"A little translation here?" Gage asked warily. "You girls are the only ones with Riley Vision. What's he saying?"

"He watches through the mirrors," Allison told him. "I don't know why he's trapped in the mirrors when the others aren't."

"So he's *traveling* through the mirrors?" Gage asked.

Allison nodded. "He's been watching us sleep." Her eyes cut to Jess's. "It's why I've been up at night."

Jess recalled when she had thought someone was watching her and shivered.

"Bryan," Dr. Brandt said. "Concentrate. Concentrate on sending Riley away."

Bryan closed his eyes and he mouthed the words *go away* over and over. Riley paced in and out of view a few times.

Allison got to her feet and walked over to Bryan. She leaned close to him and whispered something in his ear. For a moment, Jess thought Bryan would pull away from Allison's touch. She might not have caused the knives to hover or made Riley appear in the mirror, but Bryan was a bit freaked out. He listened, and nodded.

"Go away!" Bryan said, anger in his voice. Nothing happened. He repeated his words, louder this time. "I said, go away!"

"Oh, hell. Run!" Gage yelled. He grabbed Jess by the arm as he bolted for the door.

The knives rose upward, the tips of their blades facing outward. Seemingly no longer captive, Bryan was on his feet and running.

Jess screamed as a large knife flew past them and vanished as it hit the wall. She hurried into the hallway after the others.

"What just happened?" she nearly shrieked.

"They're gone," Bryan said, voice shaking. "I don't know how, but I think they're gone."

Dr. Brandt walked back into the room. Jess and the others didn't move. From inside it, he laughed. "You did it, Bryan! You did it!"

Gage reentered the room with Jess right behind him. Allison came as far as the doorway, but no farther.

Every knife was gone—vanished into thin air. Bryan stood beside Gage, his face an ashen gray.

Jess looked into the mirror. Riley was still there. "I'll leave. For now," he said. "But not because of him." He glanced Bryan's way. "Because you're not ready. Make no mistake, my Jess. You *will* be ready. *All* of you. Soon." He turned and walked off the edge of the mirror and out of view.

"He's gone," Jess said.

"The question is whether we can get him back," Dr. Brandt said.

"What?" Gage looked at him, incredulous. "Get him back?"

"He's *not* gone!" Allison cried. "Just because Jess or I don't see him doesn't mean he's not there."

Everyone stared into the mirror.

"*Is* he still there?" Bryan asked.

Jess studied the glass. "I think he's gone. But Allison's right. He probably moved to a different one."

"Then we'll smash all the mirrors," Gage said.

"That won't do any good," Allison replied. "Don't you guys get it? He's in the house! He's in the walls and ceilings. He's in the attic, the basement. Even the floors!"

"We'll have to do something about that," Dr. Brandt said. "But first, we need to draw him out."

CHAPTER TWENTY-ONE

The next afternoon, Jess sat on her bed and fiddled with her cell phone. She should call home. She hadn't made a single phone call since coming here. If she didn't call soon, her mother would not only be calling *her*, but Dr. Brandt, too. Yet, she didn't *want* to talk to her mother. Oddly, she didn't want to talk to *anyone* outside of Siler House. She'd have to lie about the experiment—tell her mother half-truths. If her mother knew what was going on, Jess had no doubt she'd be on the next plane to Savannah. It didn't matter that Jess was eighteen.

"Are you going to call her, or what?" Allison asked as she sat at the dresser, painting her short fingernails a bright shade of pink.

"Yeah, I suppose."

"It's the house," Allison said. "Have you noticed?"

Jess frowned. "Noticed what?"

"Exactly," Allison said softly. She shook her head and sighed. "Why am I *not* surprised? Look at what's happened so far. We've experienced some weird things in the basement. We've seen things in the mirrors. You've seen ghosts. Bryan has been making small objects disappear, and then there's the thing with the knives."

"I've noticed. Sure, there's been a lot of weird stuff going on," Jess said.

"*Weird?* Siler House is a lot more than *weird*. Don't you see? No one is running for the doors. Dr. Brandt hasn't brought in his peers."

Come to think of it, Allison was right. Jess started to mention that the reason she hadn't called home had been because her mother wouldn't believe her and frankly, Jess hadn't felt like explaining everything to her. After all, Jess's imagination was one of the reasons they'd sent her to a psychiatrist to begin with. What would her mother think if she told her any of what had happened? She'd show up, chew Dr. Brandt out, and cause a scene in general. That was the logical part about why she hadn't called home. The rest? She was at a complete loss to explain why they hadn't all packed their bags last night.

She couldn't explain why she wanted to stay—why it was still important to help Gracie and Emma instead of just getting out of here. Of course, there *was* Gage. He was part of the reason she wasn't ready to give up and go home, too.

You could still call him from home, a little voice in her head told her. Jess ignored it, knowing it wouldn't be the same between them once they left Siler House.

Allison was right, even though it defied logic. Somehow, the house was keeping them here. Not in the physical sense, but through some other means.

Allison tested one fingernail. "No one in their right mind would stay here after the incident with the knives. No one normal, that is."

Jess laughed. "When did any of us turn normal? Maybe that's why we're all drawn to stay—because Siler House magnifies what we are, what we could be, and somehow, deep inside, we all want that." She regretted her choice of words the minute she'd let them slip out. Of course Allison didn't want the demons to come back. Allison was here because she had nowhere else to go. For the next several weeks, she was still a minor. She'd sort of given up hope that anyone would come for her, and even if the house let her leave, Dr. Brandt wouldn't.

"I don't know. I mean, I believe you, but I wonder if somehow, it's only *us* that's keeping us here. It'd make more sense."

"If it's *just* us, why isn't Mrs. Hirsch gone?" Allison replied without so much as a blink in response to Jess's words. "Why hasn't Dr. Brandt called in more of his scientist friends?"

Jess shrugged. "Because Mrs. Hirsch is just plain scary at times? And I've always thought Dr. Brandt was at *least* as crazy as we are."

"No. It's because we all live here day and night. The maids and the renovation crew come and go. We're all starting to be drawn more to each other, too," Allison said.

Was Allison hinting about Jess's meeting with Gage last night? This morning over breakfast, they had been staring at each other a lot. If Gage felt anything like Jess did, there was going to be a *lot* of staring until they were able to find time alone again. Jess squirmed at the thought. It was hard to not think of how Gage's touch felt last night, despite the whole incident with Bryan. It's not like she hadn't had boyfriends before, so why did Gage make her so nervous?

Admit it. Allison is right. The house is getting a hold on all of us.

But the house wasn't getting her all dizzy over some hot guy with six-pack abs and a kissable mouth. Jess shook her head. "We've all got something in common. We've all been spending a lot of time together."

Allison raised her eyebrows and grinned. "Is that so?"

So, Allison did suspect something had happened with her and Gage last night. Fine. "That has nothing to do with the house or ghosts."

"I mean *all* of us, Jess. Not just this thing between you and Gage. Although I'm sure it's helping with that, too. It's like our connection with one another is getting stronger. Our connection with this *house* is getting stronger. It's like that saying, we're moths to a flame."

She'd known exactly what Allison was going to say.

. . . moths to a flame . . .

"*Are* we all crazy? Has Siler House made us crazy?"

"For staying, yes. I can't explain why we're still here either, Jess. I'm scared, and yet, believe it or not, I know I can't leave. It's like I'm waiting for something—the right moment. I don't know."

Jess fumbled with the phone again. "It can't have that kind of power over us."

Can it?

"So, *why* aren't you calling your mom?" Allison asked.

Jess sighed. "Honestly? I just don't want to deal with all the questions. You know parents. They read into things that aren't there. You're right. I do need to call her. Maybe when I'm done practicing my channeling. I think I'll ask Dr. Brandt for the Ouija board. Then, I'm going upstairs to the music room."

"You'll need two people," Allison said. "One on either side, with the board resting on your knees."

"Speaking from experience?"

Allison nodded solemnly.

"I've only used a Ouija board once. I was by myself," Jess relented. "Nothing happened. I guess I was doing it wrong."

"I used one a few times. It started as a dare with a few friends," Allison confided. "At first, nothing happened, either. I guess we forgot to close the portal and that's when demons came. After that, I just sat and asked the board questions on my own. The demons answered." Allison got up and went to the bathroom, closing the door. "I'm not helping you," she shouted from the other side.

Jess stared at her phone again, then called her mother. The phone rang a few times before Paul answered.

"Hey, Paul!" Jess said as cheerily as possible.

"Hey, Ghost Hunter! How's it going?"

"Everything's fine, except we haven't seen any ghosts," Jess lied.

"Oh, bummer. I know you were looking forward to it. Everything else okay?"

"It's great," Jess said. "Allison and I are getting along really well, and the house is incredible. I was just checking in. How's everything there?"

"Everyone's doing just fine," Paul replied. "Your mom and sister are at the mall. I'm sure she'd love to hear from you. Try her cell."

"No, that's okay," Jess said. "I don't have a lot of time. We're all . . ." She fumbled for an excuse. "We're supposed to meet downstairs in a few minutes. Tell her I'll call her later in the week or I'll send her an e-mail or something."

"I'll tell her. Lily misses you. We all do. Just take care and enjoy yourself, okay?"

Jess smiled. Lily. Was it wrong that she really only missed her baby sister? "Yeah, I will. And I miss you guys, too."

Something shifted under the bed. "Call you guys later," Jess said and ended the call. The shuffling sound returned. Her runaway imagination warned her the knives might be there, swishing back and forth, waiting for her to step off the bed.

It's not knives.

Don't look . . .

Unable to stop herself, Jess peered over the edge of the bed and finding nothing there, she stepped carefully onto the floor.

Something stirred under the bed again and she took a few safe steps away from the bedskirt.

"Jess!" a child's voice whispered. Her heart in her throat, Jess bent down and carefully lifted the bedskirt, nearly tumbling backward at the sight. Gracie looked out from under the bed, then slid the Ouija board forward.

She wasn't afraid of the girls, but that didn't make her any less nervous. Jess still rationalized that good ghosts could be trapped in the same location as evil ones. If Grams appeared inside Siler House right now, Jess would still be jumpy. No, what scared her was that the girls had shown up *under* the bed.

"Geez, Gracie! You scared the crap out of me!"

Gracie's bottom lip took on a pout. "We didn't mean to scare you. But *she* scares *us*. We're sorry Allison won't help you. She doesn't want to help us, either."

Jess took in a steadying breath. "It's okay. I'm fine now. Hey, we were just talking—"

"We said we'd help," Gracie interrupted, still staring unblinkingly at Jess. She pushed the board forward another inch. "Don't be mad we took it."

Jess's hands shook slightly as she took the Ouija board and planchette Gracie offered her. She'd explain about taking the board to Dr. Brandt later. Maybe he wouldn't notice if it was gone for a few hours. "Thanks," Jess managed to say.

Gracie smiled, then scooted backward, disappearing behind the bedskirt. From underneath the mattress came the sound of Gracie and Emma's echoing laughter.

CHAPTER TWENTY-TWO

Gage watched as Dr. Brandt set another item on the coffee table in front of Bryan. This time, he'd brought up one of those creepy-ass dolls from the basement.

"Try it again," Dr. Brandt urged, focusing the video camera on Bryan.

Bryan rubbed his temples. Clearly, the aspirin he'd taken for his headache hadn't kicked in.

"You've got your own work to do, Gage. You're not concentrating," Brandt said.

Gage stared at the dead crow in the shoebox. "Sorry. Maybe it's been dead too long."

The truth was, Gage had no intention of trying to resurrect the damn thing. Not the birds, the squirrel, or anything else Dr. Brandt brought him. Hell, he had no idea if he even *could* anymore.

But the last thing he was going to do was find out in front of Dr. Brandt. He agreed with Allison—the dude was acting strangely. His obsession with Riley, the ghosts and demons, not to mention his ever-increasing fondness for Siler House. It was all too weird for comfort.

Besides, look what it had gotten Bryan—Brandt was pushing him way too hard. Of course, had Bryan not made those knives disappear yesterday, they'd all be in some serious shit.

"Focus, Gage." Dr. Brandt went back to filming Bryan.

Bryan's eyebrows furrowed, and he pursed his lips as he stared at the doll.

"Dude, you look constipated," Gage said.

"Enough!" Dr. Brandt snapped. "Bryan, keep trying. It's very important you learn to do this. It's important to all of us."

All of us? Gage frowned. As far as he was concerned, Brandt was turning into a world-class douchebag. Forcing Bryan to practice until he damn near passed out or got a nosebleed wasn't cool. What was up with Brandt, anyway? At first, he couldn't take enough notes. Now, he took very few. Wouldn't EPAC be pissed off when they found out?

A drop of blood fell from Bryan's nose onto the table, quickly followed by a couple more. He swiped at his nose, while still giving the session his all. But his *all* wasn't working. Whatever juice Bryan had yesterday, he didn't have it today.

"Seriously?" Gage said.

"*Seriously*, Gage," Dr. Brandt shouted. He set the video camera down on the table. "You need to go practice outside somewhere. Now!"

"I'm all right," Bryan said, not looking even *close* to it.

Gage put the cover on the shoebox and stood. Fine. He didn't want to sit here, anyway. He couldn't have concentrated if he'd wanted to. "Bro, it's not worth it, okay?"

Bryan leaned his head back and pinched his nose closed in a failed attempt to stop the bleeding. A small trail of blood leaked between Bryan's fingers.

"Suit yourself," Gage said more to Bryan than Dr. Brandt. If Bryan wasn't going to walk away from this, Gage couldn't force him. Bryan had wanted to try it just one more time—to prove to himself he'd actually made the knives vanish. Maybe Bryan would listen to Jess, but even then, he doubted it. Bryan had pretty much stepped aside when it looked like she and Gage might hook up.

Dr. Brandt handed Bryan a napkin. Bryan held it to his nose. "Really, I'm fine," he finally said. "Doc Brandt is right. I think this is important right now."

"Sure," Gage said in disgust as he started to walk away.

"You forgot your book," Dr. Brandt said.

Gage turned and snatched the book off the table. "Call me when Bryan has an aneurysm."

"Dude, I'll be fine," Bryan insisted.

"Yeah, whatever, man. I'll catch up with you later." He headed for the door again.

"Gage!" Dr. Brandt called out. "Jess is practicing her channeling skills upstairs in the music room today. She'll be by herself. Go talk to her. If you aren't in the mood for your studies, maybe you'll be in the mood for hers."

Was Brandt encouraging him? Or just pacifying him while Bryan bled to death at the dining room table?

Bryan glanced at Gage. "Dude, if you don't go, I will. Girls get all sympathetic over injured guys."

"Sure. Why not? You know where to find me." He headed up the stairs, taking two at a time.

Gage had to hand it to Brandt—only one thing had any possibility of taking his mind off Bryan for a while, and that was spending time alone with Jess.

CHAPTER TWENTY-THREE

Jess sat in the middle of the music room floor and placed the Ouija board in front of her. On it, the illustration of disembodied heads seemed so creepy in comparison to the happier, glowing Ouija board she'd used a few years ago. In the top left corner next to the word YES was a picture of the sun, only with a man's mustached and goateed face. The sun wasn't quite smiling, but close. In contrast, in the upper right corner, the face on the moon appeared to have an annoyed or disapproving expression. Letters were arranged in arcs across two rows. Beneath them were numbers one through zero. And printed underneath the name were the words *The Mystifying Oracle*.

Be careful, Jess.

It was just a board.

A witchboard. That's what they used to be called.

What if Allison was right? What if she called the darker spirits in Siler House instead of friendly ones?

"Are you going to do this or not?" she whispered aloud in the empty room.

Taking a deep breath, she placed the planchette on the center of the board and lightly rested three fingers of each hand on the base. Staring at the open hole at the top of the planchette, she called out. "Gracie? Emma? Are you here?"

No answer. No movement from the planchette. She wiped at her forehead. Despite the air conditioner running almost day and night, the room was sweltering. August was usually the warmest of the summer months in the South, and this year, it seemed determined to break all records. Back home in Asheville, the temperature would be nearly ten degrees cooler and at least there would be a breeze. The air in Savannah felt as stagnant and thick as the moss draping the oaks.

Jess glanced around the room. "Could you guys at least cool it off in here a little?" The strong presence of a ghost sometimes meant a drop in the air temperature. "Gracie? Emma? *Anyone?*" She paused. An eerie silence filled the room as though the house were listening.

On a whim, she whispered, "Grams? Dad?"

The words seemed to hang in the air, expectantly. It'd been the first time she'd called to them since coming here.

There was no reply, not a single word, not a breeze or solitary creak. Feeling foolish, she stared at the board. The moon and sun continued to frown and smile, respectively. The women in the bottom corners were still conjuring spirits. The planchette's triangular shape sat on the board like some alien fly, patient and still. She tried to visualize the planchette moving, spelling out the words: *I'm here.*

Your imagination. Your misplaced imagination.

Admit they're gone. Both Grams and your father are gone, Jess. They've moved on.

No. They wouldn't leave her. Not forever. Not without saying—

Her eyes glanced to the bottom of the board and the two words written underneath the line of numbers. GOOD-BYE.

The word rekindled a familiar ache inside her chest. Regardless of what the board was, or did, it *was* her best hope. The girls had promised to help, and they'd given her the board. That had to mean something. This was her best hope of being able to say those two words to her father. She desperately wanted to see him, tell him one last time that she loved him and wished him well—wherever he was.

Dad. Grams.

I miss you guys so much. You have no idea.

It almost felt too good to be true. Was this all there was to it? To find an old board? One that had . . . *aged*? The board was old enough. Dr. Brandt had said that although it wasn't the one Mrs. Siler had used in her séances, the planchette was. Ghosts and spirits often attached themselves to objects. If there were ever a fact guide for ghosts, she was sure that tidbit would be in there.

And if it wasn't fact?

What if nothing happened?

God, Jess. You really are losing it. You're sliding down a slippery slope. It's commercially produced, for heaven's sake. There's a trademark symbol—

"Need an assistant?"

The words broke her concentration and Jess glanced up to find Gage walking toward her. She inhaled deeply, regaining control, or at least the illusion of it. She adjusted her shirt, hoping the action would offer some relief from the heat. Despite the warmth, Gage gave off a cool appearance, even dressed in a T-shirt and jeans. She wondered if he ever broke into a sweat, and an image of his bare chest glistening in the summer heat made her look away and focus on the Ouija board instead. "Aren't you supposed to be resurrecting a bird or something?"

Gage grinned as he sat on the floor next to her, leaving barely a breath of air between them. Jess's pulse picked up a notch.

"Sorry. No phoenixes from the ashes today. I like the idea of resurrecting *something*, though. Like our time under the sheets?"

Wow. Jess drew in a breath and struggled for something appropriate and witty, or even a little sexy, but not a single word formed. She could only stare, stupidly, like some silly thirteen-year-old with a celebrity fan-girl crush. Okay, so Gage was hot, but there were plenty of hot guys.

None of whom made her feel weak in the knees like Gage did. She forced herself to focus on the board.

"You look like you're a little busy at the moment, though."

"No!" Jess nearly shouted. "I mean, I really could use some help here."

"So, then," Gage said, and coughed.

It was bad enough he was hotter than the seven rings of hell, but he knew the effect he had on her. Probably had a lot of practice.

"I've never done this before. What should we ask it?"

"I think we're supposed to put the board between us," Jess replied somewhat reluctantly. Not that she wasn't up for trying to work the board with him right by her side, but supposedly, that's not how the board worked.

Gage scooted across from her, sitting cross-legged, and positioned the board across their knees. Jess scooted in until her knees touched his and placed her fingers on the planchette. Gage did the same, letting his fingers rest against hers.

Breathe, stupid. He'll think you're a clueless idiot.

"Ask away." Gage's eyes met hers. "Ask if it knows where Riley is right now."

Jess returned her focus to the board and concentrated. The question wasn't her first choice, but it'd do. "Where is Riley right now?"

The planchette moved over the letters slowly, their fingers floating along with it.

H O U S E

"Did you see that?" Gage asked.

Jess nodded. Shocked, it was all she could do. She'd hoped that the board would work, but seeing it in action was something else entirely.

"Ask it something else," Gage urged.

"Is Riley in this room?"

Again, the planchette moved across the board.

Y E S

Jess's heart began to race. She glanced at the mirrors the Silers had installed along the walls, but Riley wasn't in them. Suddenly, she didn't want to be in here. Not with all these mirrors.

"Ask it about demons. Ask the board about Allison."

Jess wondered if it was a wise thing to do, but nodded. "Are there demons here?"

For a moment, the planchette didn't move. Slowly, it spelled out an answer.

S O O N

Jess sucked in a breath. Maybe this wasn't such a good idea.

"Which ones?" Gage asked, solemn, as they exchanged glances. The planchette didn't move for him.

Resisting the urge to wipe her sweating palms on her shorts, Jess repeated his question. "Which ones?"

The planchette moved up, then down, creating a figure eight over and over again.

"He wants to channel a specific demon," Allison said as she walked into the room.

Jess and Gage looked up from the board, surprised. The last place Jess figured Allison would venture into was a room with a Ouija board. The planchette stopped its repetitive figure eights.

"What are you doing here?" Jess asked. "I thought you didn't want any part of this."

"I don't." Allison inched carefully closer as though the board might suddenly lunge for her.

She nodded toward the board. "But he does."

"Who?" Gage asked. "Who wants to channel a demon? Riley?"

Allison nodded again. "Yes. A really *bad* one."

Gage frowned. "They're *all* bad, Allison. Which demon?"

"The one who possessed him when he was alive?" Jess guessed.

Allison nodded once more.

"Well," Gage pressed. "Does the demon have a name?"

The planchette began to vibrate on the board, although neither she nor Gage was touching it. Jess swallowed hard, trying to keep down the fear building inside.

This was so not a good idea.

"They *all* have names," Allison replied shakily as she eyed the board. Jess had no idea how Allison was still here, why she hadn't turned and run by now. "I'm not doing that, by the way."

"Does the demon have a name?" Gage asked. If he was frightened, he didn't seem like it. "What or who are we dealing with?"

The question finally broke Allison. "Don't ask for its name!" she shrieked. "*Never* ask for a demon's name when using the board! *Never!*"

As if responding to Allison's outburst, the planchette resumed figure eights again, faster and faster.

"See what you've done?" Her face had gone completely white.

The board rattled slightly.

"Allison," Jess said quietly, trying to calm her. The board was feeding off their energy. It was all Jess could do not to push the board away from her, but that might upset Allison even more, and if the board *was* feeding off her emotions, that wouldn't be good.

Allison backed up a few steps. "Now you've done it." Tears began to flow down her cheeks, but at least her voice had returned to its normal pitch. "They're angry."

"*Who?*" Jess implored. "The demons? Riley? Who?" She could only stare at the board now.

"Make it stop!" Allison demanded. "Jess, just make it stop. Tell the board good-bye!"

The planchette continued its figure eights. It took all her will not to get up and run.

She's right! Tell it! Tell it!

"I don't know much about Ouija boards, but I think Allison's right," Gage said. His eyes were wide now, all pretense of calmness gone.

"Good-bye," Jess said weakly.

The planchette didn't stop.

"What do you know about all of this, Allison?" Gage's eyes were focused on the board as if it were a venomous snake. "What's it doing?"

Allison shook her head. Her voice was quiet. "You won't believe me. No one would."

How could Allison be calm all of a sudden? Because that is what Allison did. She shut down. She'd found someplace to hide within herself and she wasn't coming out until she felt it was safe again.

"Try me," Gage insisted.

"I shouldn't have come up here. I knew it." Allison took another step back. "Something's wrong with the board."

"You *think*?"

"He's not alone," Allison announced as she stopped at the doorway. One of her shoelaces on her sneakers had come untied, but she didn't seem to notice. Allison wasn't home.

"Riley isn't the only one here," she said, eyes glassy. "We need to go."

That was all Jess needed to hear. The time for false bravado had passed. She scooted backward, letting the board fall to the ground. Gage followed her lead. The planchette clattered to a stop, still on top of the board. With a quick jerk, it returned to its center, however. Jess yelped. The board vibrated a few beats as though some epic struggle was going on for control of the planchette.

Finally, the planchette began to move, gliding slowly over letters.

J E S S

Gage grabbed her arm and pulled her up.

Again, the planchette abruptly returned to the middle before hovering over three more letters in quick succession.

R U N

CHAPTER TWENTY-FOUR

The next afternoon, Jess and Allison sat under the shade of the oaks while the boys tossed a football. Jess hated the nearly unbearable heat and humidity. Yet, discussing the house, the project, and the Ouija board incident seemed safer to do on the back lawn than sitting in the Great Room—however wonderfully air-conditioned that might be. The maids were in today, and the painters were finishing up in some of the guest rooms.

Catching Gage's throw, Bryan paused, wiping his forehead. "You'd think with a house that size the renovations would've included a pool."

Gage peeled off his shirt, which almost made Jess forget about Riley and whatever else was going on inside Siler House. Almost.

"We could leave," Bryan said. "Call our folks and tell them to come for us."

Scowling, Gage shook his head. "Not mine. They'd remind me this is my best chance to talk with Ben. Besides, I made them a promise I'd stick this whole experiment out."

"I've tried," Allison said. "But they won't even take my calls." Her eyes met Jess's and she recalled their earlier conversation about how Siler House was drawing them all in. It was sick, like some dysfunctional relationship or addiction. Yet Jess felt helpless against it. It was happening to the others, too.

"I'd never hear the end of it," Jess said. "And my mom would harp on me to go back on medications."

"Better than being here," Allison said.

"It's not so bad." But Gage's voice was far from convincing. "Well, if you take out the whole thing with Brandt and the history of the place and all."

"HA HA!" Allison replied sarcastically.

"All I know is that I'm getting tired of practicing," Bryan said. "Quarters, pens, books, junk from the basement. My headaches have headaches and I'm tired of all the nosebleeds, too."

He shrugged. "At least Dr. Brandt doesn't seem interested in pushing us as hard. Yesterday and the day before, he was so determined. All he did was tell me to try harder, to focus. Now, it's like he doesn't care if we practice or not. All he did this morning was walk around the house touching things. He's acting like he's in some museum or tourist shop."

Jess had noticed the same thing.

"What about EPAC?" she asked. "Does anyone know if he's talking to them?"

Everyone shrugged or shook their head.

"Well, no matter how you look at it, we're still an experiment," Gage said. "But I don't think Brandt had planned to be another test subject."

Bryan spun the football in his hands. "You think EPAC knew?"

"Dude, I don't think *anyone* knew," Gage replied. "There's something really wrong with this place. EPAC and the doc thought we were going to be the only ones affected. They couldn't have been more wrong."

Bryan ran a hand through his hair. "No wonder this place has been shut down for so long. So now what? What are we going to do about it?"

"We're here until Siler House and Riley think we're ready," Allison said.

Jess forced herself to breathe. "Do you really think the house can keep us here?"

Allison nodded. Then Gage, then Bryan. They felt the same way she did.

"They call it Stockholm syndrome," Bryan told her. "It's when captives start sympathizing with their captors. We know we should leave. But we also want to stay. We can't explain why, but we do."

Jess glanced toward the gates, wishing she didn't already know it was true—that the damn house really had trapped them. She suspected that even if they walked up to the gates right now, no one would be able to go through them. She hadn't even tried. She'd been afraid since the Ouija board incident, and yet something about walking up to the gates scared her, too. The house had gotten to them all. It should have been impossible, but then half of what they all were here for should be impossible, too. How had she ever loved this place? "So now what?"

"We wait," Allison said. "We wait until Siler House thinks we're ready, or until it decides to kill us."

"It won't kill us," Jess said. "Wouldn't it already have done that?"

Bryan made a scoffing noise. "What do you think it's going to do, Jess? What do you think it would have done to me with those knives? To any of us?"

Jess hadn't wanted to think about that. She'd tried to put it out of her mind. But the house did have plenty of opportunities and yet, here they all were—among the living.

"Hey! Ease up, okay?" Gage said, his tone defensive.

"Jess is right," Allison said. "Riley was just playing with us. Riley or the house could have killed us had either of them wanted to. But that doesn't mean they can't. Or won't."

"I don't get it," Bryan huffed. "So if we're all being held here, then why doesn't EPAC step in? If Dr. Brandt isn't reporting back, then why the hell aren't a bunch of cars with tinted windows and men in suits invading the place?"

Gage shrugged. "It means he *is* reporting back to them. Just like we're doing with our folks. He's telling them what they want to hear to some degree or other. He's just not telling them everything."

"This EPAC . . ." Jess tucked a strand of flyaway hair behind her ear. "What's going to happen?"

Bryan kicked at the base of the oak. "It isn't good; that much is clear." He looked at Allison. "You know, don't you?"

"Yeah" she said. "I know enough. Maybe too much."

Gage took a seat next to Jess, but his eyes never left Allison. "Enlighten us."

Allison picked at the ground, breaking off a blade of grass. It grew like crabgrass here, broad and thick. "I didn't say anything before because, you know . . ."

Gage motioned with his hands for her to hurry up and tell the story. "Yeah, yeah. We'd have thought you were a hot mess of crazy the way you freaked out all the time. It's okay, Allison. Tell us. Tell us everything and don't leave a thing out."

Unfazed by Gage's impatience, or maybe comforted in the knowledge he'd believe her, she continued. "When they called a priest and exorcised the demons in me, there were these men who came. One of them said he was from an organization that'd help me control the demons and their power. In turn, I might be able to help them. Talk about crazy, right?"

"Help them with what?" Jess asked.

"No idea, and they wouldn't say," Allison replied. "Before long, they were talking to my parents, who wanted the hospital to keep me because they were afraid of me. Next thing I know, I'm being sent here as part of some experiment. I get the feeling that once this is all over with I'm not going home."

"You don't know that," Jess said reassuringly. "Maybe your parents—"

"*My parents don't want me*. I understand what Riley went through on this one." She lifted her head and offered them a weak smile as she blinked back tears. "That's what scares me. That I'll become like him." She paused and no one spoke, instead waiting for what she'd say next. "Anyway, after what I did, everyone was afraid of me. I don't blame them."

Gage spoke softly. "It'll be okay, Allison. Just tell us what you did."

She stared up at Siler House, taking in the entire structure, checking every window. Jess looked too, but no one, human or otherwise, looked back.

Allison resumed picking at the grass. "The longer we stay, the more it takes."

"No," Bryan said softly. "Tell us about what happened, Allison. Not about the house. Tell us what happened before you came here."

"EPAC isn't the only one who needs our abilities. Siler House wants it, too. Dr. Brandt and EPAC haven't figured that out. Yet. But they will. When Siler House takes us, it'll take us all. The demons said so."

Bryan knelt next to her. "You said they weren't with you anymore. You *said*—"

"I told the truth," Allison interrupted. "The demons told me *before* I came here. They told me they'd be back. They said they'd come and take the others, too."

"So they told you about *us*?" Gage asked.

Allison shook her head. "No, not like that. They just said there would be others with me. Others who could see. The demons are cryptic, just like ghosts, which is why I don't trust them. Why I think they're *all* bad. None of them ever comes out and tells you anything straight." She glanced at Jess as though this bit of explanation was for her benefit alone, and Jess supposed it was.

"But it had to be you guys they were talking about, right?" Allison searched their faces.

"Go on," Bryan urged.

"At first, when the demons were inside me, I just thought bad things. They were awful thoughts, but that's *all* they were. People do that from time to time, right? I didn't think it was the demons then. I thought it was depression or stress. Every day, my thoughts became less my own and more like someone else's—like a *lot* of someones. By then, they'd taken control. They told me to do things."

"What things did you do?" Bryan asked.

"*I* didn't do anything," Allison said. "Well, *technically* I didn't do anything. I watched. I set fire to a girl's house. She'd been bullying me. Her whole family was inside. They couldn't get out." Her smile was almost bittersweet. Her eyes were also distant, and it made the hair stand up on the back of Jess's neck despite the heat.

"I climbed a tree across the street and watched everything from there. I heard them screaming. The flames . . . they were so . . . *beautiful*." She plucked another blade of grass and blinked, snapping back to the present. "I didn't even need a match."

No one moved.

"The firefighters tried to save them," Allison went on. "The flames were too much. When the firemen went to put out the fire, I ran at them, screaming. They all thought I was friends with the family inside, but I was just upset they were putting out the fire."

Allison looked at them. "I tried to tell them the demons would be angry."

Jess rubbed her arms. Allison was still one of the most unsettling things about Siler House.

Allison pulled her legs up against her chest. "They locked me away even though no one could prove I'd done anything wrong. The arson investigator determined the cause was faulty wiring. I knew better. They put me away for observation because I kept telling them I set the fire, even though the real me hadn't meant to. The logical, moral me was horrified I could do such a thing. At first, I don't think they believed me. Until I killed one of the orderlies."

Allison tugged at her hair as she stared off into nothing. "I warned him. *Told* him I didn't like needles. I fought him off. He went to get help and I . . . *they* . . . the demons, snapped his neck. From somewhere inside, I begged and pleaded for them not to kill him. I curled up on my bed and stared at his body. After a while, I sort of *hid* somewhere inside my head. I call it my ivory tower."

She laughed, a tear escaping down her cheek. "Run away, Allison! Hide!"

Jess clasped a hand over her mouth. Her heart ached for Allison, and yet she understood why her aunt had recoiled the way she had that first day.

Allison wiped at the tear. "That's where I stayed. Hidden in my ivory tower." She laughed at this, but no one else joined her.

"I don't know the details or how it happened, but after a month in the psych ward I woke up, free of the demons. A priest was in the room. And those men in suits. The only reason I'm here instead of some mental ward or detention center is because of EPAC. Because of this study. So see? I don't have anywhere to go."

Tears ran freely down her cheeks. "I hate myself. I hate what they made me do! I lost . . ." She shuddered and choked back a sob. "I lost everything. Everyone. You guys are all I have. The only ones with half a chance at understanding me because you're all different, too. I can't leave and I can't let this place get you. I don't know how I can stop it, or even *IF* I can stop it. What if the demons come for me first? What if Riley gets to me? What then?"

Jess went to Allison and wrapped an arm around her. In that moment if didn't matter that she was afraid of her. "I'm so sorry, Allison."

"Oh, shit," Bryan said. "I get it. Holy shit, I *get* it. You think that part of the experiment is to—"

"It's speculation, but yeah. They'd use Allison as some sort of weapon," Gage interrupted. "She can start fires and snap necks without lifting a finger. Look at her. Who'd suspect?"

Allison nodded. She turned to Bryan. "As long as they think they can control it. As long as they can find a way to banish the demons at will." She turned her eyes to Jess and Gage. "As long as they can find them, conjure them, and be able to communicate with them whenever they want."

Jess understood, too. "Allison isn't the only one, is she?"

"Damn!" Bryan rubbed the back of his neck. "If what you say is true, Jess locates the ghosts and is the communicator. Allison brings in the wrath of hell. And, if anything goes wrong, Gage is the re-animator. Dead troops? No problem. Gage brings them back with a different soul inside. The ones Allison or Jess bring."

"Why do they need me?" Jess asked. "If they've got Allison . . ."

"Ghosts are drawn to *you*," Allison said. "And they can't always count on me. Demons aren't known to let their hosts live very long. You're the backup."

Gage's forehead wrinkled in concern. "So, it's like you're the conduit, but Jess is the magnet?"

Allison nodded and eyed the house. "Yeah. We might all be able to see ghosts, but without Jess, the odds go way down. Again, it's speculation, like Gage said. You guys could just be the control factors in the group. The point is, they have plans for me. Plans I want no part of."

"Can they do that? Can they force her to do things for them?" Jess asked.

"Possibly," Gage replied.

"What do we do?" Bryan asked, pacing now. "We just can't sit here and wait for this to go down."

"Easy," Gage said to him. He shrugged. "We give them what they want. We do a séance or we use the Ouija board. Except we all fake it. We blank our minds; we don't call for anything or anyone." He gave Jess a quick glance. "Not in front of them, anyway."

Bryan laughed. "You're kidding, right?"

"What else are we *supposed* to do?" Gage asked. "The spirits are getting stronger. What do you think will happen? You think that if the ghosts get stronger, then EPAC or Brandt will let us walk out of here? They'll think they've struck pay dirt. You heard Allison. We end this. In front of Brandt, we fake it the best way we can. But when we're together, we practice. We exterminate everything here that's supernatural. If the reading and sightings vanish, there's no experiment. There's no reason for them to want us."

"What if something else comes for us in the meantime? What if it's Riley?" Bryan asked.

"Then we'll crank up the juice before that happens." Gage turned to Allison. "Look, I know you don't want any part of this and I don't blame you. None of us do, either. Not like this. You saw what happened to Brandt. You and Jess saw this Riley dude. Now, you're telling us that he's getting stronger the longer we're here and we've got to be able to protect ourselves somehow. I think that means you and Jess need to keep your eyes open. We could use some help, though." His gaze moved to Jess. "Maybe those two girls you keep seeing are your first recruits. They should have one hell of a grudge against Riley."

"They've been dead forever," Allison argued. "And they've been here for too long."

Gage shook his head. "What's that supposed to mean? We either sit here and do nothing and wait for this douchebag Riley to come after us, or we take our best shot at ending this experiment and getting out of here. I'm all for getting the hell out of Dodge."

Allison nodded, but looked defeated.

"After we show Brandt and EPAC we don't have any mojo, we'll try our own séance," Gage continued. "Without anyone else looking. One shot. Just Jess's dad and those two girls. Don't bring *anything* else back. No matter what. Everyone got that?"

Jess shook her head along with the others. "What about—"

"We can't go looking for Ben," Gage replied sharply. "I don't want my brother to set one ghostly foot in this place."

CHAPTER TWENTY-FIVE

Gage looked over the edge of the book Brandt had given him. Jess smiled, her eyes lingering on his mouth. He raised an eyebrow and let a slow grin spread across his face as if to say, *back atcha*.

The grin widened when Jess sucked in a breath of air. He liked having that effect on her. She looked away, and he tried to focus on the book. Again.

Pretending to read about powers of the mind and all sorts of weird voodoo stuff wasn't easy. This crap just wasn't his thing. In fact, it was downright freaky. His mind kept wandering. What he wouldn't give for him and Jess to be able to go exploring in the house somewhere. Like one of the guest rooms. Of course, it would be Jess he'd actually explore. The rooms? Not so much.

Stay focused on getting us out of there. Not on Jess's body.

Gage cleared his throat, forcing himself to look away from Jess's legs and back at the book.

The short practice sessions Brandt had asked them to do when they gathered in the evenings were both the easiest and hardest part of their plan.

The easy part? They'd all agreed to put on a good show in front of Brandt, who sometimes watched them, although lately he was more and more preoccupied. Occasionally, Brandt would spend the time reading one of the books on ghosts, voodoo, spells, or whatever. He never used to do that. He'd still pore over the computer, reading research on paranormal psychology, ethereal case studies, and who knew what else. But mostly, he just stared off into space or wandered around the room touching things while they practiced their individual skills. Brandt took notes, but Gage didn't think they had a lot to do with anything he'd asked them.

"You okay, Dr. B?" Gage asked.

"Hmm? Yes, I'm fine, Gage. Fine." Brandt looked confused. "Why do you ask?"

"No reason. You just seemed a little lost in thought, that's all."

"Just going over a few things in my head," he replied. He got to his feet, excusing himself as he moved past Bryan and wandered into the dining room.

Bryan had been careful not to make anything larger than an empty teacup or saucer disappear. At least, not when Brandt or any of the staff were around. He had the most to prove, or since the night with the knives, to *dis*prove. Lucky for them all, Brandt seemed less interested in Bryan than he was in anyone else.

Allison, being *Allison*, remained uncooperative when under Brandt's scrutiny. Not that she was all that eager to call upon demons even when they got together without Brandt, but at least she was willing to discuss them.

Then, there was Jess. Jess made practicing difficult. Well, actually, just being around her was difficult, especially when she was so close he could feel the heat from her skin as she sat next to him on the sofa. Allison sat on the other side of Jess, which meant that tonight, Jess was sitting a little too close for Gage's comfort.

She was looking at him again. He could feel it. He let out a short huff of laughter and shook his head. They'd have to end this little game soon. Either that, or by the time they finally hooked up, they'd likely kill each other.

But, when it came down to this whole experiment thing, he had to hand it to her—Jess was putting on the best show of all. She'd sometimes close her eyes, her brows pulled together in a slight frown as though she were doing her best to talk to the other side. Except now, when she was just set on torturing him.

Jess leaned forward to grab her soda from the coffee table. She'd surprised him, the way she'd so casually answered Brandt's questions about Gracie and Emma. She'd told Brandt the truth. Sort of. That Gracie and Emma had been visiting a little more over the past couple of days.

What she *hadn't* told Dr. Brandt was that the girls had come around a *lot* more. The only room Jess hadn't seen them in was the storage room across the hall from where she and Allison were staying. Riley was making more of a presence, too. No one mentioned that, either. They'd all taken to placing towels over the mirrors in their rooms.

It'd been easy to fool Brandt, but Gage wondered if it had been *too* easy. The doc was hard to read.

Right on cue, as if he knew Gage was thinking about him, Brandt stopped staring at those freaky faces in the dining room's molding and turned to Bryan.

He took a couple of steps back toward the connecting Great Room. "How have your headaches been, Bryan? Any nosebleeds?"

"Huh?" Bryan looked up from the potted plant he was pretending to try and make vanish.

"The headaches? The nosebleeds?" Brandt repeated.

"They're gone," Bryan said. "Of course, I haven't been able to make anything disappear lately."

Gage hid a smile. *Way to go, Bryan! You lie like a pro!*

Brandt nodded, either buying into the lie or not caring. "Well, keep trying." He turned to Jess. "I need you to bring out the others, Jess. There must be more ghosts here."

"I saw the man on the stairs again," Jess replied.

"Tell us about him," Brandt urged, suddenly interested. Gage wanted to groan. They'd almost been free of him for the night. Why did she have to go and say anything?

Jess sighed and shook her head. "He's just a shadow. And he either can't talk to me or he won't."

Brandt nodded. "You should ask the Ouija board who he is."

Gage didn't dare look at the others. None of them was very fond of the Ouija board after the other night when it had told Jess to run, then hurled the planchette into the wall. Despite that, Jess had used it again at Brandt's coaxing. They'd asked about Jess's father, and Gracie and Emma. No one asked about Riley, the demons, or even the ghost of a patron saint. And there had been no more planchette mishaps since then.

But if Allison had demons on speed dial, Jess had ghosts. There had been more ghosts around—two women who might have been maids when the Silers lived here had been spotted roaming the halls.

Jess nodded in response to Brandt's suggestion about the man on the stairs. "I'll ask."

"And Gracie and Emma?" Dr. Brandt inquired.

"They're not as transparent as they used to be."

Yet another sign the house was getting stronger. Gage wondered if Brandt was drawing the same conclusion.

Brandt took a seat in one of the chairs. "It's encouraging that Gracie and Emma are showing themselves to you and Allison. But we need them to show themselves around *me*."

Gage exchanged glances with Bryan. Sure, the doc had been the only one who hadn't seen them yet, but the way he'd said it seemed . . . off.

Jess simply nodded. "I'm trying to convince them. They're just shy."

Brandt stood and paced a few steps. "We need to bring out Riley. From our combined experiences, he's the most willing. Draw out a few more ghosts, Jess. Then, we'll hold a séance for Riley."

With that, he walked away, leaving them alone in the Great Room. He'd been disappearing a lot lately. Two days ago had been the first time they'd noticed it, although even Allison thought some of Brandt's earlier disappearances were because he'd been spending time in the basement. Everyone exchanged glances.

"The basement," Allison said, echoing Gage's thoughts. "Again."

Mrs. Hirsch passed through, eyeing them. She'd been looking at them differently since the knife incident. Not that Gage could blame her.

He forced a smile and wiggled his fingers in mock greeting.

"Hey, Mrs. Hirsch," Bryan said. "How's it going?"

Bryan. Always the cheery, polite one. Mrs. Hirsch's hand tightened on her key ring and the other hand fumbled for the pendant she wore around her neck, but her stare remained as icy as ever. Instead of answering, she nodded briefly before continuing through the Great Room and up the stairs.

Gage thought it was weird that she continued her rounds even though she could see all of them were right here. He'd have gotten used to it by now, except Mrs. Hirsch was just flat-out hard to get used to. Then again, she probably thought the same about all of them.

"Well, that was pleasant," Jess said, once Mrs. Hirsch had gone upstairs.

"Yeah, well, she's a real people person," Gage replied.

"I've got something for you," Bryan said, reaching under the chair and pulling out a paper plate with a dead mouse on it.

"Ew!" Allison said.

Gage held up a hand. "No thanks, bro. I'm still full from dinner."

Bryan shot him a serious look. "It was an easy find. Do you want to practice while Brandt's gone or not? Mrs. Hirsch won't be back down for a little while." He shrugged. "Not that she'd think much of it, anyway."

Bryan nudged the plate and the mouse rolled over on its other side. "You bring it back, I make it vanish. Just like the lizard and the frog."

Gage exhaled. He didn't feel like doing this anymore. He wanted to do something . . . normal. Go out, watch TV. Anything. "We're getting to be a real circus sideshow act here."

For whatever reason, dead things hadn't been too hard to find on the estate grounds. He'd been successful at reanimating a few of them, and Bryan had been equally successful at blinking them off into his version of the Bermuda Triangle.

Jess's leg brushed against his again, making it damn impossible to think of *anything* else but her bare skin on his, how inviting and soft her mouth had been when they'd last kissed, how she had tasted as he'd kissed her neck, how she'd felt pressed up against him . . .

"I need something to drink," he said, getting to his feet and heading to the kitchen. He opened the fridge, letting its cool air wash over his skin, then took a bottle of soda and unscrewed the cap.

"It's getting to us all," Allison said behind him.

Gage lifted a brow and scoffed. *You have no idea, sister.*

Allison retrieved the orange juice from the fridge. The bottle was almost empty. "The house," she said, removing the cap and not bothering with a glass. "The longer we're here, the more it intensifies our emotions."

Gage took a swig of soda. "Tell me about it."

Which was the wrong thing to say around Allison because she would. Repeatedly. Enthusiastically. It was the one thing that made them all not want to listen to her. It wasn't that they didn't believe her. How could they not? It was just that Allison took things to an extreme. Gage eyed the doorway. Jess might already be heading upstairs . . .

"It won't be long," Allison continued, clueless as to the real reason behind Gage's discomfort. "We've got to hurry this up somehow. I feel it. The evil in the house. It's like the demons are at the door and Riley is about to let them in."

"Yeah, I know," Gage replied. "We're doing the best we can, okay? Stick to the plan."

"You don't get it," Allison said, her voice strained. "You're not the only one who has eyes for Jess. Riley does, too."

Allison's observation didn't faze him. He figured the way he and Jess had been lately, everyone would have to be blind not to see he was attracted to her. And it didn't surprise him that Riley or any other male would find her attractive, too. Still, Gage was used to competition from living, breathing rivals. Not ones he couldn't see.

He pushed away from the counter. "Yeah, I sort of got that. But he's not her type."

It wasn't as though he didn't care—he did. He understood what Allison was really saying here—that Riley would probably go for Jess first.

"Don't be a smart ass," Allison said, leaning in. "I'm scared, Gage. Not just for me, but for Jess. Even though this EPAC committee probably wants me the most, Siler House wants *Jess* the most. It'll stop at nothing to get her."

"Look, not everyone handles their stress around here by freaking out. I use humor. Deal with it, okay?" He was sorry the moment he'd spoken. He took another swig of soda. "Sorry. I guess we're all stressed. Look, about Riley. We're not going to let that happen, Allison. I promise. But what else are we supposed to do about it right now? Because if you've got a better plan, I'm listening."

Why not? Unless he was ready to just march into the Great Room and toss Jess over his shoulder and carry her off—which wasn't going to happen—he might as well hear Allison out.

Voices from the other room began to carry into the kitchen. It was getting late, and Bryan and Jess sounded like they were going to call it a night, after all.

"Well?" Gage asked. Allison might be a bucket of crazy, but something in her expression told him she'd clearly thought this over, probably quite a bit since she didn't sleep much at night anymore. He was game to hear her out.

"Okay," he said. "Let's go talk to the gang."

"We need to talk about a lot of things, but this can't be done during the day, Gage. We need to do the séance, but not with Dr. Brandt around. Something's wrong with him. We need to talk about this. Tonight. But not in the house."

Gage thought it over and nodded. Sure. Made sense, God help him. Who knew where Riley was these days? And, if they couldn't see all the ghosts all the time, it might be better if their ethereal ears weren't around for a change. They'd have to sneak out after Brandt had gone to sleep and Mrs. Hirsch made her first set of rounds, and be back inside before her next. Good thing he'd already made a note of when those times were. Of course, it'd been for different reasons, but what the hell.

"We all meet by the oak, three in the morning." He tossed the bottle cap into the trash and walked out.

"What do you think Brandt is doing down in the basement?" Bryan asked Gage once they were back in their room.

"No idea. We could follow him the next time." Gage sank onto his bed. Brandt was either up to something or his train had left the station. But either way, the doc was beginning to worry him. It was as though he was on something, like he was spacing out on them.

The house? Could it be the house has gotten to him that much? Or is he shutting down, like Allison does sometimes after she overdoses on freak-out?

"I'm curious, but I don't think we should push it," Bryan replied. "Whatever he's doing in the basement, it means he's not spending as much time with us. Gives us time to practice."

Gage stared up at the ceiling. "We're going to have to be ready whenever he wants to do this séance. I hope Allison holds it together. If she doesn't, there's no telling what she'll bring over."

"Think she can fake it?"

Gage shrugged. "She's not going to try to actually summon Riley, and neither am I, but we can't be sure it won't work, anyway. We've been pushing our luck with the Ouija board. I don't know if whatever's holed up on the other side is going to stay there if we end up doing a séance and the Ouija board is present."

"What does Jess think?" Bryan asked. "Does she think Allison can do it? Close the door to anything that might want to drop in on her and stay a while?"

"Not sure. We haven't had a lot of time to talk about that," Gage said.

Bryan laughed softly.

"It's not like that. Yet. Unfortunately. We just haven't had a lot of time to ourselves at all. Much less to talk about Allison."

Bryan laughed again.

"Shut up."

Bryan grinned. "Fine. Truce." He hooked a thumb over his shoulder. "Hey, I'm going to the kitchen for something to drink. Want another soda or something?"

"No, I'm good," Gage replied.

"Suit yourself," Bryan said as he headed out of the room.

Gage lay on his bed, hands propped behind his head.

Jess. He couldn't get her off his mind. Not just because she was turning him on all the time. But because she took his mind off everything else for a while—Ben, his parents, this house. Everyone looked to him to help make things right when he really didn't have a clue at all how to do that.

He felt badly for Jess at times. All she wanted was a chance to see her dad once more—to tell him she was sorry for not being there when he'd died. To tell him she loved him. Sometimes, he lay awake at night wondering if there was some way to help her with that. Other nights, like tonight, it was just hard not to think of her in . . . other ways.

Gage rolled over and punched his pillow a few times.

CHAPTER TWENTY-SIX

"Can't sleep again?" Jess asked. Not that tonight was any different than every other night. It was no wonder Allison always looked so tired. Jess didn't think her roommate slept more than a few hours at a time.

Allison shook her head. "You'd think I'd be used to it by now." She pushed the sheets back and sat upright. "Sorry. I know I'm keeping you awake."

Jess sat up and sighed. "No, not really. I'm not real sleepy, either. Feel like going to the kitchen and maybe getting a cup of tea or something?"

Allison retrieved a book from the nightstand. "I think I'll just sit here and finish this."

"What are you reading, anyway?" Jess asked.

Allison opened the book. "*Oliver Twist*."

Jess raised her eyebrows. "Really? *Oliver Twist*?"

Allison shrugged. "Beats thinking about Riley lurking in the mirrors."

"We've covered the mirrors. He can't see us." Jess took a seat on the edge of Allison's bed, hoping she might change her mind about going downstairs. Since the incident with the knives, Jess didn't like wandering the house alone at night. Not that having Allison with her would do much good. If anything, having a demon magnet for a roommate should have meant keeping *away* from her. But not one demon had manifested itself yet, and Allison was a pretty good Riley gauge.

Allison didn't look up from her book. Not a good sign she would give in and go along. "Doesn't mean Riley's not still there and getting really ticked about the towels over all the mirrors. I bet he's thinking of some other way to watch us. The walls and floors only tell him where we are."

Jess got to her feet and took off her sleepwear shorts and top and put her shorts and T-shirt back on. "Come on! Come downstairs with me. Please?"

Allison shook her head.

"Well, I'll be back in a little while then," Jess said, resigned.

"Be careful if you do any exploring. Don't go into any rooms where we haven't covered the mirrors."

"I won't," Jess replied. "I promise. See you in a little while. Want me to bring you anything?"

Allison's attention had already returned to her book. "No. See you later."

Jess let herself out and headed down the hallway. Mrs. Hirsch had taken to leaving the lights on by the staircase and on each floor's landing. Since the knife incident, Mrs. Hirsch wasn't keen on anyone walking the halls at night. Especially alone.

It turned out she didn't run into Mrs. Hirsch at all. Only Bryan, who was raiding the pantry for a late-night snack.

"Jess!" Bryan said, seeming surprised.

"Couldn't sleep either, huh?" She opened one of the cabinets in search of a mug. It hadn't occurred to her one of the guys might be down here. Too bad it wasn't Gage instead.

"Potato chip?" Bryan offered.

Jess smiled. "No, thanks. I'm just going to have a cup of tea."

Bryan leaned against the counter as he ate. "Allison keeping you up again?"

"She's awake, but it's not her," Jess replied as she filled the cup with water and put it into the microwave. "Just couldn't sleep is all." She rummaged through the pantry for tea. "No decaf," she said. "Guess regular will have to do."

"But won't that keep you up?" Bryan asked. "I mean, that stuff has caffeine in it, right?"

Jess laughed. "Yeah, it does, but that's all that's here. I'll have to ask Mrs. Hirsch if we can get some other kinds." She added the tea bag to the cup.

"Do you want sugar or milk with your tea?" Bryan asked, heading to the refrigerator.

Jess raised an eyebrow.

"My mom," he explained. "She's a tea drinker. She usually puts milk and sugar in hers. I guess it's a thing."

"Sure," Jess replied with a smile.

Bryan set the milk on the counter while Jess retrieved the sugar bowl.

"So, I guess three of us have insomnia tonight," Jess said, as she stirred in the sugar. She didn't want to mention the real reason she'd been restless the past couple of nights—Gage.

Bryan laughed. "I think *all* of us have insomnia. Gage is wide awake, too. He just wasn't hungry." Bryan grinned. "Say, maybe you should check in on him."

Jess nearly spilled her tea. "What?"

His smile grew wider. "You heard me."

She looked over her shoulder, half expecting someone to be standing close enough to hear them, but mostly to hide the fact she felt a blush coming on. *"Bryan!"*

He stuffed the bag of chips back into the pantry. "Oh, don't give me that 'Bryan' crap. Come on." He headed out of the kitchen, stopping only when he realized she wasn't right behind him.

"Would you prefer I go get him?" Bryan asked, still grinning. "Because I'm sure he'd love to see you. You could just . . . sit on the sofa and talk."

Jess was about to say that might be a safer idea, but Bryan was already back in the kitchen. He took the cup from her hand and dumped the tea into the sink.

"Hey! What'd you do that for?" Jess asked.

He rinsed the cup out, quickly dried it with the dish towel, and placed it back into the cabinet.

"Bryan!" But by now, his attitude was infectious and she couldn't help but laugh.

"It's clean enough," he said, taking her by the wrist and pulling her from the kitchen. Jess would like to have thought she offered some resistance, but realized that was laughable at best. She let him lead her through the Great Room and up the stairs to the second-floor landing.

Jess waited while he scoped the hallway, but even she could tell Mrs. Hirsch wasn't around. Whenever the house-keeper was checking out a locked room, she always left the door open while she was in there. The lighting in the hall wasn't great, but Jess didn't notice any open doors. Mrs. Hirsch was probably on the third floor, or in the music room.

Or in the basement with Dr. Brandt.

Bryan walked back to her. "Coast is clear. I can go get him, and we can all go back downstairs," he whispered. "Or, you can stop in and say hello by yourself. Your call. Whatever you're comfortable doing."

Jess let the thoughts of how heated things were getting with Gage fill her head. She recalled how perfect his lips felt on hers, how warm his hands were, how she'd run her hands under his shirt.

She was still thinking of these things when she realized Bryan was going into his room. Damn! She'd missed her chance to be alone with Gage. She padded down the hall after Bryan.

"Gage," Bryan called out quietly as he opened the door. "You have a visitor." Bryan turned and smiled when Jess walked up beside him.

"For God's sake, put each other out of misery," Bryan whispered in her ear.

Gage rolled off the bed wearing nothing except a loose pair of well-worn and equally faded gray sweat shorts. Add to that the sight of him shirtless, and she didn't think she'd ever catch her breath again.

He looked puzzled at first, but then that grin, the one that melted her into a puddle, spread across his face and Jess didn't care that she was staring at him in full appreciation.

Gage's eyes met hers, then he glanced at Bryan.

Beside her, Bryan laughed softly. "I'm just going to go get a snack," he said. "Another one. I'll be back in . . . half an hour?"

Gage's attention turned to Jess once more. Everywhere his gaze fell, she felt as though her skin had become electric. He stepped into the doorway, standing so close she had to lift her head to look at him. Her eyes lingered on his mouth and everything else but her need for him faded away.

Gage's eyes held hers. "Better take your time, bro."

CHAPTER TWENTY-SEVEN

How many times and how many ways had he pictured this playing out? A hundred? More? He loved how Jess's hair hung loose to just below her shoulders, the way the lighting in the hallway gave her a warm, seductive glow. He loved how long her legs looked and the way her denim shorts rested low on her hips, baring a little midriff. Her ivory shirt draped just right over her breasts, and Gage couldn't help but notice her nipples beneath the fabric. She wasn't wearing a bra. The sight was enough to drive him out of his mind. But nothing sent him over the edge like the way Jess was looking at him.

Undress me, her eyes, not to mention two very attentive body parts, said. *Like the way I want to undress you. Now.*

And if that didn't get him moving in *all* the right directions, nothing ever would. He closed in, pushing her against the wall with the length of his body, making sure she had no doubt of the effect she had on him. His mouth found hers and she greedily kissed him back, a soft groan escaping her mouth as her hands traveled across his abs and back. He reached down to cup her perfect ass in his hands, pulling her even more tightly to him.

Jess responded by pressing her breasts against him.

The girl was torture. And yet, he wanted to be sure, wanted *her* to be sure. Normally, he wouldn't have cared, but Jess . . . Jess was different.

He kissed her ear, her neck. "Are you . . ."

Jess grinned up at him, then she wrapped her arms around his neck and lifted her legs gracefully around his waist, positioning herself against the front of his shorts.

"Shut up," she said breathlessly. She kissed him harder, more intently, biting lightly at his bottom lip.

God, how he needed her. The feel of her against him was enough to make him want to groan out loud. He turned and carried her back into his room. Jess untangled herself from him, setting her feet down on the floor. Gage closed the door behind them as Jess tugged forcefully at the band of his shorts, pulling him to her once more.

She leaned into the wall as Gage pressed himself against her, harder than ever this time, kissing her and letting his hands travel down her shirt, reaching underneath it and up to her breasts. He took them in his hands, his thumbs brushing her hardened nipples.

Jess pushed him away, and he was about to complain until she tugged her shirt over her head, tossing it to the floor. He grinned, taking in the sight of her. She came to him again, running her hands through his hair, down his shoulders and arms, then slowly over his chest and abs before traveling farther south. His heart thudded hard as first her lips and then her wet, warm tongue brushed his chest. He leaned his head back and closed his eyes as a low growl escaped him. Damn, the girl was on fire, and Gage was more than enjoying the heat.

He fumbled with the button on Jess's shorts, and finally managed to unzip them. She helped him slide them over her hips and then stepped out of them, wearing nothing but pink cotton panties.

Gage walked her backward to the bed, his eyes holding hers as he pushed her onto it, then eased himself on top of her. Jess wrapped her long legs around him once more and arched her hips.

"I've been waiting for this, Jess."

Jess smiled at the low rasp of his voice as he said her name. She wanted to spin him up, tease him as much as he'd teased her, not just now, but over the past week and even before, when thoughts of him had begun to invade her dreams.

His mouth was warm, delicious and kissably soft, while the feel of his body against hers sent waves of heated desire through her midsection . . . and lower. The heat of his breath against her neck and the touch of his hands as he explored her body was almost too much.

Jess had been daydreaming of this, but never had she expected it to feel as good as it did at this very moment. And oh, God, if she thought Gage could do wonders with his hands, his mouth and tongue were even better. She reached down to his shorts, sliding them over his hips, taking in the sight of him. Was there *anything* about him that wasn't sexy as hell? Suddenly, she didn't want to tease anymore, didn't want him teasing her, either. Yet, that's what he did as he tossed his shorts from the bed and positioned himself between her legs, pressing hard against her panties as he went back to kissing her. She struggled against him, thinking that he was going to make her beg. He kissed her throat, her chest, her stomach as he slid off her underwear.

Omigod! He's amazing!

"Gage . . ."

He looked at her and he was wearing that damned cocky grin of his. Then her breath caught as his eyes held hers and the grin faded from his face.

In that moment, nothing else mattered. Not the house, the ghosts, the experiment. Just his groan of pleasure as he entered her for the first time.

Telling Bryan they'd needed more time had been a good move. Jess couldn't help but stare into Gage's eyes, hoping this night would never end. After their first frenzied rush, Gage had made sure to take things more slowly the second time, his touches soft and tender, fueling her need for him and sending chills along her skin at the same time. Nothing could have been sweeter, more passionate.

And oh! What moves the boy had.

He paused, pushing up off her a little. His eyes were closed and his jaw set as he attempted to adjust his breathing. The feel of him inside her and the small beads of sweat on his skin only ignited her further. She wrapped her hands around his hips, urging him on until they were both over the edge in ecstasy.

He kissed the tip of her nose before rolling off her. He might not be long-term boyfriend material, but Gage was a god in his own right, and certainly in Jess's mind.

After a few minutes, he tucked an arm under her and stared into her eyes. "So, we live about an hour and a half away from each other. That's not so bad." That devastating grin that turned her inside out spread slowly over his face again. "That is, if you ever *needed* anything."

Jess laughed and gave him a playful shove. Gage not only knew the right moves, he knew the right words. That was a dangerous combination. Too dangerous, actually. She'd dated his type before. The afterburn had turned her off from dating for a while. Still, her hand rested against his chest, wishing that there might be a time when all this was done and she *could* make such a call.

"Careful," he said, still grinning, gorgeous hazel eyes flashing. "Bryan's due back any minute."

"You're incorrigible," Jess said, grinning back. She ran a finger along his abs. The house wasn't the only thing around here that was addictive. "Yeah, I'd like us to stay in touch."

"You know it's inevitable."

Jess laughed. "What's inevitable?"

"Me," he said simply. "I'm going to win your heart yet."

"Uh-huh, right." There was no way she was going to let him know that, in part, he already had.

He kissed her softly. When they broke apart, he brushed back a strand of her hair. There was tenderness in his eyes at first, and Jess thought she just might get lost in them. But Gage being Gage, that grin crept back and tenderness was replaced with mischief. And *that* she could always get lost in.

"We still have a couple of weeks." He kissed a trail down her neck to her breasts.

Oh yeah, Jess thought. This experiment had just gotten a lot better.

CHAPTER TWENTY-EIGHT

Jess crept back into her room just before one o'clock. She'd expected Mrs. Hirsch to be standing outside Gage's room or at the very least, to catch her on her way back to her own, but she must have been elsewhere. It was odd not to have run into her, but Jess wasn't complaining.

Allison was still awake, still reading her book.

"If we go to sleep now, we can still get a couple of hours," Jess said as she exchanged her shirt and shorts for a sleep shirt.

Allison looked at the clock and yawned. "Yeah, I suppose. Did you run into Mrs. Hirsch?"

"Never saw her. Found Bryan in the kitchen, though." She didn't mention the part about Gage.

Allison frowned. "That's weird she didn't run into you guys. She's been by here a few times. I can hear the floorboards creak in the hallway. For a while, she was up and down it so much I thought she was looking for you in one of the rooms again. I almost checked."

Jess crawled into bed and fluffed her pillow. "Nope. She never found me." Before Allison could ask *why* Mrs. Hirsch hadn't found her, Jess turned out the light, and rolled over. "Sleep quickly," she said.

"Maybe it wasn't her, then."

"What?"

"Maybe it was one of *them*."

Jess turned back over. "Them? You mean the girls?"

"No, it was only one set of footsteps and too heavy for a couple of girls." Allison adjusted her own pillow. "Anyway, they're gone now. See you in a couple of hours."

Great. Even when Allison wasn't really trying to creep her out, she was creeping her out. Jess looked at the dresser where a large bath towel covered the mirror.

Don't think about it. Gage's mirror was covered, too.

Jess lay on her side, listening to the sound of crickets and bullfrogs, which were in full chorus, and trying not to think about any of the other sounds that might be one of the resident ghosts. Or Riley. What if he found a way out of the mirrors like Allison said?

What if he hadn't needed them all along?

Stop thinking about it. You'll never get any sleep.

But exhaustion and thoughts of Gage won out and Jess drifted into perfect, dreamless sleep.

Until she felt a cold hand on her arm. She jerked, wondering if it was three o'clock already and Allison was shaking her awake. Sensing someone standing beside the bed, she bolted upright. The twins. They'd startled her so badly she couldn't even scream. God, she *hated* it when ghosts snuck up on her. They were like cats, mostly quiet and stealthy.

"Shhh!" Gracie whispered. "We don't have long."

Jess tried to collect her thoughts. Her heart was beating wildly in her chest. She looked at the nightstand clock. Two thirty. "What are you doing here? What's wrong?"

"We want to show you something." Emma stuck out her hand as though she expected Jess to take it.

Jess glanced over at Allison, who was still asleep.

"I don't think—"

"It's *important!*" Gracie whispered. Her face wrinkled in concern "Please, Jess. *Please!*"

Reluctantly, Jess got out of bed and threw on her shorts under her sleep tee. She reached out to take Emma's hand in hers, knowing very well that it'd slip through her grasp.

But it didn't. Not entirely. While she couldn't say that *she* was holding Emma's hand, Emma's hand was definitely holding on to Jess's. There wasn't the feeling of Emma's skin on hers, just a cold *something* in her palm. Allison's warning that the house and its occupants were getting stronger was an understatement.

Emma smiled up at her, and Jess tried not to show her nervousness. She'd never been able to touch a ghost before, and one had never touched her—not even Grams. Jess had thought about it, and often wondered what it'd be like. It was like touching death itself.

Emma tugged at her, sending biting cold into her hand. What would Allison think when she found Jess already gone?

225

She allowed Emma to lead her out of the room as they followed Gracie down the hall. The girls walked ahead, going down the stairs and vanishing through the front door. Jess held her breath, then unlocked the door and opened it slowly, hoping it wouldn't creak.

Stepping out into the night, she closed the door carefully behind her. The girls stood waiting, the moonlight shining through them. Their expressions were pinched, as though worried. Despite the warm air, Jess shivered.

Gracie turned and walked down the steps and her sister followed. Jess followed, too. "Where are we going?" she asked.

"You have to *see*," Gracie replied without stopping.

Jess quickened her step. She wondered if Bryan and Gage were already out here and something had happened. "Wait! See what?"

"What he did," Emma replied, her tone sullen.

"What *who* did?"

"Don't worry, it's none of your friends," Gracie called back to her. Her words might have reassured her if Jess didn't hear such sadness in them. Why would they want to show her something that clearly upset them so much?

Jess followed them across the moonlit lawn to the rear of the house, toward the little fenced-off cemetery where Gracie and Emma were buried. Jess expected them to stop there, but the girls walked past it, straight to the edge of the woods. There, they stopped and turned to face Jess.

"Why are we out here?" Jess asked.

226

The girls exchanged expressionless glances. "We told you," they said in unison. "To see."

Jess looked around. There wasn't anyone else out here. Everything looked just as it had in the daylight—quiet and undisturbed. "I don't know what you mean."

"You will," Emma said.

"In there," Gracie added. She pointed to the dense line of trees bordering the back lawn.

"In *there?*" Surely the girls didn't wake her in the middle of the night to go wandering off into the woods.

The girls nodded.

Jess eyed them cautiously. She didn't like the idea at all. "Girls? What happened in there?" It was almost a rhetorical question because Jess felt certain she knew *exactly* what had happened. Riley had killed them.

"We died in there," Emma said, confirming Jess's suspicions.

Jess glanced at the woods. It seemed even darker now, like it could swallow her whole if she stepped inside. "Well, then, it doesn't sound like a good idea for me to go there."

"You have to see what happened," Emma said. "We'll be with you, Jess. *Please?*"

"Don't worry." Gracie placed her hand in Jess's, sending another shiver up her arm.

"You said you'd help us. We just need to show you what happened," Emma pleaded.

"When you see, you'll understand," Gracie pressed. "We can't be at peace until you see what needs to be done. We've been separate all these years. He separated us."

Separated?

Jess looked into Emma's pleading eyes. Trust them? Or turn and run? The others would be out here soon and wonder where she was. On the other hand, if the girls could revisit the place they'd died, revisit what horror had fallen on them, then Jess could try to find her strength and go with them. Maybe the act of finally showing someone what had happened would bring them peace. Maybe it'd be a step in helping to send them on, freeing them of Riley and Siler House.

She had no idea if this was true or not, but maybe all the girls needed was for someone to understand the horror of what had been done to them—why their lives had been taken at such a young age. She'd never crossed over a ghost before. But she'd read and heard of stories where ghosts just needed a form of closure before they let go of the past. Siler House had sat empty for so long that the girls had no one to tell.

Until now.

They continued to wait patiently. Emma's lips were pursed together, her forehead wrinkled with worry in anticipation of Jess's answer. "Please, Jess. *Please.* We can't truly be together until you see."

Standing on the edge of the woods was like standing on the edge of another world. Trees stood like some spectral army against a backdrop of black. Stepping inside meant wearing the darkness like a cloak. It would envelop her, making her invisible to Gage and the others who expected to find her on the back lawn.

Turn back.

Emma took Jess's hand into both of hers and tugged.

"How far?" Jess asked.

"Not far. You'll be back before Allison and the others come looking for you," Gracie said.

"Okay," Jess said, not feeling that it was okay at all.

The girls smiled and led Jess into the woods.

CHAPTER TWENTY-NINE

True to their word, the girls hadn't ventured too far into the woods before coming to a complete stop. The bright moon shone through the treetops, allowing Jess better visibility.

"Is this where you died?" Jess asked, unable to keep the slight tremor from her voice. There wasn't anything unusual about the area they'd stopped in. Just a bunch of trees with woodland debris at their bases.

The girls exchanged another glance.

"This is where it happened," Gracie said. "Are you ready to see?"

Jess didn't answer. Her heart raced and her mouth had gone dry. She wasn't ready, but what could she say?

"You have to touch the earth," Emma explained. "You have to touch the spot where it happened. You'll see it then."

"And you'll see it *when*," Gracie added.

Jess shook her head. "I don't think that's all it takes." Her reply was more of an excuse to turn around and go back than anything else. She wondered what might be underneath the decaying leaves. Crawly bugs, snakes, and the like were the least of her worries.

"But it is enough," Gracie's form flickered in the moonlight. "For you." As Emma let go of Jess, the cold chill slid up from her hand to her entire body, freezing her into place.

"You've always been able to see things, Jess. See *us*. Ghosts. But you don't know how to channel it. Yet. Touching the area our bodies were in will help. You'll be closer to us and you'll see through to the other side," Gracie explained. "You'll be able to see things in our world."

Emma nodded. "It's what you'd call the veil."

Jess frowned, but the girls' expressions remained emotionless. What if by helping the girls, Jess could make it easier to find her father on the other side?

Be careful what you let in, Jess.

But this wasn't a portal or some veil. She wasn't letting something or someone else in. She was just looking through it to some other side.

Like some sort of one-way mirror. No. Don't think of it like that. Don't think of Riley and whatever else is there.

Part of her wanted to scream, to run away. Yet, some other part wanted to see this—wanted to know if she truly could see even further into the unknown.

It's the house. Allison is right—it's doing something to us.

It can't. You're not in the house. Don't blame it for what you want to know. You can do this. You've come this far. It's just dirt. Dirt! Just sticks, leaves, and Georgia clay. You've let ghosts touch you and you can't even touch a patch of dirt?

Jess shook her head, trying to clear her thoughts. "Okay." Shaking slightly, she knelt down to the moonlit earth, the girls standing on either side of her, and placed her palm on the ground. At that same moment, the girls rested their hands on Jess's shoulders. The cold of their touch bit into her, and she cried out in agony. Her vision grew fuzzy. A sense of frigid air and darkness swirled through her.

Jess blinked and found herself standing alone in the woods. It was daylight now and the air had a different smell—more earthen and pine, and something else, too.

. . . *you'll see it* when.

When. As in time. Jess understood where she was, but more importantly, she had a good idea *when* she was— August 1909.

"Gracie? Emma?" she whispered. No answer. Up ahead came the sound of someone shoveling dirt. She wanted to call out again, but didn't dare. If all she had to do was see what happened, then maybe she'd return or wake up.

Heart hammering, Jess made her way toward the sound. His back was to her as he fervently dug into the earth. Same dark hair, same tall, thin build.

Riley.

Gasping, she ducked behind a tree, mentally cursing herself for making noise. Surely he'd hear her. But he didn't. He grunted as he continued to shovel sprays of earth.

He was digging their graves!

After a few minutes, Riley stopped and tossed the shovel aside. He walked out of her line of sight, behind a thicket of trees, and then returned with a blanket and a wicker basket.

He set the basket down and spread the blanket out neatly between a couple of trees.

What the hell?

Riley took a seat on the blanket and extracted silverware from the basket, along with a red apple. He bit into the apple and looked up into the trees, taking in nature and the sky above him.

She cursed him for being so nonchalant about enjoying a picnic before burying Gracie and Emma's bodies. She should have been glad that he'd been caught, except he'd still gotten away with it—the girls remained his captives long into their deaths.

Finishing the apple, he tossed its core aside. After taking a moment to pick his teeth, he got up and went back to where he'd been digging, putting his back to Jess once more.

Riley reached down and pulled at something—a flash of white skin caked with dirt. Dizzy with horror and disbelief, Jess nearly fell backward. He wasn't digging a grave for Gracie and Emma.

He was digging them up.

Jess fought to catch her breath and stay on her feet as Riley dragged the girls from the ground and onto the blanket, propping up each against the base of a tree. Muddy dirt, twigs, and leaves covered them. Dark stains along the neckline of their dresses indicated they'd bled heavily.

Jess wanted to move, to order her legs to take her away from here. But the shock and fear froze her in place. Her stomach began to rebel and she gagged, then wiped at her mouth, fighting against it.

He'll hear you!

Riley knelt down between the girls and examined each girl's neck where he'd clearly slit their throats.

He began to sing. "He cut off their heads with a carving knife, have you ever seen such a sight in your life!"

Again, Jess's stomach lurched hard enough that her eyes watered.

Run. Run!

Her traitorous feet remained motionless as though stuck in quicksand. Jess was helpless to do anything but watch. Her breath came in quick, ragged bursts and she fought to not pass out. If she did, Riley would find her. Even now, she was certain he had to hear her, hear her breathing and the pounding of her heart.

Riley stopped his singing and bit into Gracie's cheek, tearing away a chunk of flesh. He chewed slowly and swallowed. Jess's eyes watered again and she retched, unable to silence the sound, but nothing came up. Her heart pounded so hard now she swore it would burst. Her vision began to swim, yet her eyes remained glued to the grisly scene. Her knees buckled and she fell to the ground.

Turn your head, look away.

Omigod! The smell!

The girls might only have been gone a day or two, but given that they'd been buried in shallow graves in Savannah's summer heat, they'd already started to decompose badly. Jess retched again.

Riley leaned closer to Emma and took a bite out of her, too.

And then Jess blacked out.

It was dark when she woke. Riley was nowhere to be seen. Neither were the girls. Relief poured over her when she recognized she was seeing the here and now. But relief began to ebb as the full realization of it all crashed down on her. She'd returned to the spot where the girls had taken her—the place where they'd told her to touch the ground—the place where Riley had dug up their bodies.

The place where Riley had begun to eat them.

"Oh my God! Oh my God!" Jess scrabbled backward a few feet. Her hands! Her hands were covered with dirt, her fingernails caked with mud. Her eyes settled on something smooth and hard poking out of a small section of earth. That hole hadn't been there when she first arrived. Somehow, in her time-travel trance or whatever it was, she'd dug up this spot . . . the spot Gracie had told her to touch. The shape was unmistakable—the eye socket of a human skull stared up at her; the rest remained interred in the earth.

He separated us.

He cut off their heads with a carving knife, have you ever seen such a sight in your life?

Jess scrambled backward again, meaning to stand, but her legs were unable to support her weight and she fell backward, onto her bottom. "Oh my God!" she cried as she scooted farther away before finally getting to her feet.

How could Riley do that? How could anyone be capable of such a thing? He'd not only killed them, but buried their bodies, and then he'd come back later to . . . to . . . *eat* them. Why did they have to show her that part? Where were they? Had it worked? Had Gracie and Emma moved on?

Jess's head buzzed with questions and fear.

If the girls *had* moved on, Riley wasn't going to be happy about that. If they were finally free of Riley, there'd be hell to pay.

But the more she thought about it, she knew Gracie and Emma were still here. They'd told her they had been separated. That's why they couldn't move on. And heaven help her, but Jess knew what they'd have to do. But right now, she had to get out of these woods.

Jess ran, blindly, hoping she was headed in the right direction.

CHAPTER THIRTY

Gage had expected to find Jess with Allison when he and Bryan snuck out of the house. Allison had been alone, though, pacing on the lawn and looking rather anxious. Her already pale skin seemed even paler in the moonlight.

"She's not with you?" Allison asked. The subtleness of her question didn't go unnoticed. "No." Gage shook his head. "Didn't she come back to your room?"

"She did, but when the alarm went off, she was gone. I thought she might be with you."

"Shit!" Something was wrong. Gage scanned the yard, hoping Jess just couldn't sleep and was already out here.

Bryan frowned, looking as worried as Allison. "I hope she's not still in the house. You don't think—"

Allison's eyes went wide. "I don't think so." She whirled to look up at it.

Gage looked, too. It seemed different than before, darker. More ominous. He rubbed his eyes.

It's going down. It's done playing. Riley and Siler House are knocking over the dominoes.

"We've got to find her. Something's not right." Gage walked on, hoping his first thought about Jess's whereabouts was correct, that she was out here somewhere and just hadn't seen them yet.

"Maybe Dr. Brandt caught her, or Mrs. Hirsch," Bryan offered.

"No," Allison said. "I don't think so. It's one of *them*."

Allison said what he'd been thinking: Riley. He didn't want to think of Jess trapped inside a room with that monster. But she was known to go off exploring. What if she'd ventured into a room with an uncovered mirror? If Riley could make knives appear, Gage had no doubt he could close and lock doors, too. With Jess's ability, he didn't think it'd be long before Riley found a way out of a mirror, or a way to get Jess *in*.

He had to keep calm. He could feel the paranoia trying to creep in. Gage resisted the urge to run back and search for Jess inside the house, to scream her name as he went from room to room.

The basement.

The music room.

Stay cool, man. She's not in there.

He closed his eyes, recalling Jess—how her hair smelled of shampoo, how her skin had felt like silk under his touch. No, she was out here. Somewhere. He could feel her.

"Maybe she's already out back, waiting on us." Gage was running now, hoping with all his might they'd find Jess by the oak tree.

"She'll be okay," Bryan said, catching up with him. "I know she means a lot to you. We'll find her."

Anger began to stir inside him, replacing the hint of panic. He'd be *damned* if he was going to let something happen to Jess.

"That bad, huh?" Bryan said, eyeing him on the run.

Gage glared. "We're friends."

"Yeah, I saw that," Bryan said with a smirk.

They rounded the house and headed toward the oak. Gage had picked this spot because the tree and nearby area were cloaked in shadow, making it impossible for anyone to see them from the house.

When they reached it, Jess wasn't there.

"Damn it!" Frustrated, Gage scrubbed his face as he scoured the yard for any sign of her.

"Gage, I think it's okay," Allison said as she joined them. "I don't know where, but Jess is out here. I can sense her, too. I told you we were all connected."

She walked toward the graves. Gage didn't follow.

"She's right," Bryan said. "Chill, okay? We'll find her." He studied Gage's face. "Gage, she'll be okay, I promise, man."

Gage clenched his jaw and scanned the grounds one more time. Where the hell was she? The estate grounds were huge.

Come on, Jess. Come on, sweetheart. Where are you?

Bryan shifted uneasily. "You know, I'm starting to buy into this collective thing. I mean, I didn't at first. I thought Allison was nuts. But now? I dunno, man. It's like I can pick up on all of our . . . vibes or something lately. What do you think?"

Gage looked at him without saying a word. He wouldn't admit it, mostly because it sounded girly, but he understood exactly what Bryan was saying. It was like they had some weird connection growing between all of them—and it seemed stronger almost every day.

Not just between them, either. The house, too. That part couldn't be good.

"There!" Allison pointed toward the woods. "It's Jess!"

A dark figure emerged, running toward them. Jess. Gage breathed a sigh of relief and he quickened his step. What was she thinking, going out into the woods at night by herself? "Jess?" he called.

Reaching them, she flung herself into Gage's arms. "Are you okay?" he asked.

She nodded yes, then shook her head no. "I know how the girls died," Jess sobbed, clinging to him tightly. "I saw what he did."

Gage stroked her head. "It's okay, Jess. It'll be okay." He gently pushed her back so he could look at her. Her eyes were wide with fright. "What happened?"

Jess took a long, shuddering breath.

"It's okay," Gage repeated. "Come on. Tell us about it." He led her back toward the shadowed concealment of the oak tree and took a seat, pulling her up against his chest. Bryan and Allison took seats nearby.

Jess leaned into him, her body tight with fear as she filled them in about the girls leading her into the woods, the strange vision, and how she'd woken up next to partially unearthed bones.

"So, you're saying you don't remember digging anything up?" Bryan asked.

Jess shook her head. "No. But how can that be?" She picked at her fingernails, which clearly had dirt under them. She turned to Allison. "How can that be?" she repeated, as if not wanting to admit that she'd either been under Gracie and Emma's influence or had done something without the slightest recollection of it. But Gage knew the real reason—Allison was the only one of them who'd ever been under the influence of something or someone else. Jess was looking to Allison for answers, and damn if Gage didn't agree with that.

Allison had grown quiet. She wasn't blocking them out or shutting down as she sometimes did. Allison had heard every word Jess had said. She was probably just trying to figure out a tactful way of saying the obvious. That Gracie and Emma had become strong enough to take over Jess. They might not be demons, but they'd essentially done the same thing. Possession.

Jess, sweetheart, you're playing with fire.

He gave her a little squeeze. "Hey, maybe it's not such a good idea to talk to the girls for a while."

"I agree with Gage," Bryan said. "Skills or not, I think we're above our pay grade on this one. They're stronger than us if they can take you over like that."

Jess stiffened. "We've been saying it's the house keeping us here, but I think it's more than that. Allison was right. Siler House is sick. But it didn't start that way. It has something to do with Riley. What if we bury the skull I found with the rest of their bodies? They said they'd been separated. Maybe if we bury it—"

"They'll be at peace," Bryan finished. "They'll stop haunting Siler House. And us."

Allison laughed bitterly. "And you *believe* that?"

Bryan shrugged. "I don't know, maybe Jess has a point. Maybe part of breaking Siler House's hold is to set their souls free from Riley's control."

Allison got to her feet. "They're *spirits*. Spirits who are drawing their strength from Jess. I don't trust ghosts. Not one." She turned her face up toward Siler House.

"We could still use them to help us get rid of Riley," Jess said. "They might not be what they appear, but how could they side with Riley? Evil or not, that doesn't mean they don't want him gone."

Gage sighed. This wasn't going to go down easily or end well. He could sense that and wondered if the others could, too. Sure, he'd be happy to use Gracie and Emma to get rid of Riley, and then he'd be just as happy to send them packing, too. Good riddance.

Allison turned to Jess and knelt down inches in front of her. "If they're such saints, Jess, then where the hell are their cute little girl angel wings?"

Jess tensed. "I never said they were angels. Never. But you're the expert on demons. Am I right?"

Allison didn't answer.

Jess pushed away from Gage and got to her feet. Damn. This *was* going to wind up in a fight.

"Jess—" he said, reaching for her.

She shoved his hand away and stood over Allison. "You said Gracie and Emma weren't demons. Is that still true?"

Allison stared up at Jess in that emotionless, freaky way of hers.

"ARE THEY DEMONS?" Jess demanded.

"No," Allison admitted.

"Okay, then," Jess said, taking a few steps away, her arms folded across her chest. "Look, I'm not saying I'm turning into their big sister. I'm just saying that if we are over our heads here, and since the girls *aren't* demons, we see if we can use them against Riley before we put them to rest. Why don't we just give it a try?"

Allison rolled her eyes.

Jess sighed and threw her hands into the air in exasperation. "Why would they help Riley, Allison? Why would they want to help the person who killed them and then *ate* part of them?"

"But then why show you that, Jess?" Bryan asked. "I mean, what's the point? Why not just tell you?"

Jess sighed. "Because ghosts don't operate the way you and I do."

Gage thought the twin dead girls were just creepy, no matter what their intentions. Hell, for that matter, *all* dead things were creepy—especially when they came back.

Allison finally got to her feet. Gage watched carefully, but it didn't seem like Allison was in a catfight mood.

"Okay," Allison said, her voice soft and calm. "We'll see if they can help us against Riley. But then we get rid of them, too."

Jess nodded. "Fair enough."

"But it'll have to be in the daylight," Gage said. "No wandering around in the woods at night."

Allison's gaze returned to the house. "I wish there was another way to get out of here. Let Siler House and everything in it be someone else's problem."

"That *is* the problem, though, isn't it?" Jess said. "The house isn't going to let us leave."

"No," Bryan admitted. "I tried. The day after that whole knife thing. I got as far as the gates, and . . . I dunno. It was weird. It was like I had this . . . panic attack or something."

"You tried to leave?" Jess asked.

Gage shrugged. "Can't blame him, really."

Allison nodded. "We're bound here. Bound to each other until we break whatever's holding us."

Jess relaxed as if all the wind, all the fight had gone out of her. "Sounds like we need to just do this thing with Riley and the girls. Get it over with. The sooner, the better."

Allison let out a nervous laugh. "You know the house is going to be so pissed, right? It's going to be *so* freaking pissed."

"Yeah, I think so, too," Jess agreed.

Gage dusted himself off. "Well, good to see you two are BFFs again."

"So, what's the first step, Gage?" Bryan asked, motioning toward the house. "Because if the ghosts are taking control of Jess, Riley isn't too far from freeing himself from wherever he is, either. And since Jess is the most susceptible to ghosts, he'll be coming after her first."

Gage gave them a half-cocked smile. "We're going to do what we came here for. We're resurrecting Riley. And then we're going to hand him a one-way ticket back to hell."

Bryan snorted. "Yeah? How are we gonna do that?"

"With a few things I snagged from Brandt's room. He printed out some voodoo crap about vanquishing spirits. I guess in case things got out of control. There's a small bag of weird stuff still in his room, too."

"So, we've got to get back into his room without anyone seeing us." A line of wrinkles claimed Bryan's forehead. "Sure. But I think he'd miss the whole box, so what do we need from it?"

Gage shrugged. "Weird stuff, like a small piece of wood tied to cardboard. It's from a rowan tree or something. There's a rabbit's foot, some smelly flower stuff rolled up into a turd-sized joint-looking thing, and what looks like a four-leaf clover in a glass vial."

"Sage," Jess informed them. "The stuff that looks like a super-sized joint? It's called sage."

Bryan laughed. "And you think that's going to work? A four-leaf clover? Some herbs? Man, that's the worst plan I've heard yet."

"Probably," Gage said, clapping a hand onto Bryan's shoulder. He doubted any of that was their silver bullet. If he was right, the end-all answer was standing right in front of him. "But that's why we have you."

CHAPTER THIRTY-ONE

Jess swatted at another mosquito. Funny how she couldn't stand the little bloodsuckers when she'd first gotten here, but now found them almost preferable to being inside. She stood in the dark with Gage, Allison, and Bryan, facing the back of Siler House. It loomed over them as they contemplated the best way to end this—the best way to free themselves from its stranglehold.

The house *had* become an addiction. And like an addict who's suddenly come to terms with his or her dependency, finally admitting it was both frightening and also provided an overwhelming sense of relief.

Bryan laughed. "It's weird, don't you think? The house can keep us from leaving, but it can't stop us from feeling like rats in a snake pit?"

"Because it likes it," Allison replied. "It likes our fear."

Jess shuddered. Had she ever really loved it here? She'd been so willing to find all the good in the house. The house was beautiful. Jess thought it would have been so much easier if it had been otherwise. Looking at the house, there was nothing that warned people away. Siler House was something shiny and appealing until you saw the ugliness it hid underneath the paint and floorboards. She had seen it too late.

Gage paced a few steps. "Our first move *is* the most unnerving. We've got to have a little one-on-one with Riley."

Jess grimaced inwardly. This was her part. "I guess that means I'm the one who has to get his attention."

She stole a glance at Allison, but she was either focused on what Gage had to say or was ignoring her.

Gage nodded. "You *and* Allison."

Allison looked at them all with an expression of resolution and hurt. She'd made it clear she didn't want any part of this, but probably understood there was no other choice. Allison was the only one of them who knew how to do this. She was the only one who'd ever had to deal with malevolent things—demon or spirit. She'd been the one to shout to the rafters that the house and everything in it meant them harm.

"Okay," Allison said, sounding tired. "But after we bring him into the open, it's anyone's guess what'll work to get rid of him forever. Or even if there *is* a forever. In time, he might still come back. Like the demons."

Bryan lifted his head from his hands. They were all tired. Maybe too tired to be working out such a plan. But the longer they waited, the more advantage Riley and Siler House gained.

"So, how do we get him out of the mirrors?" Bryan asked.

Gage shrugged. "No clue."

Allison turned her head to Jess. "Use the Ouija board— do the whole séance thing. We have to call Riley, but *only* him. When he's over, we have to clear the space—we have to tell the board to quit and we have to snuff out the candles and break the séance."

Finally. Allison realized they had to use the board.

"And then?" Bryan asked. "Is that when it's my turn?"

They all stared at him. Jess felt sorry for him. It was a lot to bear.

Bryan scoffed. "So, it's all on me, then. We've got to hope I'm strong enough to nuke Riley and anything else he brings with him. But we don't even know I can get rid of ghosts . . . or whatever the hell he is."

"You're our best hope and you'll have help," Gage assured him. "The rest of us will have this banishing spell memorized. And we'll have all those herbs and things from Dr. Brandt. We'll perform the ritual while you do your . . . thing."

"Then we go after Gracie and Emma next," Jess said.

Gage nodded. "We get a shovel from the renovation crew, we go get that skull, and we bury it in the cemetery. Hopefully, that'll put Gracie and Emma to rest, once and for all."

Bryan scratched his neck. "Once we start this, there's no going back. We bust that lock on the fence and dig up those graves, someone's going to notice."

"You think they won't notice *until* then?" Allison burst into hysterical laughter. Jess knew she was thinking of all the things that could go south in a hurry.

Jess wrapped an arm around her. "It's okay," she whispered. "We'll get through this. All of us."

"We have to do this after the last of the maids and the renovation crew have left for the day. We can't risk involving anyone else," Gage said. "As for the property, whatever damage is done, it's done. We'll just have to work fast the next morning before anyone shows up."

Bryan swatted a mosquito. "We should do it when the crew won't be here, or the maids." He cocked his head and shrugged. "That means Friday night. The maids and the crew don't show up on the weekend."

"That gives us only a day to prepare," Jess said. "What about Dr. Brandt and Mrs. Hirsch? What do we do about them?"

Gage rubbed his eyes. "If we include Dr. Brandt, we don't have to worry about what Mrs. Hirsch thinks."

Allison shook her head, her soft strawberry blond hair sweeping against her slumped shoulders. "But—"

"How else are we going to do it?" Gage snapped. "There's not a chance we can do all this without one or both of them finding out—ahead of time, or worse, during."

Bryan's gaze cut to Gage. "Brandt's been wanting to bring Riley over. This way, we just keep him close."

Something about Brandt was off, Jess felt sure of it. "Allison's right. I don't know if that's the best idea."

"Got any ideas how we can do it without him?" Gage wanted to know. "Because I'm listening."

Jess knew he was tired. They all were. Their nerves were on edge. Everyone wanted Gage to be the one to fix it, to have a plan, and like the others, he had nothing. First, they'd have to collect the supplies without Dr. Brandt's knowledge, then set up in a room where he, or more likely, Mrs. Hirsch wouldn't walk in on them. Their absence would ensure someone would wonder what they were up to. And while Dr. Brandt seemed occupied with the house and who knew what else, even he'd be curious. He could walk in at the wrong time.

"Fine, but I don't trust him," Jess said.

"Won't he go back to EPAC?" Bryan asked. "If we succeed and he's there—"

"He tells EPAC we're marketable. I know. I know," Gage finished.

"Not if we meet in the middle of the night again," Allison suggested. "Of course, we'll still need to worry about Mrs. Hirsch. Or we can do it your way and take our chances with Dr. Brandt."

"We could hope he realizes this is something neither he nor EPAC can control," Jess said, not really buying into it.

"He spends time down in the basement right after lunch," Bryan said. "And since he doesn't go up to the music room before then, maybe a couple of us could set up the room fast. No one will think much of it since Jess practices up there, anyway."

"Works for me," Gage said.

Allison shivered. "I'm scared."

Bryan smiled nervously. "At this point, I think we all are."

The worry was easy to see on Allison's face. She hadn't needed to tell them. Her eyes were owlish, with dark crescents underneath, her skin pale, and she was gently rocking back and forth. Allison was close to shutting down.

Jess recalled Allison's words, how she described hiding in her ivory tower. *Run away, Allison! Run away!*

Jess turned to her. It was bad timing, but she had to know. "When we do the séance, how will we know Riley's all we've brought back?"

Allison continued rocking. "We'll know. *I'll* know."

She's going to break. Allison isn't going to be able to hold this together much longer.

And if she did break? If Allison lost it before they could cross Riley over *and* banish him to who knew where for who knew how long? What then? And what were the odds only Riley would be waiting on the other side of that door? Allison would be weak, vulnerable. Even more than now.

Jess feared the worst was true.

The demons would come for Allison. Maybe for all of them.

CHAPTER THIRTY-TWO

The sun shone a bit too brightly through the window the next morning. Jess would have liked to sleep longer, but someone was knocking lightly on their door. Head pounding from lack of sleep, she rolled over and looked at her roommate, hoping she'd answer it, seeing as her bed was closer to the hallway. Allison was sleeping like the dead. There was another, louder tap on the door.

Ugh!

"Just a second!" Jess called. Wiping her bleary eyes, she forced herself from the bed and stumbled to the door. Allison merely grumbled something and rolled into her pillow. Jess raked a hand through her hair and opened the door a crack.

A woman wearing the standard Siler House maid uniform stood before her. Jess didn't recognize her, but that didn't mean a lot. Since they'd been here, three maids had either given notice or just walked off the job—like the gardener had done last week.

The woman smiled. "Dr. Brandt sent me to check on you and Miss Giles. Are you two all right? It's after nine o'clock and he wondered if you were joining him for breakfast."

Who was this cheery in the morning?

She opened the door a little farther. "Where's Mrs. Hirsch?"

The maid gave a slight shrug. "I don't think she's in today. Should I tell Dr. Brandt you'll be down shortly?"

Another polite smile.

"Not in? She *lives* here. I mean, she's been staying here with the rest of us."

"Sorry. I'm sure you could ask Dr. Brandt."

"Tell him we'll be down in a few."

With that, the maid turned on her heel and headed back down the hall.

"Who was that?" Allison asked, voice still heavy with sleep.

Jess closed the door. "I don't know. One of the maids. Another new one."

Allison looked at the clock and leapt from the bed. "It's after nine! Mrs. Hirsch will be up here next if we don't get downstairs!" She slid out of her sleepwear and grabbed last night's pair of shorts from the floor.

Jess stretched, trying to shake off the sleep that wanted to reclaim her. She changed out of her sleepwear as well, also putting on last night's clothes. After breakfast, she'd come back and take a shower. A nice, long one. "The maid said Mrs. Hirsch wasn't here today."

Allison stopped brushing her hair and turned to face Jess, surprise evident on her face.

"Yeah," Jess replied, sliding on her sneakers without bothering to unlace them first. "That's what I thought, too. It's why I want to hurry up and get downstairs. Don't you think it's a bit *too* weird?"

Allison nodded as they left the room. "Think she saw something and quit? It'd sure make things go more smoothly."

Jess nearly laughed. "If she didn't quit after seeing what happened with Bryan and the knives, she never will."

"You never know. Mrs. Hirsch walked around at all hours. *Alone*. She's likely to have seen anything. Maybe *she* found some way to leave. We could hope, right? For her sake?"

It was possible, but Jess still didn't feel right about it. Mrs. Hirsch just wouldn't have quit. And if they were stuck here, then Mrs. Hirsch had to be, too. The house had affected everyone who stayed here around the clock.

What if she had gone the way of Dr. Brandt? What if she was so taken by the house that she'd holed herself up in one of the rooms?

What if she'd uncovered one of the mirrors?

Jess envisioned Mrs. Hirsch, a crazed look on her face and a large, shiny knife in her hand.

. . . She cut off their heads with a carving knife, have you ever seen such a sight in your life . . .

Stop it! Just stop it right now!

Her mother's words rang in her head. *Your imagination. Your misplaced imagination.*

"When's the last time you saw her?" Jess asked.

255

"Yesterday. Last night, maybe? You don't think Riley or the house . . ." Allison trailed off.

Jess forced a smile, trying not to recall Allison's words about how pissed the house would be once it realized what they were up to. "No. I'm sure she's around here someplace."

She gave the second-floor hallway a quick glance as they passed it. No Gage or Bryan. "I saw her when she went through the Great Room, but that was it."

"She was in the hall right after you left to go downstairs," Allison said. "I heard a couple of the doors open and close— you know, like she always does when she's on patrol."

"But did you actually *see* her?" Jess asked as they headed into the dining room. Dr. Brandt sat at the table sipping coffee, an empty plate in front of him.

Allison shook her head. "No, but I'm sure it was her. It's what she always does."

"Hey!" Bryan said as he exited the kitchen with a plate and coffee.

"Coffee sounds really good," Jess said, deciding that coffee outweighed everything this morning, including Mrs. Hirsch's whereabouts. Allison followed her into the kitchen.

Gage had already poured himself his own mug. Jess watched as he took a sip. Only Gage could make sipping a cup of coffee sexy. He hadn't even bothered to comb his hair. Jess resisted the urge to run her hands through it to make it even messier. It was a strange thought in the midst of all they had going on today, but thinking of them together, alone again with nothing else to worry about, sounded like heaven right now.

"We could use bigger mugs." He smiled as he walked past Allison. He leaned in as he neared Jess. "Not that I'm complaining about the lack of sleep," he said quietly.

Before Jess could reply, he left the kitchen.

She poured some coffee, added milk and sugar, tossed a Danish onto a plate, and followed Allison out of the kitchen and into the dining room.

"So, what happened?" Bryan asked Dr. Brandt. "Did she say?"

Dr. Brandt gave a slight nod to Jess and Allison and waited for them to take a seat. Once they were settled, he said, "Bryan was just asking about Mrs. Hirsch. She's not going to be joining us for a week or so. Family emergency."

He turned to address Bryan, his demeanor calm and casual. His face was a mask, totally unreadable. "No, she didn't explain."

"That was sudden," Gage added. "We just saw her last night."

Dr. Brandt offered a thin smile. "These things happen. That's why they call them emergencies."

"So she just up and left?" Jess said. "How is that possible?"

"I imagine she left right through the front door," Dr. Brandt answered.

He doesn't know? He honestly has no idea the house is keeping them? Liar!

But what if it wasn't keeping *everyone*? What if it was keeping just *them*? She'd only assumed it kept everyone who stayed, but what if it was selective?

Brandt pushed his empty plate aside and folded his hands on the table. "I think the time has come to do the séance."

Brandt's gaze fell on all of them, one by one. Allison stopped chewing, Bryan nearly spit out his coffee. Jess dropped her Danish back onto her plate. Only Gage seemed unfazed.

"Tonight," Brandt finished.

Jess looked down at her plate.

"After dinner, there won't be any staff present, and there won't be any of the construction crew here. And with Mrs. Hirsch gone, it's just the five of us. We might not get an opportunity like this anytime soon." Brandt grinned again and Jess didn't like it. Had he heard them last night? Maybe he'd been listening to them through an open upstairs window.

"I think it's safest this way, don't you agree?" Brandt pulled a yellow notepad and a pen from the leather portfolio beside his chair. It'd been a while since he'd actually written anything down.

"We'll need to record it, of course," he went on, not waiting on anyone's acceptance or refusal—not even Allison's. He looked up, though he continued to write. "I leave that part to you, Bryan. You already know how to operate the video camera."

Bryan nodded casually. "Sure."

Dr. Brandt went back to scribbling on the notepad. The four of them exchanged a quick glance.

Now what? their expressions seemed to say. Would Brandt have them send Riley back or would he insist they try to control him somehow? Did he actually believe Allison could handle that?

No, Jess decided. If Gage and Allison were right, and she believed they were, then Brandt would want, no, *expect* them to control the situation.

Well, crap!

"We'll meet down here at ten," Dr. Brandt said. "We'll gather the equipment and set up in the music room. Then, we should go over what we'll each be expected to do. We'll hold the séance at midnight."

His gaze fell on Allison as though waiting for her to protest.

If it was at all possible, Allison appeared even more pale than usual. She set down the last of her Danish. Allison put her hands in her lap and began to wring them underneath the tablecloth in an attempt to hide her anxiety. She offered Brandt a thin smile.

Jess wanted to reach over to Allison, to offer her comfort.

Good, hold it together, Allison. Just hold it together.

Bryan swallowed his food and cleared his throat. "Why the music room?"

Dr. Brandt shrugged as though this was obvious. "Because that's where Jess has had the most sightings of Gracie and Emma. It's where she's been practicing the most, and I think that's where the house's energy is the strongest."

And that settles that, Jess thought. Now they had to think of a contingency plan that included Dr. Brandt.

CHAPTER THIRTY-THREE

Neither Jess nor Allison talked about the séance as they showered and dressed for the day. Jess thought it was best to keep Allison's mind occupied on other subjects. It wasn't like they could do anything about the séance during the day, anyway—not without putting the maids and the workers in jeopardy.

Besides, the less Allison had time to think about the séance, the better the chances that she could hold it together when they needed her to. Coming up with other subjects to talk about wasn't easy. Jess realized how many of their conversations had revolved around Siler House, death, demons, and ghosts. Even talking about family felt too connected to their situation right now. Jess sighed. Time to bring out the tried and true topics like celebrities, movies, and ex-boyfriends.

And for the rest of the morning, Allison did seem to be more at ease.

Dr. Brandt had stayed in his room that morning and came out only for lunch. Even then he seemed preoccupied. He squeezed another slice of lemon into his iced tea.

"If Mrs. Hirsch isn't here, what are we doing for dinner?" Bryan asked.

"Spaghetti," he replied. "I think we can handle that, don't you?"

Bryan nodded.

"You don't need to practice today if you don't want to," he added. "I'll be in my room, if any of you need me. Otherwise, I'll see you for dinner."

He stood and walked a few steps. "Take the day off. Go. Have fun."

Jess nearly laughed at this. It was as though he were sending them off to the movies or a dance club somewhere. She felt Gage's eyes on her and her face warmed a little. Yeah, she knew what kind of fun *he* was thinking about. For a moment, the same idea crossed her mind. She desperately wanted something normal to hold on to while they still could. With Brandt at the séance, anything could go wrong. Not that it wouldn't have without him, but now? Jess let thoughts of Gage fill her, trying to imagine a time in the future when they weren't here, but were still together. The daydream comforted her.

"Weird," Bryan said, interrupting her thoughts.

"What is?" Gage asked almost absently.

Bryan motioned to Dr. Brandt's place at the table. "He just left his plate. He never does that."

They all stared at the half-eaten sandwich, the crumbs, and nearly empty glass. Brandt had always been so meticulous at mealtime. He'd made sure the table was cleared and that everything was back in place before they did anything else—talks, practice sessions, phone calls.

Jess frowned. "What do you think?"

"I think he's being sucked in worse than us," Allison replied. "And I don't like it."

"Yeah? Well, that makes two of us." Gage got to his feet and cleared his place at the table. "But there's not much we can do except keep watch."

It didn't take much for the four of them to put away the sandwich fixings they'd taken out of the fridge.

Jess put the last of the dishes in the dishwasher and closed it. "Now what?"

Allison set the dish towel on the counter as though its weight were more than she wanted to bear. Shoulders slumped, she sighed and stared off into nothing. "The house already knows. There's nothing we can do." Slowly, she turned to face them. "So we might as well hang out in the Great Room, or go hang in our room."

"Your room sounds like a plan," Gage replied.

On the way upstairs, they passed two maids who were just finishing their duties on the second floor. Once they'd reached their room, Allison curled up on her bed, leaving space for Bryan. He took a couple of pillows and propped himself up beside her.

Jess sat on her bed and tried not to think of the last time she shared a bed with Gage. He reached over and took her hand, smiling faintly.

She couldn't help but return the smile.

Bryan glanced around the room, clearly feeling a bit awkward. "So, why do you guys think Brandt's spending so much time in his room and the basement?"

Several things ran through Jess's mind. Was Brandt holding his own séances? Was he using the Ouija board?

"Could be anything," Gage mused. "Working on paperwork, sending e-mails to EPAC—"

"He could be figuring out a way to bring back Riley on his own, or talking to ghosts we haven't seen yet," Bryan theorized.

Jess hadn't thought about anyone else seeing ghosts without her present. But the house *was* getting stronger, and since it had a way of affecting them all, it was entirely possible that Brandt was seeing or talking to someone Jess hadn't come across yet.

She thought of the times she'd walked into a room and sensed someone behind her, even when the room was empty. And the man on the stairs—the apparition that was nothing more than a shadow.

Other people besides Gracie, Emma, and Riley have died here.

We'll probably be next.

She closed her mind against that thought.

Allison had fallen asleep. "I can't believe she's sleeping," Bryan said.

"She's on overload," Jess replied. "I don't think she can do this, guys."

"We don't have any other choice." Gage shrugged. "Unless you've got something?"

Bryan shook his head.

"Let's just let her sleep. Maybe it'll help," Jess offered.

Gage stifled a yawn. "We probably could *all* use a nap."

Jess agreed. They hadn't had a lot of sleep last night, and if they were going through with this plan, it might be best to catch a couple of hours sleep. Gage cradled her against him and pulled a pillow under their heads. Bryan rolled over, his back to Allison.

Jess lay there, listening for the sounds of the house or the maids, but other than an occasional creak of a floorboard or a bird chirping outside, it was quiet. After a while of listening to the soft, peaceful breathing of everyone else in the room, Jess's eyes closed.

When she awoke the room felt warm and stuffy. The clock on the nightstand indicated it was after five. They should be going downstairs for dinner.

She glanced at the others, who were still asleep.

Let them sleep, she thought. *Just a few more minutes. If they're sleeping, they're not thinking about Riley or the house.*

Jess got up slowly, so as to not wake Gage. She loved the way the late afternoon sun shone on him, basking him in light. Resisting the urge to bend over and give him a kiss, she went to the dresser for her hairbrush.

For a second, she thought the towel covering the mirror had moved.

It's the ceiling fan. Just a draft.

Towel or no towel, being so close to the mirror gave her an uneasy feeling. What if Riley could sense how nervous she was, even with the towel between them? Jess knew he was there, right on the other side . . .

Stop it. Stop scaring yourself!

She snatched the hairbrush and moved to the window instead, quickly brushing her hair as she went. Beneath the oak tree, in the shadows, stood the figure of a man. A ghost, from the way he flickered. It made it impossible to see his face, but she swore it was . . .

The hairbrush tumbled from her hands.

Couldn't be. Not here.

Her father. She pressed her face against the glass. The figure might be the right height, and even the right weight—before he got sick. Blue jeans. White T-shirt. Short brown hair.

She rubbed her eyes and looked again. Between the glare from the glass and the way the sun glinted through the tree limbs, she couldn't be sure it was him. Then again, she couldn't be sure it wasn't. Whoever the apparition was, he didn't look like he'd died in the early 1900s.

Dad?

If was him, she wanted to scream at him to get away, to leave Siler House.

Damn it! Step away from the tree. Step into the light where I can see you!

It *couldn't* be him. He'd have shown up before now. There were others here—Jess had sensed them. Brandt had told them about the people who'd died while the Silers lived here, but he never said that others *hadn't* died here since. Was this one just now showing himself?

No one has lived here since then. That meant . . .

. . . I saw a man on the stair today . . .

Get a grip, Jess. It could be anyone.

If it were her dad, surely he would never have let her come here if he knew about the house. She'd never thought about it before, but could ghosts travel long distances? Did they always know where their loved ones were? Or, since they were in the veil, were they limited in their knowledge of things?

Allison's words ran through her head. *They know where to find you.*

The figure pointed toward Gracie and Emma's graves. Then it pointed to her, then back to the graves once more.

The hair rose on the back of her neck. What was he telling her? That'd they'd be dead like Gracie and Emma? Or was he telling her to hurry up and bury that bone?

From somewhere behind her, a floorboard creaked, and Jess spun around, expecting to see . . .

Riley.

Gage?

Except everyone was still resting. No one stood behind her. The sound came from the hallway. Someone was pacing the hallway just outside the door. Jess looked back out the window, but the shadowy image was gone.

She turned back toward the room. Allison was awake now, and the two of them stared at each other as though they were trying to decide why Dr. Brandt was pacing outside their room. The maids would already be gone for the day.

Allison carefully got out of bed, but her movements still managed to wake Bryan.

"Huh?" he said in a muffled voice.

"Nothing," Allison said quietly. "Just Dr. Brandt."

Gage woke and rubbed his face. Bryan got up and walked to the door. He opened it slightly at first, then all the way. He stepped out into the hall, then back in.

"He's gone."

Jess shivered.

"We probably should head down for dinner," Gage said.

"Yeah," Bryan agreed. "We should go."

"I like Bryan's idea," Allison said. "Leave."

If they only could. Just walk down the stairs and keep going. Jess looked out the window one last time. The sun sparkled between the branches of the oak. But not a single person—dead or living—was anywhere to be found.

"Jess, you coming?" Allison stood in the doorway. Gage and Bryan waited behind her. Although she'd slept a little last night and soundly again this afternoon, the dark circles under her eyes were still pronounced and her face still pale.

Her eyes darted between Jess and the mirror.

We both sense him. We both know he's there. Ghost or demon? Or maybe a little of both?

Jess crossed the room, not daring to glance at the mirror.

CHAPTER THIRTY-FOUR

The more he thought about Brandt at the séance, the more Gage realized it was a *really* bad idea. Hell, the séance with just the four of them was dangerous enough. They had to leave. Or at least try. Maybe together it was possible.

After dinner, Gage led the way as the four of them walked to the front gate. Allison and Bryan hung back, already convinced any attempt at leaving was useless. Gage quickened his step. They didn't have long. Brandt wouldn't stay in the basement all night. Or his room. Sooner or later, he'd know they weren't in the house.

Brandt might not be like Riley or Siler House, but he wouldn't agree to them leaving. Not now.

Not that *he* could stop them.

Only the house could do that.

But they had to try. He had no doubt the séance would work. The only doubt Gage had was whether they'd survive the aftermath. Brandt was up to something and whatever it was, he didn't think it would help their plan.

They reached the gates and stood there, staring at them as though electricity ran through each iron bar. On the backside of one of the brick pillars to the right of the gate was a covered box with a button inside it.

"Press it," Jess said.

The others watched as Gage reached for the button. Why did he feel as though it really would electrify him if his finger made contact?

He paused.

"See?" Bryan said. "It won't let us leave."

Allison was nodding in agreement, her arms drawn up against her chest.

"It's not going to bite us," Gage said. "Relax."

"So, press it then!" Bryan insisted.

Gage stared at the small silver button covered by an aluminum overhang.

It was just a button. Not a keypad like he'd expected. Nothing with a combination to try and figure out.

Press the damn thing already!

He tried not to think of the house or Riley or anything else for that matter. His finger reached just a little closer.

Almost there.

Allison shoved him aside.

"What the hell, Allison?" Gage snapped.

Ignoring him, she stepped forward and pressed the button. Mashed it several times, to be exact. They all looked at her, with shock or adoration, Gage wasn't sure. Maybe a little of both.

Who knew the girl had it in her? Sure, she was prone to outbursts now and then, but usually nothing involving going up against the house.

But the gates didn't open. No electric current. Just *nothing*. The gate stood before them. Closed.

Gage jabbed the button himself this time. No sound of anything mechanical clicking into place as it prepared to open the gates, only the persistent choir of nighttime crickets and bullfrogs.

Bryan tried his luck next, followed by Jess. No dice.

"I told you," Allison said. "The house isn't going to let us leave."

Anger began to boil inside Gage. "To hell with that." He gripped the gates and tugged. When the gates didn't budge, he tried pushing them. Going over the top was of no use— the bars were all vertical—nothing to get a leg up on.

He stepped back. "Maybe it's just broken. Or Brandt's done something to it from inside the house." He eyed the gate and the surrounding wall. "We'll go around."

"In the woods?" Jess asked. "At night? I don't think so."

No one else spoke, which probably meant they were agreeing with her. Even Gage had to admit he wasn't fond of the idea.

That's stupid! Think of what's inside that house and then grow some stones, chicken shit.

But he knew he couldn't leave. If Jess wouldn't go with him, he wouldn't leave her behind. Not even to go find help.

Who knew how long it would take to find someone? If they thought Riley would be pissed once they freed the twins, how mad would he be if one or even two of them got out and left the others behind? What would he do then?

No. They had to stay together.

"Dude, as bad as it is, we don't have a choice," Bryan said. "We've got to go back. Just get this over with."

"It's had us from day one, hasn't it?" Jess asked.

Bryan shook his head. "Meaning?"

"She means," Allison interrupted, "that the house got inside our heads from the first day we stepped foot in the place. We let it. We were either all open to it, or instantly afraid of it. Either way, Siler House played us. It played us against ourselves and our weaknesses."

"The bond we share," Jess said, taking Gage's hand into hers. "It's using that, too, isn't it?

Allison nodded. "It'll hurt any one of us if it thinks another won't do as it wants."

Gage glanced at Jess and gave her hand a little squeeze. He wouldn't let anything happen to her. House or Riley be damned, he wouldn't. He'd figure something out.

Allison smiled as though reading his thoughts. "But it's bigger than the two of you. It's bound the four of us. I don't know how I know, but if something happens to one of us, it'll make the others weaker. At least, that's how the priests broke the demons inside me. One by one."

Bryan frowned. "You mean, divided, our abilities are weakened somehow?"

She nodded. At one time, he'd have blown off Allison's words. It wasn't that he didn't believe her; it was just that everything had always sounded over the top with her.

Gage sighed heavily and nodded.

He turned and looked up at the house. It sat against a steel-gray sky. Looking at it was like seeing something different for the first time. Something evil like some dark, growing cancer. For once, he thought Allison's take on the house was an understatement, or maybe that's because she was trying so hard to reel in the crazy. But even he could see that the place wasn't just brick and mortar. The house really had fooled them all. It was a living, breathing entity of its own. It didn't matter if it'd become that way the day Riley came to live here or if it had evolved into a monster since then.

"It's like it's watching us," Jess said as they walked away from the gates.

Gage looked up at the windows. They'd left enough lights on, but he didn't believe any amount of lighting could chase out the darkness that walked the halls within Siler House.

CHAPTER THIRTY-FIVE

"Screw it. I say we take care of Gracie and Emma first," Gage said as they headed back.

What? Jess stared at him, incredulous.

"I've been thinking about this," he went on. "If this doesn't go down the way we want, we won't have time to cross over the girls."

He had that determined look on his face, the one that said his mind was set. He also looked mad. She'd never seen him like this before.

"Besides," Gage went on, "it'll piss off Riley, and right now, that's fine with me. It might even work in our favor."

Jess frowned. "You *want* to piss off Riley? Are you nuts?"

Gage picked up the pace as he headed for the back lawn instead of the front door. "I refuse to let that little prick have us run around as if our heads have been handed to us. If we're not thinking clearly, Riley and Siler House will have the upper hand."

"So, how's getting Riley angry going to help?" Bryan wanted to know.

"We turn the tables. If he's angry, *he's* the one not thinking clearly," Gage replied.

Bryan laughed. "Yeah. And when he's flinging knives or taking over one of us, what are *we* going to do?"

Gage stopped once they reached the oak, his face tight and eyes dark. "You think it's going to get any easier once we've pulled Riley through? It's not. And right now, he and this fucking house have us running scared. You think he's not going to pull out all the tricks? You think he's going to follow all those baby-game monster rules you had when you were a kid? That if we don't stick a leg or arm out of the covers the monster under the bed has some code of ethics where they won't eat us alive? I've got news for you, guys. Pissed or not, he's coming after us. And he's not going to play fair."

Like the others, Jess stared at him. She considered what he'd said and had to admit he had a point. They needed an advantage. But what? "If we put Gracie and Emma to rest now, we lose any chance they'd help us with Riley."

Gage let out a small laugh. "Sweetheart, if they could do something to stop Riley, I'd bet they'd have done it by now."

That was true, too.

"I say we go dig up some bones," Gage said.

Bryan sighed deeply. "When?"

Without so much as a pause, he replied, "Tonight. Now."

"*Now?*" Jess nearly shouted in protest. "No way, Gage! No. We're *not* going in there." She expected a reaction, some wisecrack, some angry retort. But Gage simply looked at her, unwavering, determined. The thought of stepping foot back into those woods, going back to the spot where Riley had killed the girls, was too much. She drew her arms up against herself. "No, Gage. Just . . . *no*. Especially in the dark. Not a chance."

Gage shrugged. "You don't have to, then. Stay here with Allison. Bryan and I will go. Just tell me where to look."

"Gage, that's impossible!" Bryan said. "How are we supposed to find the same spot? We need Jess to show us."

All eyes turned to her. They were asking too much on this one. Her mind scrambled to find some excuse. If she didn't, Gage and Bryan were going to do it, anyway. She didn't like the idea of them out there, either. "Guys, I can't. *We* can't! It's dark. We don't have a shovel or even a flashlight."

"It's the only way, isn't it?" Allison said in that resolved, trance-like voice she got into now and then that set Jess's bones on ice. "I don't like it either, but what choice do we have? The sooner we do this, the better."

"Why can't we do this in the morning? We'll find some other way to get him angry," Jess protested. Great. Three against one. There was no winning this one, no matter how she tried. She'd thought Allison would be on her side, but now, Allison just looked . . . *defeated*.

Bryan leaned one shoulder against the oak tree and closed his eyes. "Jess, you know Gage is right."

Gage nodded. "Besides, even if we could wait, we're burying a kid's skull . . . in the cemetery, which is sectioned off with a padlocked iron fence. Brandt might be getting a little weird on us, and the dude's all about the experiment, but I don't think he's going to stand by and let us dig up Gracie or Emma's grave tomorrow."

"I'll go fetch the shovel." Bryan shoved off from the tree. "I noticed a couple of them just by the side of the house. They must belong to the renovation crew."

Gage leaned in and kissed the top of Jess's head. "Stay here with Allison. We'll get the shovels and some flashlights and be right back."

He and Bryan set off across the lawn. Jess opened her mouth to complain, but to what end? The others were set on doing it now, and eventually it had to be done.

Jess wanted to tell him to not go. Instead, she called after him, "Be careful. Don't get caught."

By anyone.

Or anything.

He turned, walking backward. "Never," Gage said as he offered that devastating grin of his before turning once more and walking off toward the house.

Jess stared after him, never realizing until now just how large Siler House truly was.

Allison stood next to her. "How's he going to get the flashlights with Dr. Brandt in the house?"

"No idea. But he'll be right back with them. They'll be okay."

She hoped.

"It's getting more dangerous." A small breeze blew wisps of hair across Allison's face, but she didn't seem to notice. "For all of us. It wasn't Brandt or some faulty switch that stopped us at the gate. It was the house." She turned her head in Jess's direction. "It watches us. It's watching now."

Jess stared up at the house, taking it in. It was bleak and cold against the night sky, void of color.

You see what it wants you to see.

She swallowed past the lump in her throat. Just days ago, Jess would have argued Allison's point. Not tonight. Not ever again.

CHAPTER THIRTY-SIX

After what seemed like an eternity, Jess heard Gage and Bryan's voices. Gage flicked a flashlight on and off, letting them know they were okay. She and Allison had been sitting quietly at the oak's base, neither talking much.

Relieved that they'd returned, Jess got to her feet as they approached. "I see you didn't have any problems getting the flashlights."

Gage shook his head. "None. Brandt wasn't in his room. The door wasn't even closed."

"Where was he?" Allison asked.

"We don't know." Bryan shrugged. "We never saw him. We just got in, grabbed the flashlights, and took off."

Gage turned to her. "Want to give us some direction?"

Jess let out a long sigh. They'd be forever if they went in by themselves. Or at least, longer than Jess was comfortable with. Who knew what else was out there.

She felt a chill despite the temperature. "I'll show you. Just everyone stay close, all right?"

They each nodded.

Gage handed her a flashlight. "I'll be right beside you."

She silently chastised herself for going along with this. "This way." She motioned for them to follow and headed for the woods, her heart pounding so hard her chest ached.

The woods looked every bit as eerie as it had when she'd last been here. Although the flashlights helped, their stark circles of light only managed to illuminate how much scarier everything looked in the dark. Shadows danced and shifted, giving Jess the illusion that whatever had been in her flashlight's path a moment before had darted into the nearby darkness.

She stayed in the most open of areas, just as she and the girls had done. Twice, she doubted her sense of direction until finally Jess spotted a familiar, shorn tree trunk with a hollowed base in the middle of an otherwise empty path.

"Over here," she said, taking a right. Wordlessly, everyone followed her another couple hundred yards. Jess stopped when she recognized the two small saplings whose limbs crossed the pathway in front of them like an arch.

It's just ahead. Only a little farther.

Adrenaline coursed through her.

"Are you okay?" Gage asked, concern evident on his face. Behind him, Bryan scanned the area with his flashlight. Like Gage, he'd put on a brave face.

Jess let out a quick breath, willing her heart not to explode from fright. "Yeah. We're almost there."

Gage walked ahead of her, taking her slowing pace and choice of words as a sign that she wasn't willing to lead any longer, although she wasn't any more thrilled to have him walk into the area, either. She stayed close as he pushed onward.

"Here," she said once they'd reached the spot. She scanned the area with her light. Leaves and twiggy debris covered the ground, but one area stood out the most—a cleared patch of upturned earth. A small, whitish item that, in this lighting, could be anything—a pale leaf or a rock—protruded from the ground.

Or bone. She knew it was bone.

"There." She wiggled the light, coming to rest on the object.

Gage knelt down to examine it.

"Is it a skull?" Allison inquired. She hadn't ventured as close as the boys, staying a good distance away.

Gage brushed away some of the dirt. "No idea until we dig it up."

The guys dug up the area, uncovering not one but three bones, although one was nothing more than a long fragment. Rib? Part of an arm bone? Jess refused to get too close for fear she'd see the vision again—see Riley biting into Gracie's cheek.

Bryan held the first bone under his flashlight for all of them to view, but it didn't take much to know what it was—a section of skull.

Moving closer, Allison reached in to touch it, then apparently thought better of it. "Why did they leave behind some of their bones?"

"No idea," Bryan replied. "But it doesn't really matter, does it? We've just got to get them back to the gravesite and bury them."

He and Gage collected the bones and they began to walk back. Allison hurried behind them. Not wanting to be last to leave, Jess quickened her pace. She hadn't noticed it the first time she'd been here, but the place didn't feel right. It felt . . .

Evil?

When she could see the clearing, it was all she could do to keep from running.

"We've been gone a while," she said as they emerged from the woods. "Do you think Brandt has been looking for us?"

"Probably," Gage replied. "But we'll worry about that later. Let's get these bones buried before Brandt comes out *here* looking for us."

He walked on, stopping in front of the padlock on the iron gates surrounding the girls' gravesite. He reached into his back pocket and extracted a small Allen wrench and a modified paper clip and immediately went to work.

He gave the lock a quick tug, and it opened. He glanced at her again, a cockeyed grin on his face. "Always come prepared for the job."

Jess laughed and smacked him playfully on the arm.

Bryan grabbed the two shovels they'd left leaning against the fence, pushed past them, and swung the gate open. A gust of wind kicked up as they stepped inside, and Jess recalled the figure pointing toward the graves and back to her.

Had this been what he'd meant? Were they doing the right thing?

Bryan and Gage began digging up a patch of earth at the base of the monument. Gracie and Emma's statues had taken on an eerie glow in the moonlight and Jess shivered. It was as though the girls were watching them from their carved pedestals. The sound of the shovel seemed louder than what she'd expected. Brandt had to hear them out here. She glanced at the house, but no lights came on.

After a while, Bryan hit something with the tip of the shovel. They all exchanged glances.

"It's got to be the casket," he announced.

Gage shone the flashlight into the hole. "Hardwood. Probably mahogany or something like it, seeing as the Silers were wealthy."

"Which grave?" Allison asked. "Is that Gracie's or Emma's?"

Gage glanced up at the monument. "No idea. Maybe Gracie's. Of course, we don't know whose bones we have, either."

"Now what?" Jess asked nervously. She hadn't thought about that part. "Can we just bury the bones on top or do we . . ."

. . . *break open the coffin?*

From the looks on everyone's faces, they were wondering the same thing.

Bryan leaned on the shovel. "Unless someone has a manual for this kind of stuff, we're just winging it. I mean, we don't know whose bones we're even burying here. Unless we open up both caskets and can figure out who's missing a rib or whatever that is, and part of their skull, it's a crapshoot."

Gage pitched the handle of his own shovel from hand to hand. "In or out of the casket, it doesn't matter. We're only going to bury the bones on top. Which means this one is as good as the other. Mind handing them to me, Allison?"

Allison shook her head and took a step back from the bones resting at her feet. "I'm not touching them."

Gage shot her a hard glance, tossed the shovel down, and picked up the bones. Jess understood both sides here—Allison's reluctance to touch the bones, and Gage's irritation after he and Bryan had been digging in the August heat while she and Allison merely watched.

"Aside from not knowing who's missing what, is there a reason we're not putting the bones back in the coffin?" Jess asked.

Using his forearm, Gage wiped sweat from his forehead. "Because, for whatever stupid reason, I paid attention to some crap on TV once—about burials. We have no way of knowing if the girls were embalmed with arsenic or not. It was common around the turn of the century. I can't remember an exact year, but Gracie and Emma were buried close enough to the time frame that I'm not willing to take any chances."

He carefully set the bones on the coffin's top, then picked up his shovel and started tossing dirt back onto the coffin. "Hell, for that matter, I have no idea if this stuff leaches into the soil."

Bryan scoffed. "You're kidding, right? It's probably ma-hogany, like you said. You think arsenic might have seeped through the caskets and into the soil?"

A sheen of sweat covered Gage's muscular arms. "Sorry. Can't answer that. I'm not a mortician. I'm not a chemist, either, but I don't think coming into contact with a poison-ous substance at a haunted house is a good thing."

Jess watched as the bones disappeared beneath the spray of orange earth.

"Should we say something?" Jess asked.

"Like what?" Bryan asked.

She shrugged. "A prayer?"

She recalled the first time Gracie and Emma had shown themselves to her, their faces so frightened and pale. She thought of how young they were when they'd died. How they had promised to help her.

How they creeped her out at times.

As Gage continued shoveling dirt onto the gravesite, Jess recited a childhood prayer. It was the only prayer she could think of.

"Now I lay me down to sleep. I pray the Lord my soul to keep." She paused. The next part didn't fit.

If I should die before I wake . . .

Jess knelt once Gage had thrown the last of the dirt onto the grave. "I hope you two are at rest now. I hope you're free of Riley and this place. Take care, Gracie and Emma."

Allison handed her some flowers she'd picked nearby and Jess placed them on the broken earth.

CHAPTER THIRTY-SEVEN

Gage had expected Dr. Brandt to ask where they had been and what they'd been up to, seeing how dirty and grimy they were—especially him and Bryan. He didn't know how Brandt could miss it—they all *looked* like they'd been digging up graves. But Brandt merely glanced up from his spot on the sofa, eyeing them briefly, then ordered them to get cleaned up before the séance.

Weird. Too weird.

"Snap, snap!" Brandt said cheerfully. "The room is ready for us except for the candles. I just need to get them from the basement."

"I'll help," Gage offered. "It won't take me but a few minutes to clean up. Bryan can use the shower first."

Dr. Brandt seemed genuinely surprised by his offer, which confirmed Gage's suspicions. He was hiding something. Had he been doing a little practicing of his own—without them? Allison had thought he might be, and Gage agreed. Until tonight, Brandt was the only one actively working on crossing Riley over into their realm.

Then why do the séance with us at all?

Easy. Because despite his efforts, Brandt had failed. He hadn't told them about his work in the basement because they'd . . .

What? Stop him? Ask him why he was conducting séances without them?

"No," Brandt said, his voice no longer cheery. "I'll get the candles. Get cleaned up. And find separate rooms. It'll take too long if you have to wait on the others." He glanced at Jess and Allison, who were waiting on the bottom stair. "Besides, the renovation crew broke a window and left everything a mess. I don't want anyone injured."

"Okay," Gage replied. "It's a good idea. We don't have much time left before midnight."

Brandt stood patiently in the Great Room. With a final glance, Jess and Allison headed up to the third floor. Bryan waited for Gage and they went to their own floor together.

"I'd bet anything he's been holding séances without us," Bryan said once they were out of earshot. "He's been acting weirder every day. You think he's using the Ouija board and trying to channel Riley?"

"No doubt," Gage replied. "The question is who answered. Riley or some other spirit in the house? He's clearly not himself."

"What do we do, then? Do we go on with the séance?"

"Yeah. Right after we knock his ass out cold."

Bryan laughed. "Dude. We can't just knock him out."

"He'll be *fine*. We need something to tie him up with, though."

"Yeah, well. I'll think about it. I'm going to go to the next room and shower," Bryan said, grabbing some clean clothes. "Maybe if we're done fast enough we should check out what he's been up to."

"Good plan." Gage avoided telling Bryan that maybe they didn't really want to know what Brandt was up to—that it didn't matter because he didn't think Brandt was entirely Brandt anymore.

CHAPTER THIRTY-EIGHT

Jess collected her hairbrush, a few toiletries, and a fresh change of clothes. Allison hadn't taken part in Jess's earlier explorations and wasn't comfortable showering in a strange room. And at this point, neither was Jess. She promised herself she'd hurry—she would just shower and change. She would dry her hair when she got back to the room.

Allison was already in the shower.

"I'll be back," Jess shouted into the bathroom.

"Okay," Allison shouted back. "Hurry, will you?"

"I will." Taking a deep breath for courage, Jess padded down the hall quickly. She chose the room at the end of the hall, the one she was most familiar with. Not that it would make any difference. By now, Siler House knew exactly where they were at any given time.

Stop thinking about stuff like that.

Her hand paused as she reached for the doorknob. With a quick glance back to her own room, Jess opened the door and let herself in, leaving the door open—just in case.

As if it would do any good if Siler House or anyone in it decided to come after them. The room was empty. No sign of ghosts of any sort. No demons. No Riley. Just a normal room.

Keep thinking that. Normal. Everything's normal.

Jess made sure the towel in the bathroom covered the mirror before undressing. After waiting for the water temp to adjust, she stepped into the shower. She washed in what she thought was record time. Grabbing the towel, Jess ran it over her body and then over her hair. She dressed, tugging her short-sleeved shirt over her head and resisting the urge to bolt from the room.

Normal, normal, normal. Everything's just fine, Jess.

Heart pounding, she quickly scooped up her things and hurried from the bathroom.

Don't look behind you. Just keep moving. There's nothing there. Nothing there.

The door was still open, but it felt as though it were a hundred yards away. In her mind, she pictured the door slamming shut in front of her.

Stay casual, Jess.

Her eyes focused on the door as she crossed the room, letting out a sigh of relief once she was back in the hallway.

Exploring Siler House used to excite her. She'd loved to go from room to room, taking in the furnishings and atmosphere. Now, everything about the place made her uneasy.

Very uneasy. The sooner they did this, the sooner Riley was gone, the better. Of course, what about afterward? Would the experiment be over? Or would EPAC have more in store for them?

You'd better hope you'll get out of here at all.

The hall was as empty as she'd hoped. Still, the eeriness of it made her break into a run to her room. She opened the door and stepped inside.

Allison gave her a smile of relief. "Glad you're back."

"Something happen?" Jess asked, trying to sound composed.

She was back in her room. Allison was here. Yeah, like that was a whole lot better—the girl who could become possessed at any moment.

She's not. It's Allison. Just Allison.

"Everything's fine. If you're going to dry your hair, you'd better hurry. You can use my dryer. I left it plugged in."

Jess nodded. "Thanks."

Why did it feel as though something was about to go wrong? Terribly, *horribly* wrong? And how had Allison suddenly become the calm one?

Jess closed the door to the bathroom as she dried her hair, leaving it slightly damp to save time. She unplugged the dryer and walked back into the bedroom. Allison was sitting on the edge of her bed facing the doorway.

"Sshhh!" she said, turning her head back to Jess.

Jess crept over to Allison. Outside the door, someone paced the hallway.

"It's like the other night," Allison whispered. She scooted back on the bed and wrapped her arms around herself.

The pacing continued and Allison's fear was escalating. She buried her head in her palms and began to whimper. Which was why Jess had to go and open the door. By now, she believed there were things that wanted to hurt them in Siler House. But realistically, it could also be Gage or Bryan, or Dr. Brandt.

Or someone else entirely.

Each creak of the boards set Jess's nerves on edge.

She went across the room. They couldn't jump at every shadow. They'd be a wreck by the time they had to do the séance.

"Don't!" Allison pled. "It'll know which room we're in."

More footfalls sounded outside the door.

"Whatever it is, it *already* knows which room we're in."

The doorknob turned back and forth, but no one entered. Jess held her breath, but Allison . . . Allison was curled up on the bed whimpering.

Enough of this! It's scaring the shit out of her.

And me!

But it's going to make Allison crack completely.

The pacing resumed. Jess took a final step forward and the pacing stopped.

Open it. It's right on the other side of the door. Just open it!

As Gage had put it, if they weren't calm, they weren't thinking. Right now, Allison wasn't thinking. They'd need her for later. They couldn't afford for her to make any mistakes in telling them how to guide Riley over into their realm.

What if it's Riley?

It's not.

If he were free of the mirrors, he wouldn't be walking the hallway waiting for an invitation. Her hand hesitated only once. Gathering up every ounce of courage she had, Jess grabbed the knob and flung the door open.

No one was there. There should have been. There should have been someone standing right outside the door. For some reason, part of Edgar Allan Poe's "The Raven" came to mind—the part where Poe kept hearing the tapping on his chamber door, but when he answered, *quoth the raven, nevermore.*

Stop it! You're freaking yourself out even more because Allison is on the edge, and she's going to take you with her.

Jess scanned the hallway and gasped. Mrs. Hirsch walked from one of the rooms. She switched the key ring from one hand to the other before looking in Jess's direction, then raised the chain around her neck—the one with the pendant she always wore. She held it as though showing it to Jess, then tucked it back inside her uniform and walked off toward the stairs. Without a single word.

Jess exhaled and leaned against the doorway.

When had Mrs. Hirsch returned?

Jess stepped out of the room in time to see the woman's shadow on the landing wall.

"Mrs. Hirsch!"

The first step creaked and the shadow on the wall headed downstairs.

Jess jogged down the hall.

"Mrs. Hirsch!" Jess shouted. "Wait!"

What was with her, anyway? Jess came to the top of the stairs.

And came to a complete stop.

The stairwell was empty. Mrs. Hirsch couldn't have gone down the steps that fast. Jess ran halfway down the stairs before a few things occurred to her. The ghosts at Siler House were becoming less and less transparent or *glitchy* as they'd once been. In fact, the last time she'd seen Gracie and Emma, they hadn't been transparent at all. The only other explanation was that Jess was getting better at seeing ghosts. Probably a combination of both.

The hallway behind her seemed too open, the stairwell too treacherous. All Jess wanted was to get back to her room. She raised a trembling hand to her mouth. Dr. Brandt had lied to them.

Something had happened to Mrs. Hirsch, because what Jess had seen was her ghost.

CHAPTER THIRTY-NINE

Footsteps and voices echoed up the stairwell. Gage, Bryan, and Dr. Brandt. Jess blinked. Her pulse still wild, head still reeling, she tried to unscramble her thoughts. Did Brandt know? If so, why hadn't he told them?

Unease pooled in her stomach. She needed to talk to everyone, everyone *except* Brandt. But there was no time. They were coming up for the séance. Brandt would know something was up if she asked to speak to everyone else— alone.

Something is terribly wrong here. Something is wrong with Brandt.

The three of them met her at the landing. Bryan panned the video camera to Jess.

"And this is Jess, our resident Ghost Whisperer." Bryan waved at her from behind the camera lens.

She forced a smile in his direction.

"Is Allison ready?" Brandt asked casually.

Jess nodded. "Yeah, she's ready. I just need a moment with her before we start."

Brandt glared at her. His eyes were different. Darker. Colder, although not as cold as the chill that scurried up the back of her neck. "Five minutes." He grinned and Jess wanted to recoil. "Do *not* make me come for you."

Bryan was recording the whole thing and Gage's face was tight. So they knew something was wrong. They just didn't realize *how* wrong.

"It's a shame Mrs. Hirsch isn't here," Jess said. Hopefully, the guys would pick up on her comment. She couldn't see Bryan's reaction from behind the camera, but Gage gave her a questioning frown.

Brandt waved a dismissive hand. "Given our task, I think it's better she isn't here." He walked ahead to the staircase leading up to the music room.

Gage stayed alongside her, letting Bryan and Dr. Brandt get ahead of them. "We need to talk—"

"I saw her ghost," Jess whispered, interrupting him. "He knows. He has to."

"What?" Gage shook his head. "Are you *sure?*"

Jess nodded.

"Son of a *bitch.*"

"The clock is ticking, Ms. Perry. You and Ms. Giles now have four minutes," Brandt called back to them.

Gage took her gently by the arm and they ducked into her room. "Four against one. We can take him down, tie him up until after the séance."

"We don't have time," Allison said. "It's too close to midnight. It's important that we start this as soon as possible." She unfurled herself and slowly swung her legs over the edge of the bed. "If we're going to do this, we need to hurry."

Siler House had already broken Allison. Shoulders slumped, she wouldn't meet Jess or Gage's eyes. If she checked out now, they were lost. Jess had no clue why it was important they start the séance as soon as possible, but it didn't matter. She either trusted Allison at this point or she didn't. "You can do this," Jess encouraged. "I have faith in you."

Allison smiled briefly and moved past them, looking like someone walking death row on execution day.

Brandt had set up the music room. He'd placed four folding chairs around a card table in its middle. Candles burned atop the baby grand piano in the corner and the lights had been dimmed. The odd glow coming from Bryan's camera and the candles' flames reflected eerily off the mirrors. Brandt had taken down the sheets they'd hung over them.

Another larger, floor-length mirror trimmed in ornate gold had been propped against the far wall. Like the others, it was uncovered.

Brandt sat at the card table, the Ouija board already in place.

Allison gasped and Jess placed a hand on her arm to calm her. *Keep going. Just keep going, Allison . . .*

"Have a seat," Brandt said rather coolly. "Jess and Allison should sit next to each other." He motioned to the two empty chairs across the table. "Gage, sit next to me. Bryan is recording the séance and won't be participating directly."

Gage leaned in and whispered into Bryan's ear. Bryan frowned.

Allison's expression resembled that of a rabbit cornered by wolves and Jess felt sorry for her. "We need you, Allison. Stay strong. You can do this. We'll follow your lead. Just tell us what to do."

"The candles," she said, her voice faint. "The color is wrong."

The candles? The mirrors were uncovered and Allison was concerned about the color of the candles?

"What about the candles?" Gage asked.

"They're not white," Allison stressed.

Jess frowned. "What does that mean?"

"They should all be white. White is pure."

"Well, some are close," Gage offered. "Most of them look yellow. Except for the couple of red ones. At least they're not black."

"At least they're not black," Allison echoed.

Don't space out on us.

Allison's words and that damn song echoed in her head.

Run away, Allison! Run away!

See how they run! See how they run!

Brandt observed their conversation and reactions, Jess noticed, but never said a word. The apprehension in her stomach had turned into greasy panic. She took a deep breath and pushed the unease down.

When they had taken their assigned seats, Brandt leaned forward. "Here are the rules. We concentrate on Riley and

Siler House." He glanced at Jess and Gage. "No one else. Not your grandmother or father, and not Ben."

He leaned back. "Of course, if someone or something *else* presents itself to Allison, then the choice is hers."

"But that'd be opening her up to—" Jess interjected.

"Yes! It very well might, Ms. Perry. And as I stated, we leave that choice up to her. Is that clear?"

It was. All too clear. To everyone. Brandt belonged to Siler House now. Jess reconsidered Gage's offer to deck Brandt and tie him up. She gave Allison a sidelong glance.

Allison watched Jess carefully, and slowly shook her head. "No," she mouthed.

And that ended that idea.

"Good," Brandt replied, taking everyone's silence for agreement.

He templed his fingers. "Riley is stuck in the mirrors because of a séance Catherine Siler and a chambermaid held after the failed exorcism. One of the maids knew a little voodoo and cast a spell designed to bind Riley's soul to a mirror. The women held the séance, calling upon Riley. When he presented himself, he caught his reflection in the mirror. Once he was trapped inside, Catherine Siler had the mirror dumped into the Savannah River, away from Siler House."

Jess shook her head. "Then why is he still here?"

"Because, according to the journals Mrs. Siler kept, the demon who possessed Riley told him how to escape into the house itself. Unfortunately, he's limited to the mirrors—any mirror brought into the house."

Gage shrugged. "So, why can't we just break the mirrors?"

"That would be destruction of property, and I'm not sure that would do any good in freeing Riley. He has to be invited back into our realm. I chose the mirror in the corner because it's an original and closest to the one Riley was first trapped in." Brandt's gaze shifted between them. "We want him to feel comfortable, right? Any more questions? Or shall we get started?"

Yeah, Jess thought. *Tell us about Mrs. Hirsch.* She wasn't sure what had happened, but she sure bet Brandt knew more than he was telling.

The time for questioning Brandt had passed. He'd already said what he was going to about Mrs. Hirsch. If she was here, she might answer to Allison.

Allison's eyes grew wide and fixed in the dim lighting, her breathing becoming quick and shallow. Jess reached over and squeezed Allison's hand.

"We do exactly as I say," Allison told them without looking up.

Brandt smiled. "That's my girl." He rubbed his hands together with enthusiasm. "Now, shall we begin?" He placed two fingers lightly on the planchette. Gage and Jess did the same. Allison's hand shook as she joined them.

Allison took a deep breath. "Ouija, are you here with us? Can you help us?"

The planchette jerked right, then began spelling its reply.
J E S S

"It wants you to ask the questions," Allison said.

Jess blinked. "Me? But you're the one with experience."

"I'll tell you what to say and what to do. But you have to be the one to open the connection. You're the one the house wants most."

Brandt handed Allison his pad and pen. "Write the questions down, then put your fingers back on the planchette."

Jess's mouth went dry. This was supposed to be Allison's job. The plan was spiraling out of control. First, Brandt intervening, and now this. She forced herself to swallow. Eyeing the others, Jess asked Allison's original question. "Ouija, can you help us?"

Y E S

Jess read Allison's question. "We are channeling the spirit of Riley, who lives here, in Siler House. Riley, are you here?"

Without hesitation, the planchette shot to Y E S.

"He's not alone," Allison said. "Oh my God, he's not alone. There are others."

"How many?" Brandt demanded.

"Two more," Allison answered. She looked as though she might be sick.

"Who?" Brandt asked. "Who's with Riley?"

"Is Mrs. Hirsch with you, Riley?" Jess asked. Brandt shot her a hard glare, but she didn't care.

N O

Brandt grinned.

Allison scribbled something down on paper. *Which spirits are with you?*

Jess concentrated on the planchette. "Who is with you, Riley?"

"No!" Allison shrieked. "That's not what I wrote!"

The planchette jerked once and began going over letters so quickly that keeping their fingers resting on top of it was difficult. Through the hole in the planchette, Jess read:

G R A C I E

E M M A

The planchette abruptly returned to the middle.

Jess gasped. How? How could they still be here? Why hadn't burying their bones worked?

"They're supposed to be at peace!" Bryan lowered the camera for a moment.

"Keep recording!" Brandt ordered. Bryan raised the camera again.

Jess shook her head slowly. There was only one answer. "They have unfinished business."

The planchette jerked again, this time hard enough that it pulled away from their fingertips. Moving on its own, it replied.

Y E S

The piano played a familiar stanza. Jess's breath caught and her blood froze.

She cut off their heads with a carving knife,

Have you ever seen such a sight in your life . . .

Allison was crying now. Her hands, although shaking hard, reached for the planchette. "We can't let the board answer by itself."

It couldn't be. It just couldn't. This was wrong. All wrong!

"You're supposed to be at peace!" Jess nearly shouted.

N E V E R

"Come on!" Allison urged. Tears streamed down her cheeks. "We have to finish it. We have to bring over Riley before anything else crosses over."

"Finish it?" Brandt asked, his voice almost childlike.

Bad idea. Bad idea.

But what else was there?

Get ready. Get ready to grab Gage's hand and run out of here as fast as you can.

Jess and Gage placed their fingers back onto the planchette.

"Bring over Riley," Brandt demanded. "Bring him over. He's right there."

"Oh shit!" Bryan cried out. "He's in the mirror. Guys, he's in the freaking mirror!"

A dark shadow in the outline of Riley appeared in the ornate mirror.

"NO!" Allison screamed. "Don't. We can't. I didn't know! I was wrong! Please don't make me do this. Close the session! Tell the board good-bye!"

Jess couldn't contain the fear rising in her throat like vomit. "What is it? What's wrong?"

"Riley's not a ghost. He's been hiding it all along!" Allison cried. "We can't bring him over!"

"Great!" Gage said through gritted teeth. "Do it, Jess. Clear the board!"

The fear was nearly paralyzing. "Good-bye!" Jess called out.

The planchette refused to move.

"GOOD-BYE!" Jess screamed at the board.

"Force it!" Allison shouted. *"Force it!"*

Brandt removed his hands and laughed. Jess joined Gage and Allison in applying pressure to the planchette, forcing it down the board. As soon as the pointer came close to the phrase *good-bye*, the board spun around.

"What is wrong with you?" Gage shouted to Brandt. "Help us! Hold the damn board still!"

"It's too late," Brandt said. "It's too late."

"What are you talking about? Hold the damn board, asshole!"

Bryan put the camera on the table and took Brandt's spot with the planchette. The board continued to spin whenever they moved it close to the word *good-bye*.

"Tell us your name. Who were you before Riley?" Brandt shouted over the mayhem.

The board righted itself and the planchette effortlessly spelled out the reply, even though Jess and the others tried their best to prevent it.

E U R Y N O M E

A biting cold swept through the room, along with a stench Jess could only identify as rot. Reflexively, she gagged.

Brandt laughed. "I *knew* it!"

"Who is Eurynome?" Bryan asked.

"The prince of death," Brandt replied. "Devourer of corpses. And now, he's here. We can still call him Riley, if we'd like."

The planchette returned to *good-bye* of its own accord—just as the lights went out and the candles extinguished themselves.

CHAPTER FORTY

Gage had been ready to punch Brandt—take him down and subdue him somehow, without anyone's blessing. But that was before all the commotion. Jess and Allison sat frozen in their chairs, eyes fixed on the far side of the room and screaming. Bryan trained the camera on the mirror. Eurynome or Riley or whatever the hell he called himself stood inside the mirror. Gage didn't look behind them. The demon's form wouldn't appear there. Riley reached out of the mirror and took hold of its frame with slender fingers longer than any human's. He then ducked down and stepped through the frame, his face hard and malevolent.

They might not make it off the property, but he knew one thing with certainty. They had to get out of the house. Now. Or die.

Think, Gage. Focus.

On what, exactly? Go! The time for thinking is done.

The light from Bryan's camera bounced off the mirrors, bathing everyone in eerie green. Chairs clattered to the floor as they fled the room. Brandt cackled as the piano began to play.

See how they run! See how they run!

Jess! He pushed her in front of him. "Run."

They raced down the stairs toward the third-floor landing, using the railing and light from the infrared camera to help guide them. Brandt followed, and undoubtedly, Riley wasn't far behind. They couldn't hear him, but no one dared look back. Reaching the third-floor landing, Gage kept Allison and Jess in front of him, shielding them from whatever, and whoever, was behind them. Doors in the hallway began opening and Allison locked up, causing him and Bryan to crash into her.

"Keep moving!" Gage shoved Allison forward. She was moving again, which was good. She was also screaming, but then he thought they might *all* be screaming at this point. He was too scared to really notice. Former Siler House inhabitants stood behind the doors, but Gage didn't want to do more than catch them from the corner of his eye.

The house was alive now, in full swing. Lights out, doors on all floors opening and slamming shut, making them jump. They reached the second-floor landing without anyone falling and without a single Riley sighting.

He's toying with us.

Brandt was still on their heels. "Run! Riley's coming!"

Driven by fear, everything became a blur. Jess, Allison, and Bryan were up ahead, still running down the stairs.

"Run and hide if you can! Riley is coming for us all!" Brandt chanted behind him.

Gage had had enough. He turned and threw a solid punch to Brandt's face, knocking him backward and on his ass. Gage's hand throbbed, but the reward had been worth it.

"Gage!" Jess cried. "Gage! *Come on!*"

"Oh shit, dude!" Bryan yelled, panning the camera light back toward him. "Gage! Run!"

Gage looked up. Riley scurried down the walls on all fours, his dark hair hanging limply across his face, eyes burning with hate.

And hunger. The demon they knew as Riley meant to do to them what he'd done to Gracie and Emma. He was just taking his time about it. This was it, the moment Riley had waited for—their fear whetting his appetite. Somehow, Gage was moving again, stumbling, but catching himself with the handrail.

Riley disappeared into darkness once more. Bryan shone the light forward again as they ran. But Riley was still close by. Gage could hear him, softly laughing from somewhere above and behind them. Any minute now. Any minute, the demon would reach out and grab him.

They made it down to the first floor. The front door was in Jess and Bryan's reach.

"It won't open!" Bryan shouted.

"Try the window!" Gage yelled, running past him.

Jess tried the latch. "It won't budge."

Gage grabbed a vase from a table and hurled it at the window. The vase hit, shattering and spilling water and flowers. The window stayed intact.

He blinked in disbelief and cursed under his breath.

"Siler House has locked us in," Allison sobbed. "We're dead. We're *dead!*"

"The basement," Gage said.

"Are you nuts?" Bryan snapped. "*No one* runs to the basement!"

The stairs creaked and Bryan panned the camera back to the stairs. Brandt. He moved slower now and held the left side of his face, but he was still laughing.

"We do if there's a broken window in the basement. Siler House might be able to lock doors and bulletproof windows, but I hope it can't create what isn't there. Brandt said the renovation crew broke a window."

No one had to say it was a good idea. Without a word, they ran to the kitchen and the basement stairs. Damn! How he wished they'd remembered to bring a flashlight to the séance.

"Where are you, you son of a bitch?" Gage snarled. Riley's absence worried him. Where was he?

"I don't know!" Bryan shouted. He spun around in a circle, searching for Riley. The camera's light spun with him, bringing sections of the room in and out of view. "He can travel through mirrors, scale down walls. What the hell?"

"He has nothing but time on his side," Jess reminded them, voice trembling.

"He's tasting our fear," Allison said in a high-pitched tone. "Demons do that."

The basement stairs were narrow and steep, and they had to be more careful running down them. Bryan panned the camera, giving them light, however dim. The basement seemed more menacing than the last time they'd visited it. The stone walls and darkness reminded him of catacombs.

The light from the video camera made the cobwebs appear ten times their normal size. The jars that had once contained pickles, spaghetti sauce, and other items now appeared to contain other things. Insects swarmed inside one jar, while several others contained dead birds and rats. Gage tried not to look at them. He clenched his jaw and forced himself to keep moving.

They're not real, Gage repeated to himself. These were all visuals Riley and Siler House had conjured in order to frighten them. Nothing more.

Yeah, well, it's working.

Keep going. The douchebag is resorting to special effects. That's all it is. Keep moving!

Bryan panned left and right, checking out the area in front of them. To the left was an opening between the shelves. It was the route they'd taken the first time down here with Brandt. Gage wondered what was taking him so long to get down here after them. Was he searching for a weapon? Was this a trap?

Brandt had lost it—totally given in to Siler House. Siler House might have been influencing them all, but Brandt had allowed it to completely consume him.

Damn it! Why hadn't he thought to grab a knife from the kitchen? You're not thinking, Gage. And it's going to get you and everyone else killed.

Allison shrieked when light from the camera illuminated jars containing human body parts—eyes, ears, fingers. Jess retched as one of the fingers in the jar twitched.

Gage took her hand, pulling her to him. "Don't look at them. Stay close."

Bryan went ahead, shining light into the storage room. The furniture was still there. The worn chairs, the toy chest, the dresser with the creepy dolls.

And Riley's crouched frame. He hunkered by the dresser, dirty white shirt with dark stains, dark pants, and black boots. He grinned, revealing teeth that didn't belong to any human. They belonged to a demon—one that ate corpses.

But dammit! They weren't corpses yet.

Gage kept Jess close to him. Allison ducked behind Bryan.

"Allison is right, you know," Riley drawled. "I can taste it. Your fear and the stink of your sweat. I salivate thinking of how salty your skin will taste. How the fear will have flavored your flesh." He scratched at the packed dirt of the basement floor. "After it's been properly tenderized, of course."

His tongue snaked from his mouth and wriggled, as though sampling the air. "But not yet. A little more seasoning, I think."

Allison shrieked. "There, *there*!"

Bryan panned the camera right a few feet and then back to Riley, who watched them with beetle-dark eyes. "Go on," Riley coaxed. "I don't bite. Yet."

Bryan swept the camera right again. Mrs. Hirsch's body had been propped up against the broken and moldy furniture.

"I didn't kill her, if that's what you're thinking," Riley said.

Bryan panned back to Riley, who absently picked at his nails. "Dr. Brandt was kind enough to do that. I watched. Death is a fascinating spectator sport at times. Although I must confess, his execution disappointed me. He stabbed her from behind, right above the kidney. Sort of anticlimatic. However, watching her bleed out was gratifying. He had to leave her locked in one of the rooms. He was so afraid you'd find her, but you'd stopped exploring by then."

He cocked his head to the side, the movement unnatural, as though his neck were broken. "You remember the room, don't you, Jess? It's the room where you and Gage were getting to know each other beneath the sheets. I listened, hoping you two would do it then and there. Gave me the biggest hard-on. But you didn't finish. I had to wait. So worth it. Soon, it'll be my turn, Jess. Allison, too."

Trembling, Jess pressed against him and Gage wrapped his arms around her. "Never going to happen, asshole."

"Gage, Gage, Gage," Riley tsked. "You can watch if you'd like."

Thrashing and the sound of jars crashing to the floor erupted behind them. Brandt. Bryan shone the light toward

MICHELLE MUTO

the direction of the noise, then back again. Riley was gone. Gage didn't know what was worse, knowing where Riley was, or *not* knowing where he was. The basement was huge, much larger than he'd originally thought.

Once more, Gage cursed himself for not grabbing a knife from the kitchen. He didn't know if Riley could bleed, but Brandt could.

This is what happens when you lose your head. You're on the run now. On the house's terms.

Which was exactly where Siler House wanted them.

CHAPTER FORTY-ONE

"We've got to keep moving," Gage said.

He might be pretending to stay calm, but Jess knew otherwise. He was as terrified as everyone else. She slid her hand into his as he guided them in what she hoped was the right direction. The basement windows were only on one side. Of course, they had no idea what might be in their path, or which window had been broken. With only the light from the video camera, she found it difficult to gain her bearings.

Spiders nested along old basement windows. But Jess's fear of them didn't outweigh her fear of the house itself.

They moved through the area the remodeling crew had set up. The sawhorses and tools looked like wreckage from the *Titanic* in this light. Ladders, paint cans, and other items were scattered around the area.

Gage tugged at her. He'd stopped to pick up something from a makeshift workbench littered with all kinds of things—a foam coffee cup, a soda can, wrappers from a fast-food place, a pack of cigarettes. And a can of paint thinner.

Gage grabbed the paint thinner. "Pay dirt!" He held up the first object he'd snagged—a lighter. "We're gonna light this place up."

"Not while we're in it!" Bryan objected.

"No, once we crawl out the window. Keep an eye out for more stuff we can set on fire."

Jess grabbed a couple of dirty rags hanging off a sawhorse. They weren't much, but it was a start. With all the junk down here they should have no trouble setting the house ablaze. No house, no Riley. This nightmare would end.

"You're going the wrong way!" a small voice said. "The window is over here."

The voice remained bodiless for a second as Jess squinted into the dark. Gracie and Emma steadily materialized before them. "Hurry," Emma said. "Dr. Brandt is coming! You have to hurry!"

"You're supposed to be at peace," Jess gasped. The sight of them frightened her. She was done seeing ghosts. If she never saw another, it'd be too soon.

"We promised to help," Gracie said. She took her sister's hand and they ran into the darkness.

Before Jess could object or dwell on what to do, Bryan headed the direction the girls had gone. Allison appeared doubtful, but followed them across the basement. The girls ran ahead, the camera light making them appear paper-thin. Somewhere in the basement, Brandt cursed as he stumbled around in the dark looking for them. He was getting closer, though.

"Over here!" Gracie called back. "He'll be here soon!"

Emma pointed up. "There. There's the window."

Bryan panned the camera. It picked up the outline of a window frame, and a dirty reflection. Glass. The window wasn't broken.

She turned to Gracie and Emma. "It's not broken. It's the wrong window."

The girls smiled. "We know. We don't want you to go."

Gracie played with her sister's hair, fixing the ribbon in it. "We said we'd help you, but we didn't say how. We're helping you come to us. We love you, Jess. We want you *here*. With us. Forever."

"Light the place up," Bryan whispered to Gage. "If we're trapped, so are they. Fire is supposed to burn things clean, right? Make things pure again. Just light it up."

"You don't understand, do you?" Emma said.

"If you burn the house, you'll free all the darkness inside it. You won't stop Riley and you *won't* stop us," Gracie added.

Emma grinned, and for the first time, Jess saw all the malice behind that little-girl smile. "Burn the house, you'll set us all free. We can go anywhere, then."

"The bones," Jess whispered.

"Yes, thank you," Gracie said. "Too bad they weren't ours. They were Riley's. Papa killed him and left him in the woods for the wild things to eat."

This was it, Jess thought. They'd die here. Worse, they'd spend eternity here.

"Here." Bryan handed Allison the camera.

She frowned. "What am I supposed to do with it?"

"Just hold it!" Bryan closed his eyes in concentration, wincing and inhaling sharply.

Gracie and Emma began to flicker. "We won't *stay* gone. That part only works on physical things," Gracie hissed, and then they vanished.

Bryan swayed, then managed to right himself. Blood trickled from his nose.

"Two down, two to go," Gage murmured. "Come on, we've got to find that window."

"You heard them," Allison said, her voice trembling. "They'll be back. Whatever Bryan can do, I don't think it works the same on spirits."

"That's an understatement," Bryan muttered.

"Yeah, well, we'll take whatever time we've got." Gage flicked the lighter and moved along the wall with it, searching. Allison righted the camera, aiming it at eye level.

"You okay?" Gage asked. Bryan nodded.

They fumbled their way to the next window, which wasn't broken either, and the sick feeling in Jess's stomach worsened. Had Brandt lied about the broken window? Beside her, Bryan wasn't looking so good. Apparently, zapping spirits took more out of him than dead birds, keys, and abusive fathers. Jess took him by the arm to help steady him.

A support wall stopped their progress. Jess's panic was nearly unbearable now. Gage must have sensed her fear. He leaned in and kissed the side of her head.

"Don't worry. We've just got to follow this wall until we reach the next window."

Jess didn't mention the obvious. That following the wall meant going back to the center of the basement. No one spoke as they inched their way in the near darkness. It felt like an eternity. Finally, they reached the end of the wall. Now, all they had to do was follow it back toward the windows. Jess wanted to run, just bolt toward it, but without lighting, they could get turned around.

Gage stopped and flicked off the lighter. He turned to Jess and whispered. "Hear that?"

Everyone stopped and listened.

Jess shook her head. She heard absolutely nothing.

"I don't hear anything," Allison said softly, stepping past Gage.

He grabbed her arm and pulled her back. "Exactly. That means Brandt is probably around the corner."

CHAPTER FORTY-TWO

Brandt was ahead of them, somewhere around the support wall. Gage was certain of it. He moved away from the corner. "I have a plan, but I need you all to buy into this, okay?"

"Sure," Jess whispered.

Bryan simply nodded, looking pale. Gage had no way to know for certain, but if Bryan used to get killer headaches before, he could only imagine the mother he must have right now.

Allison eyed him suspiciously. He didn't expect her to like his plan any better once he explained. "I'm bringing back Mrs. Hirsch."

"What?" Bryan managed to say.

Allison stepped away from them. "No way! You want *her* to come after us, too?"

"Do you have another plan? Because we're listening," Gage asked her.

Allison shook her head. "Maybe if we run, we can get past him."

Gage was losing patience and they were wasting time arguing. "Really? That's your plan? We're not bringing back a ghost, Allison. We're bringing back a *person*. She might not even have a soul. I don't know what happens when I bring things back."

"Just have Bryan zap him!" Allison hissed.

Jess motioned to Bryan. "Look at him, Allison! Does he look like he can keep this up all night?"

Allison glanced at Bryan. Even in her fight-or-flight induced craziness she had to realize it was impossible for Bryan to nuke Brandt *and* every entity into oblivion without hemorrhaging to death.

"Look," Gage said. "We still have to get through Riley and the Evil Sisters are likely to make a reappearance at any time. If Bryan is going to use his mojo on anyone, it's got to be them. Maybe we can use Mrs. Hirsch to take out Brandt."

Allison shook her head. "She'll kill us."

Jess lightly shook her arm. "Wake up, Allison! It's not like we're going to stand around and watch! She's going to gain us some time."

"Go for it," Bryan said.

Jess nodded. "Do it."

Gage thought about Mrs. Hirsch. Saw her in his mind. He pictured her as though he were standing right in front of her lifeless body, concentrating on her as he'd last seen her alive. He exhaled through his mouth, as though blowing air onto the faces of the images in his mind. *We need you, Mrs.*

Hirsch. Are you there? We need to get out of the house. Brandt is blocking us.

Would it work? Mrs. Hirsch was much different than a bird or dog. He kept concentrating. He sensed the house-keeper stirring. Although he wasn't in front of her to see it, damned if it hadn't worked. He had no way to know her thoughts or even what she was doing. He only sensed her and her emotions, and man, was she was pissed.

"She's coming," he said at last.

He wondered if the communication worked both ways. Could Mrs. Hirsch hear him? Sense their fear? Their hesitation? Even so, what would it mean?

Allison tried to push past him. "Wait," he cautioned. "Not yet."

Allison pulled away, dropping the camera Bryan had handed her. Jess scrambled to catch it before it hit the ground. Allison bolted, forcing Gage to go after her.

"Damn it, Allison! Wait!" Bryan was right behind him, as well as Jess. Allison ran ahead, still in full freak-out mode. It didn't do much for not giving away their location, and it wasn't helping them find the broken window.

Gage feared Allison would be right. By chasing after her, they'd probably put themselves directly in Mrs. Hirsch's path—or Brandt's.

"BRANDT!" came Mrs. Hirsch's gravelly voice from deep within the basement. She didn't quite sound like she had when alive, but then, she was in a body that had been dead a couple of days.

319

More shuffling and banging noises he couldn't identify. Mrs. Hirsch sounded closer now. *"BRANDT!"*

Allison stumbled, tripping over something she'd run into in her blind attempt at escape. Gage grabbed her and she kicked and fought against him. "No!" she wailed. "Let me go!"

Something crunched beneath Gage's shoe. Jess panned down with the camera. Glass. Thank God for broken glass.

"The window!" Jess exclaimed, panning the camera to reveal their escape route.

"Jess, you should go first," Bryan said. "Then Allison. Gage and I will try to hold off everyone else."

Jess shook her head. "Get Allison through first. Then I'll go."

Allison had stopped struggling but was still crying. Without waiting, she scrambled toward the open window. It was several feet above the basement floor, and not a full-sized window. Gage hoisted her up and Allison grabbed the window frame. Once her feet wriggled through, he called to Jess. "Just run, okay? I'll find you."

She didn't seem so sure, but nodded. "You'd better."

His only thought was to get Jess to safety. That meant more than getting her out of the house, but he had to start somewhere.

Jess handed Bryan the camera and Gage lifted her enough for her to grab onto the windowsill and finish pulling herself up. Once she wriggled through, she poked her head back in. "Come on."

"Bryan's gotta go next," he said. "He's not doing well."

"No," Bryan said. "I'm the only one who can make them vanish. Go on."

"I'm not arguing with you," Gage told him. "Once you're up, you can help pull me through. Now move!"

Bryan tossed the camera up to Allison and let Gage give him a leg up.

"BRRRAANDT!"

Jess helped guide Bryan through. "Gage!"

Her warning made him turn to find Riley coming at him, his ashen face contorted with anger. Gage braced himself. There was no time to get out of Riley's way.

"Run, Jess!" Gage shouted.

"No!" Jess screamed as Bryan pulled her away.

Riley flung himself forward and unexpectedly went right through the window.

"Jess!" Gage yelled. "Jess!"

Shit! He was after Jess. More screaming. Jess's voice. Allison's. Bryan's, too.

Gage backed up and took a running leap, grabbing onto the window frame, cutting himself on jagged glass. He pulled himself up and pushed his way through.

Bryan had Jess behind him, trying his best to guard her. He was squared off with Riley. And Allison was running for the woods.

Something grabbed his foot and Gage kicked. Brandt? Hirsch? Whoever it was, they were strong. The pain in his ankle felt like they were trying to snap his leg in two. He rolled over, ignoring the pain. Brandt. He was halfway out the window. The Dr. Brandt they'd known was lost behind those crazed eyes. Gage brought his other foot down on Brandt's face a few times—hard. Brandt rocked backward with each kick, his nose bleeding and clearly broken.

Gage managed to free himself and scoot backward. He might have knocked him back into the house, but Brandt kept coming. Gage stood and an intense bolt of pain shot up his ankle. He'd twisted it, but at least he was able to put weight on it.

And the hits just keep on coming, he thought.

His only hope was that Mrs. Hirsch would do something to Brandt. At least slow him down.

Bryan and Jess hurried to his side, Bryan helping to steady him.

"I'm good," Gage said, hobbling. "We've got to go. Did you get him? Did you get Riley?"

Bryan sighed. "No. I tried. He's gone, but not because of me. Maybe he went after Allison, I don't know."

Gage forced himself to put a little more weight on his leg and they made their way toward the front of the house. They couldn't leave, not without sending Riley to the Twilight Zone first. Even then, he'd be back. "The front gates."

"We've tried that before," Bryan reminded him.

"Yeah, but this time, it'll be different. He's coming for us. I hope you've got enough juice for one more shot. When Riley comes for our asses, hit him."

Bryan frowned. "I don't know if I can get rid of Riley as long as I did the girls. He's stronger."

Bryan really didn't look well. The moonlight made them all seem pale, but Bryan's complexion looked downright gray.

Gage mustered what he hoped was a half-assed but comforting grin. If they didn't get out soon, Bryan wasn't going to make it.

CHAPTER FORTY-THREE

Jess had a horrible thought—what if Brandt killed the power to the front gate? What then? Maybe they should try the woods. Make a break for it. With any luck, they might get to the road. Maybe Allison would reach it before them. She glanced toward the line of trees only to see Allison's form heading back toward them.

"There's no way out!" Allison called.

Jess hurried to her. "What happened? Are the woods fenced off?" She didn't want to think about the other possibilities—that if Siler House was able to control the doors and windows, it would be able to control other things. Jess shuddered, thinking of what might lurk in the woods.

Allison's wavy hair was as wild as her eyes. "There's something in there," she whimpered.

Not good, Jess thought. *Not good at all*. Gage had a sprained ankle. Bryan's nosebleed was pretty bad, as was the mammoth migraine that threatened to drop him where he stood. They were still no closer to getting out of here.

Jess looked back at the house, wondering what she'd ever seen in it. Brandt had finished making his way out of the window. "Shit," she said.

The others turned to look.

"Well, now what?" Bryan asked. He'd wiped at the blood on his face, but already a fresh trickle was visible under his nose. His shirt was bloodstained, reminding her of just how much it had taken out of him to make the girls vanish.

Gage shook his head. "Sorry, man. I'm fresh out of plans."

He exchanged glances with Jess and she wondered if he was thinking the same thing. The only defense they had would be for Bryan to get rid of Brandt, after all. And the girls when they came back. And Riley, too. Jess looked at Bryan. It would kill him.

Gage stood, waiting for Brandt, ready to fight if necessary. Jess would fight alongside him if she had to.

Laughter, dark and bitter, came from up in the oak tree. Riley crouched on one of the wide, lower limbs. "A duel to the death. Who will win? My wager goes to the good doctor."

Jess glared up at him, nearly blind with fury and fright. *"GO AWAY!"*

She searched the ground for anything to throw, a rock or discarded brick, and came up with a small metal hinge most likely left over from when the renovation crew had built the new iron fencing around Gracie and Emma's graves. She hurled the hinge at Riley, hitting him dead-on. He cried out as a red burning hole appeared on his chest.

A hinge?

She glanced at the gravesite, recalled the man (Dad?) standing under the oak, pointing to her, then to the gravesite and back to her again. Riley said he didn't kill Mrs. Hirsch, even though he could have. Why? Because of the pendant. It was made of the same material as the hinge.

Iron.

Mrs. Hirsch had known all along. Hadn't Brandt mentioned that her family had owned Siler House for years before finally selling it?

Brandt grinned at Gage. "I have strength you won't believe. I guess you could say the gift was *on the house*. I can't let you leave, Gage. None of you. You understand, right? The experiment isn't over yet."

Behind Brandt, Mrs. Hirsch had crawled through the window. Would she help them or join forces with Riley?

Gage held his head up, defiant. "The experiment is over for us."

Mrs. Hirsch held something thin and shiny in her hand as she stumbled across the yard toward them, her attention solely on Brandt. Was that a golf club? A wood iron? Brandt was too focused on Gage to notice her approach.

Gage stepped back.

Brandt laughed. "Not so tough now, are you?"

"Gah!" Mrs. Hirsch brought the head of the golf club down on Brandt's head. She swung again, splitting his head open. He toppled forward, falling face first. Mrs. Hirsch continued to bring the golf club down on Brandt's lifeless body again and again, her blows becoming harder and quicker with each swing.

"The gravesite!" Jess shouted, trying not to watch the grisly scene in front of her. "The fence—it's iron!"

Allison perked up. "That's right! Demons can't cross over it!"

Jess removed the already opened lock and swung the gate open. Allison darted inside first, then Bryan.

"Hurry!" Jess screamed at Gage. The gaping red, smoldering hole in Riley was closing up. Mrs. Hirsch was still busy practicing her golf swing on what remained of Brandt's head, but she doubted that would last much longer. They couldn't risk that she'd turn on them next.

Riley began to scale his way down the tree.

"GAGE!" Jess screamed.

Gage made his way to her, although not nearly as fast as she wanted him to—his ankle preventing him from running. Her heart pounded furiously in her chest.

Hurry, damn it! Hurry!

"Close the gate!" Allison shrieked. "He's not going to make it. I'm sorry, Jess!"

"No!" Jess shouted back. She wouldn't leave anyone behind. Especially Gage.

"You can reopen it when he's closer! Do it! Close the gate!" Allison dove forward, but Bryan held her back.

"You're risking all of us for Gage!" Allison wailed.

"He'd do the same for us," Bryan reminded her.

Fear did strange things to people and Jess believed that coming here after having to deal with the possession had broken Allison permanently. She was a rat drowning in a sewer flood. She'd bite and climb over anything in her path to escape.

A shadow, because that's all Jess could describe it as, appeared on the other side of the fence. She called the entity a shadow, but in reality, what appeared before them seemed more like a void—as though all the light, all the space where the figure stood, existed in some black hole. The ample moonlight failed to penetrate it. The figure was tall and male, but nothing like the transparent ghosts she'd been accustomed to seeing. The ghost's features were impossible to see because they blended in with the night . . .

Dad?

Wishful thinking. Dad would show himself. This ghost is intentionally hiding his identity.

Still . . .

"The man on the stairs!" Allison said. "He's going to make it in! Close the gate!"

"He's not after us," Jess said.

"You don't know that! It's a ghost! They're bad, Jess. Why can't you get it through your head? Damn you!"

The shadowy figure stepped aside as Gage drew closer, then stood in Riley's path. The two shoved each other for a moment before the figure vanished. Gage limped inside the gate just as Riley's hand grasped the back of his shirt.

"Let go!" Jess yelled, slamming the gate closed. As she did so, it made contact with Riley's hand. He screamed as the iron burned him.

Riley circled the gravesite, but ventured no further. Jess embraced Gage, hugging him tightly against her. For a moment, she thought Riley had him.

He kissed the top of her head. "I'm okay. Are you?"

She nodded.

Gage turned to Bryan and Allison. "Are you guys okay?"

"I'd be better if you had something for this headache," Bryan replied solemnly.

Allison didn't look up. "I'm sorry. I thought—"

Jess let go of Gage and turned to Allison. This was as close to admitting that not every ghost meant them harm as Jess would ever hear from her. "You're going to be fine, Allison. We all are. When it's daylight, they'll find us here."

Allison sniffed. "But what if the house doesn't let them in?" She stole a glance outside the gates where the ghosts of Siler House waited and watched.

"I don't know," Jess replied.

They sat together at the base of the monument. No one mentioned they were sitting with the girls' and Riley's remains just a feet away. Gage rested with his back against the monument, cradling Jess against his chest. Allison faced the house, staring, rocking in place. Bryan finally stretched out on the ground. He needed a doctor—or something to knock him out for a few hours until his head stopped pounding.

Mrs. Hirsch continued to stare at them from the other side of the fence.

"Now what?" Jess asked.

Gage shrugged. "If Riley doesn't kill us first, we're stuck here until Monday."

"I hope the house lets them in," Jess said.

"It's got to let them in, right?" Bryan asked. "It has to."

Allison continued rocking. "Riley will think of something else. He won't wait until Monday."

Riley had resumed his place in the oak, his glowing eyes fixated on them from his perch.

"He's figuring out a way to open the gate," Allison said.

They huddled together in the dark, watching Riley and Mrs. Hirsch. Jess wondered how badly Riley and the house wanted them.

CHAPTER FORTY-FOUR

Dawn took its time chasing away the night. One by one, the ghosts returned to Siler House. Except Riley. He'd remained vigilant the entire night. He hunkered next to Brandt's body. He scooped up something with a finger and tasted it.

"Look," Jess whispered to Gage. She didn't want to alarm Allison, who seemed to be dozing. Mrs. Hirsch was pressed up against the gate, her face puffy and greenish, indicating bacteria had set in. Even from this distance Jess smelled her decay. She couldn't think of anything worse than being trapped inside a rotting corpse.

Except maybe sitting here, waiting for Riley to find a way to open the gates and kill them.

Gage was watching Mrs. Hirsch, too. "I don't know why it didn't work the same on her as Ben's dog and the animals. Maybe because I wasn't standing in front of her when I called her back. Who knows? All I do know is I'm done. I'm never bringing anything back again."

Jess nodded. "I wish things were that easy for me. I wish I had a choice—to never see ghosts again."

"She's able to touch the gates," Bryan said quietly. "Mrs. Hirsch."

"Because she's not a demon or a ghost," Allison explained.

"Riley's gone!" Bryan said. "Where did he go?"

"No idea," Gage replied. "Maybe it's a trick."

"Think we can get to the front gates before he shows back up?" Bryan asked.

Gage sighed heavily. "Even if we could, they won't open until Riley's gone. The house is tied to him."

Jess was listening to the guys talking, but her attention was also on Mrs. Hirsch.

Mrs. Hirsch lifted the pendant hanging from around her neck. With a quick yank, she broke the chain, and held the pendant out to Jess. She stood, ignoring Gage's quiet warning to be careful.

"It's iron," Jess whispered. "The pendant. It's made of iron."

"Jess!" Allison protested as Jess walked closer. "Stay away from her!"

Jess ignored her. If Mrs. Hirsch was offering her the pendant, she didn't mean her any harm.

She hoped.

Mrs. Hirsch's cloudy eyes narrowed on Jess. "Take it!"

Jess jumped at the gravelly, hoarse command, but she slowly reached for the pendant. Mrs. Hirsch grabbed her with her other hand and tugged Jess to the fence, inches from her face. Jess wanted to cry out, but the scream remained trapped in her throat. Mrs. Hirsch's flesh was cool to the touch, like Grams's hands at the wake. Her eyes remained focused on Jess.

Gage and Bryan jumped to their feet and pulled at Mrs. Hirsch's hands, trying to get her to release Jess. She ignored them and only held on tighter, making Jess cry out in pain.

"Wear it. Then be careful what you let in." Mrs. Hirsch's breath was the foulest thing Jess had ever smelled.

With that, she let go. Jess staggered backward, rubbing the red marks on her wrist. Mrs. Hirsch tottered back a couple of steps. Jess glanced down at the pendant. It was iron all right, with a raised Celtic cross.

Be careful what you let in, Jess.

Her eyes met Mrs. Hirsch's once more. She'd never told anyone what Grams used to say. Not Allison, not Gage, not even Brandt. And certainly never Mrs. Hirsch.

Gage examined her wrist.

Mrs. Hirsch narrowed her eyes. "Fix it."

"Maybe we should make a run for it," Allison suggested.

"What if it's a trick? Riley didn't just up and leave. And now we've got Mrs. Hirsch to worry about," Gage replied.

"We'll take our chances," Bryan said.

Gage rubbed his forehead. "You know I hate to ask this. Can you do it? Can you get rid of Mrs. Hirsch *and* Riley? And live to tell the tale?"

Bryan's face fell. Jess didn't think it was possible for him to look any worse. The nosebleed had slowed overnight but a small trickle remained and Bryan wiped it away with a rust-stained hand. "No. Sorry. I might be able to do it once more. But beyond that?"

"Then we've got to take care of Mrs. Hirsch first. Somehow." Jess understood the gravity of what she was saying. There was no need to clarify who Bryan needed to save his strength for.

"You mean *kill* her?" Bryan asked.

"She's already dead," Gage said. "You said so yourself—bringing someone back from the dead means they're just zombies. Besides, *look* at her, Bryan."

Jess took another look, as well. Mrs. Hirsch had been dead long enough that she'd already bloated the way corpses did as they started to decompose.

Allison had been too quiet. She was on her knees, her head against the sidebars of the gravesite, her right arm extended through the fence into the dirt on the other side. What was she doing? Once she finished, Allison joined them.

"One? You can only send away *one*?" Allison asked. Her face had taken on a determination that Jess hadn't seen before. "Think about it, Bryan," Allison went on. "If Mrs. Hirsch was willing, are you positive you could send her to wherever it is you send things?"

"I guess so."

"No!" Allison snapped. "Are you *sure*? We need to know, Bryan."

"Why is it so important?" Jess asked.

Bryan seemed to think about it for a second. "Yeah," he finally said.

Allison bit at her bottom lip and tears threatened her eyes. "Where do they go, Bryan?"

He shrugged. "I don't know. But Riley won't stay gone for long. He's a demon. Not a person."

Allison brushed her hair from her face. "Okay, then. When I tell you to do it, you do it. Got that, Bryan? No matter what."

His forehead scrunched in concern. "Sure, okay."

"Can I borrow this?" Allison asked, tapping the pendant in Jess's hand. "I promise you can have it back."

Jess reluctantly handed her the pendant. Allison gave her a smile that didn't reach her eyes. Her sad gaze fell on all of them, one by one, and finally back to Jess. "It's for the best."

Then Allison opened the gate and stepped outside.

"Allison!" Jess screamed. *"No! Come back!"*

Allison smiled faintly. "Then tell them I did it, Jess. Tell them I killed Dr. Brandt and Mrs. Hirsch. Tell them the demons came for me. It won't be a lie."

She walked over to where she'd been playing with the dirt. Mrs. Hirsch barely glanced her way, her focus still on Bryan and Gage—the person who'd put her in this position, and the one who could remedy it. Clearly, Allison didn't think Mrs. Hirsch was a threat. She'd said they couldn't trust Mrs. Hirsch, and yet Allison had walked out of the gates and passed right by her without hesitation.

What is she doing?

Jess ran to the side of the gate. In the dirt, Allison had written the letters of the alphabet. Above, on opposite sides, she'd written the word Yes and the word No. Beneath it all, Good-Bye.

"It'll work," Allison said as she knelt on to the ground. She held onto the chain and dangled the pendant above the makeshift Ouija board.

"No!" Jess said. "Allison! Get back in here!"

"Are you here?" Allison asked, opening the session. The pendant swung to the word Yes.

She mumbled something else too faint for Jess to hear. Riley appeared out of nowhere, standing right behind Allison.

"Allison, hold on to the pendent!" Jess said. "For the love of God, hold on to the pendant!"

Allison stood slowly. She leaned against the fence. "Me, Bryan. Send me."

Nothing could have prepared Jess for what Allison was doing—offering herself up for possession. The thing she feared most.

"What?" Bryan said. "No! Allison! Get back in here!"

"Do it!" Allison hissed. "Then run. I don't know how much time you'll have. I'll hold on to him for as long as I can."

"No!" Jess screamed as Allison turned and dropped the pendant into the dirt and raised her arms in welcome. "Come to me, Eurynome! Come to me, the demon we call Riley. I welcome you."

She looked at Jess once more, her eyes filled with terror.

Jess's legs wanted to crumple beneath her and she gripped the bars tightly. No, not this. Not Allison's worst nightmare come true. Not Riley. "Run away, Allison! Hide. To your tower. Don't look," Jess called out, her voice shaky and weak.

The demon swept down on Allison and wrapped his arms around her. She opened her mouth to scream and the demon covered it with his, dissolving into black smoke and insects. Allison remained in that pose, rigid and mouth still open in a scream as the demon entered her.

CHAPTER FORTY-FIVE

Bryan's face contorted as he stretched a hand toward Allison. Eyes closed, his head had dropped against his chest, blood flowing freely from his nose over his mouth. Gage could see he was giving it everything he had.

He wondered if Bryan's all would be enough. If Bryan failed, Riley would use Allison's body to open the gate.

You can do it, Bryan. You can.

You've got to.

Jess was squeezing his hand tightly.

Grimacing, Bryan cried out and fell to his knees, still working his mojo on Allison.

Allison faced them now, teeth bared. She walked toward the gate. Gage picked up one of the shovels. "Grab the other one, Jess!"

"What?" she cried. "Gage, I can't. I can't. It's Allison. She's in there."

Gage moved forward. "Well, she's going to be in *here* if we don't stop her. And just a reminder—she's got company."

Gage cursed under his breath.

The air began to crackle with electricity. Allison was almost at the gate. God help him, he was about to hit Allison with the shovel if she took a step closer.

Yellow light burst from Allison's abdomen and a roaring sound like a thunderclap echoed around them. Gage stumbled back and shielded his eyes from the light. When the cracking and popping subsided, Gage opened his eyes. Behind him, Jess was sobbing.

And Allison was gone.

He dropped the shovel. Jess was holding Bryan, who lay on the ground. He was conscious, but not in great shape. Blood soaked his shirt. How much had he bled, anyway? He'd never seen anyone who'd bled as much.

Bryan grinned up at him, weakly. "Just like the spider, dude. Chicks dig it."

Jess laughed through her tears and kissed Bryan's forehead. "You did it, Bryan. Oh my God, you did it."

But they weren't in the clear. Not yet. They still had to get out of here and off the property. With Bryan's condition and Mrs. Hirsch still hanging around, it wasn't going to be easy.

And the girls would be back. He had no doubt about that. In the meantime, Bryan could bleed to death.

"Come on. We've got to get out of here," Gage said, bending down to help Bryan to his feet.

"Is he going to be all right?" Jess's face looked as tired and worn as his. She reached through the gate, keeping an eye on Mrs. Hirsch as she retrieved the iron pendant Allison had dropped.

"Yeah, I think so. We just need to get him out of here."

Jess looked to the spot where Allison had last stood, tears pooling in her eyes.

"She's okay," he told her. He hoped that wasn't a lie.

Bryan managed to stand but it wasn't what Gage would call graceful. "We don't have a lot of time. Like the girls, Riley's absence is temporary."

Except for Allison. Gage doubted Nowhereville was temporary for Allison. Wherever Bryan had sent her, he knew she wouldn't be back. He only hoped she'd found a place where there were no demons. Not even her own.

The tears on Jess's cheek told him she felt the same. Allison and Jess had been at odds with each other now and then, but Jess was taking it harder than he'd expected. Even when confronted with the shadowed figure blocking Riley the way it had, and then Mrs. Hirsch possibly being the world's most helpful zombie, Allison still saw demons.

And Jess still saw angels.

Which is probably why he cared for her.

"Riley won't stay inside her," he said, hoping it'd be *some* comfort.

Jess could only nod as fresh tears spilled onto her cheeks.

Mrs. Hirsch stared at them from the other side of the fence. However useful she'd been, odds were good that at Siler House, she wouldn't stay that way much longer. They couldn't get Bryan out of here without getting rid of Mrs.

Hirsch first. If nothing else, she'd force them to end her form of existence, too. One way or the other.

"Keep Bryan steady," Gage said to Jess. She threw one of Bryan's big arms around her.

Limping, Gage picked up one of the shovels, earning him a frown from both Jess and Bryan, who swayed on his feet. Gage returned to them, using the shovel for a cane as Bryan wrapped his other arm around Gage's neck.

"We're going to need the shovel," Gage explained.

"What for?" Bryan asked.

"Mrs. Hirsch," Gage replied quietly. "I don't know how far we're going to get once we open the gate, but we can't take any chances. And like Jess said, we can't leave her like that."

Mrs. Hirsch didn't respond to their movement. She stared blankly as they made their way to the gate. Jess released the latch and pushed the gate open. The housekeeper continued watching, but made no moves.

"You're going to have to keep him upright." Gage eyed Mrs. Hirsch. "I'll take care of it."

"Okay." Jess accepted more of Bryan's weight. "Just help me through the gates first."

She's not going to be able to keep him on his feet, Gage thought as he helped her guide Bryan through the gates.

Mrs. Hirsch continued to stare after them. He wasn't sure whether her intelligence was now equal to a bag of hammers, or whether she was just waiting for the right time.

Five feet outside the gate. Ten. He glanced back. Mrs. Hirsch was beginning to follow them.

Fifteen. Twenty. Thirty feet. She was closer now, beginning to pick up the pace.

"Keep him upright," Gage reminded Jess. "Can you do that on your own for a few minutes?"

"No," Jess replied. "Gage, I can't."

"You have to, Jess. She's coming for us."

"Leave me," Bryan said weakly.

Gage shook his head. "Not a chance, bro."

This was impossible. Even if they got Bryan to the road, what then? They didn't have a phone. Sure, the estate was off a fairly decent-sized road, but that didn't mean anyone would stop. But he wasn't leaving Bryan behind.

"Hold on to Bryan," Jess said. "I'll take care of it."

"Jess—" Gage protested.

"Just do it!" she snapped.

Bryan shifted his weight to Gage and he winced at the extra pressure on his injured ankle.

"Give me the shovel," Jess said. Tears flowed down her cheeks, but her voice remained strong. Determined. "I'm not big enough to support Bryan. You're the only one who can help him, even with your ankle. Like you said, it'll only take a second."

Gage looked at her, then Mrs. Hirsch, who was less than ten feet away now. "You sure?"

Her bottom lip quivered. "To the head, right?"

He nodded and handed her the shovel. "Hard as you can."

He wanted to tell her she had courage, but the words seemed lost in the situation. Jess was doing this because it was a logical decision. And because she didn't want to see Mrs. Hirsch like she was any longer.

Come on, you can do it, Jess. I know you can.

He hated it that she'd have to be the one to set this right. *Fixing it*, as Mrs. Hirsch had called it, should have been his cross to bear since he had brought her back. Jess shouldn't have to go through this.

Shovel in hand, Jess met Mrs. Hirsch halfway. The housekeeper stopped and waited. Jess paused for only a second, then drew herself up and cried out as she swung the shovel hard, making a direct hit to Mrs. Hirsch's left temple.

Thwaaap!

Jess stepped backward, holding the shovel like a bat, sobbing freely now but ready to swing again if necessary. Mrs. Hirsch wobbled on her feet a second before falling to the ground.

"Fix it! Fix it!" Mrs. Hirsch's arms flailed at her sides.

Gage was ready to ease Bryan to the ground and take care of the situation when Jess raised the shovel high and brought it down hard into Mrs. Hirsch's forehead. Jess let go of the shovel and backed away. The shovel remained upright, protruding from the housekeeper's head. She lay still in the grass. Jess stared at Mrs. Hirsch, then, wiping the back of her hand against her mouth, Jess began to sob.

"I'm so sorry, baby." Anything else Gage might have wanted to say was lost on him. Jess returned to him and Bryan, choking back more tears. What could they say? Any of them?

Without another word, they made their way to the front gate, and from there, to the road.

CHAPTER FORTY-SIX

Fourteen months later . . .

Jess held flowers as she and Gage walked through Highland Cemetery outside Asheville. The weather had turned unusually cool for late October. The flowers she'd brought probably wouldn't last long.

But they'd last long enough.

"Have you heard from Bryan?" she asked. Once in a while, Bryan would call her, but mostly, he kept in touch with Gage. He'd vowed to visit them over Christmas break, but they both knew he wouldn't. They'd most likely never see him again. He only kept in touch to make sure life was still normal. To make sure it was truly over and that nothing had followed them out of Siler House.

Bryan thought they might be pushing their luck for all three of them to be in the same place at the same time. There was no sound evidence to prove his theory, but he wasn't taking chances.

Jess understood. Some days, she felt something was there—waiting. She knew Gage often felt the same, even though all of them now wore iron pendants. Gage wore his on a strap of dark leather and Jess wore hers on a chain of sterling silver. So far, her dorm roommate hadn't questioned Jess's only choice of jewelry. But she *had* noticed Jess's weird habit of covering up the mirror in their room before going to bed at night.

"Bryan called last weekend," Gage replied. "His mom is getting remarried."

She smiled. "That's good. I'm glad he's doing okay. He could use a little normal in his life."

"I checked on the house this morning." Gage didn't need to tell her which house. "It's been reopened as a bed and breakfast."

Jess shook her head. How long before the house became active again? Before people saw things in the mirrors, anxious for a chance to spot a ghost at Savannah's most infamous haunted house?

Promise me, Jess. Promise!
Be careful what you let in.

Jess sighed. "Fools."

Gage squeezed her hand. "Maybe someone else will find a way to make it stop."

"Yeah, maybe," she said. "I'll always feel bad we couldn't tell anyone the truth."

They'd kept their word to Allison, but that didn't make her feel good about it. She thought of Allison nearly every day.

"There's nothing we can do. If we had told them the truth EPAC would still be hounding us. And every paranormal specialist out there would think they had something to prove. We know that won't end well. All we can do is hope that what happened at Siler House doesn't happen again anytime soon."

But it probably would, and they both knew it. Maybe not exactly what happened to the four of them, but Riley and Siler House would never rest. Neither would those who walked its halls. The best they could hope for was that Siler House would remain standing during their lifetimes. Because, if it ever did catch fire . . .

Jess shuddered.

The authorities and EPAC remained convinced Allison was still out there, somewhere. As for physical evidence, the camera was missing. And, in the end, Dr. Brandt's final notes turned out to be more about the house and his own findings than anything about the four of them. For now, they were off the hook with EPAC.

Not that they could ever have fully controlled their abilities, anyway. Some things were never meant to be harnessed.

Jess knelt in front of Grams's grave and placed the first set of flowers there. Grams always loved roses, and while there were only a few mingling with the carnations, Jess thought Grams would approve. She lingered for a moment, then stood and rested her hand on the top of the headstone.

I'm careful now, Grams.

She took Gage's hand and led him along the pathway. The tree leaves were a beautiful gold as they danced against the clear blue sky. A squirrel bounded across the lawn in front of them.

Jess stopped in front of the second grave—her father's. Her heart still ached for him—still ached as though it were only yesterday that she had stood here for his funeral. She placed the second set of flowers on his grave. Had he been at Siler House? The shadowed figure? Had he been watching over her the whole time? Was he still here, somewhere close by?

She wanted to say good-bye, as though after all that had happened, it'd be some sort of closure, some way to make up for the fact she hadn't been there when he'd died. She used to think if she'd been given the opportunity to go back in time, to have that moment they'd been cheated out of, the pain would be different. She realized there weren't ever enough good-byes, because she'd always want one more.

Had her father been at Siler House? Jess would never know. At one time she'd only wanted answers to questions like those. Now she realized some things weren't meant to be messed with. She, Bryan, and Gage had vowed to never try to make contact with anything otherworldly again. No matter who it was.

Not all ghosts were bad or harmful, but you couldn't always open the door to one without opening it for the others.

Would their vow be good enough? No. Probably not. Allison had said that once the portal had been opened, it couldn't ever be fully closed. It was a bridge they couldn't uncross.

Jess had been glad to move out of the house and into a dorm at the start of her freshman year at the University of

North Carolina. Especially after she noticed little black spots on her sister, Lily's, dresser mirror. She'd broken that mirror. Total accident, she'd explained to her mother. Lily kidded her about seven years of bad luck. It could have just been a faulty mirror, but Jess wasn't taking any chances that dark spirits had found a way to get to them.

"I gave Lily my room," Jess said as she placed the flowers on her father's grave.

Gage nodded. "Ah! The wrought-iron headboard. Good move. When we're out of school, we'll buy our own." He grinned in that devastating way that made her heart race every time.

A blast of cold air blew past them and Jess rubbed her arms as she stood. Winter felt like it might come early this year.

Gage held her against him. "Are you cold? Want to go grab some coffee?"

"Yeah," she said smiling up at him. Things might never be the same again, but then, she couldn't expect them to. "Coffee sounds good."

He kissed the top of her head and Jess wrapped her arms around him even more tightly. God, he was still as sexy as ever.

"I told you I'd win your heart," he said, making her feel warm inside.

It was hard to believe he'd stuck around, but he had. He'd even transferred to UNC to be with her. She loved Gage and had no doubt they'd stay together. Unlike Bryan, Jess thought they'd grown closer because of what they'd been through. No one else would ever get that. They'd finally found something to hold on to in this world.

Still, she thought of Allison and what had happened that last night at Siler House. While they could have all stayed holed up behind the fence until the maids and renovation crew had shown up on Monday, she understood that Allison's nightmare would never end. It was just one more nightmare Allison couldn't live the rest of her life running from.

Jess squeezed Gage's hand and he smiled warmly at her.

Jess understood what the nightmares were like. They crept in around the edges of her sleep more than she cared to admit. Terrifying ones where Riley had managed to take her for his queen. Nightmares where evil spirits found her. In her nightmares, Riley found Bryan, then Gage.

Then Lily.

Visions of Allison's terrified face woke her often. Allison, staring at the mirror. Allison with nowhere to go and no one to turn to.

The difference between Allison's situation and hers, Jess thought as she and Gage walked under the unblemished sky, was that Jess had someone who understood, someone who'd always be there to hold her when the nightmares came.

ACKNOWLEDGMENTS

Behind every book, there's always another story—how the novel came to be. I've always wanted to write a haunted house novel. I love haunted house stories. The premise behind *The Haunting Season* has been in my head for nearly two years. I set it aside to get *The Book of Lost Souls* published, and then again to publish *Don't Fear the Reaper*. But when I sat down to write the sequel to *The Book of Lost Souls*, I dreamed of *The Haunting Season* instead. Night after night. I guess the story itself haunted me.

Getting a novel ready for publication is a lot of work and all authors need a great support network. I'm lucky to have such support. Thanks to my husband, who by now is used to weird work hours, the insomnia, the tears, the rants, the depression and elation. You are indeed my rock.

Thanks to my dogs, who had dinner served to them later than they'd like and walks that were nonexistent or cut short, but who stayed by my side, patiently and without complaint.

To D.B. Reynolds, Leslie Tentler, and Steve J. McHugh, my critique partners without equal. You guys have been more than crit partners and friends. Thanks to Courtney Cole and M. Leighton for all their input and suggestions.

To author Thomas Amo, who was also a mortician for nearly twenty years. I could never have accurately written a key part in this book without your input. I truly enjoyed our talk during dinner about embalming and burial methods. Invaluable information, bud. Thanks so much.

To Sarah Hansen, who took my breath away with the cover. To Mich's Minions, my street team—I love you guys.

Huge thanks to my rock-star agent, Scott Miller, over at Trident Media. Thanks to my editor at Amazon Skyscape, Marilyn Brigham.

And, as always, thank *you*, dear reader. Because ultimately, every author with a story to tell writes with you in mind.

ABOUT THE AUTHOR

 Michelle Muto lives in northeast Georgia with her husband and two dogs. She is the author of *The Book of Lost Souls*, an eFestival of Words winner for Best Young Adult 2012, and *Don't Fear the Reaper*, an LDS Women's Book Review Top Ten Pick 2011. Michelle loves changes of season, dogs, and all things geeky. Currently, she's hard at work on her next book.

Learn more about Michelle:
Web: www.michellemuto.wordpress.com
Twitter: MichWritesBooks
Facebook: Michelle Muto Author Page